MINOTAUR
MYSTERIES

Other titles from St. Martin's **Minotaur** Mysteries

St. Martin's Paperbacks is also proud to present
these mystery classics by **AGATHA CHRISTIE**

Murder Sets Seed

JANIS HARRISON

St. Martin's Paperbacks

MURDER SETS SEED

Copyright © 2000 by Janis Harrison.

Excerpt from *Lilies that Fester* copyright © 2001 by Janis Harrison.

Library of Congress Catalog Card Number: 00-025131

ISBN: 0-312-97725-5

Printed in the United States of America

St. Martin's Press hardcover edition / August 2000
St. Martin's Paperbacks edition / November 2001

St. Martin's Paperbacks are published by St. Martin's Press, 175 Fifth Avenue, New York, NY 10010.

10 9 8 7 6 5 4 3 2 1

This book is dedicated to my mother,
Betty Trenary,
and my grandmothers,
Lillie McGinness and Ida Trenary,
all of whom have taught me
the love of family,
and the serenity of flowers.

Acknowledgments

Story ideas come from life's experiences, but the "glue" that holds them together is credited to the following:

My husband, Don, of twenty-seven years.

My agent, Lori Pope, Faith Childs Literary Agency, Inc.

My editor, Kelley Ragland.

A special thanks goes to:

Marian Fleischmann of Sedalia Book and Toy, Sedalia, Missouri.

Gerald R. Atchison, Atchison Monuments of Clinton, Missouri.

Billie Kelly, Mulberry, Arkansas, who took the time to talk with me about the "treasure" in her garden.

Prologue

✿ "Death is drawing near," murmured Cameo, touching the tingle at the nape of her neck. The sensation was just as her ancestors had described in their journals. To experience this phenomenon firsthand was a link she cherished. A *true* Beauchamp woman could predict her own death.

Cameo Beauchamp-Sinclair rolled her wheelchair across the flagstone terrace that lay behind her beloved home. At the age of eighty the foreseeing of her passing was more probable than prognostic, but Cameo didn't dwell on that trivial detail. After years of disappointment it had become second nature for her to seize the slightest bit of evidence that she was worthy of her Beauchamp name.

A shaft of sunlight soothed her arthritic body as she gazed at the neglected gardens and orchards that had once been a source of family pride. Tears gathered in her eyes. Weeds were as tall as fence posts. Wild rosebushes rambled unchecked; their thorny branches dripped red, pink, and yellow petals on a snarl of vegetation that had no aesthetic value.

Cameo bowed her head. She possessed a fortune. Money could put the garden back to its original beauty, but it was the principle. Family had always undertaken this responsibility. However, it wasn't the deplorable state of the gardens that weighed so heavy on her heart. Haunting her was the unredeemable truth. She'd failed to keep the strain of Beauchamp women flourishing.

Make no mistake: Cameo had done the physical part. She'd produced a daughter and named her Topaz, just as Great-great-grandmother Amethyst had directed from her journal. But Topaz wasn't true Beauchamp. From the moment of conception, Cameo knew her child would be trouble. That very night after she and her husband, Hiram, had sexual relations, he'd accused her of hateful things. When she discovered she was pregnant, she'd kept her secret. She might never have told him if he hadn't taunted her about getting fat.

Cameo didn't understand this present-day mumbo jumbo about cloning, but she understood selective breeding. Find the man that fit Granny Amethyst's criteria, marry him, bring forth a daughter, and continue with the plan: Take a man's name, but never let him control the Beauchamp dynasty. Thank the angels she'd succeeded in keeping *that* sacred trust intact. Hiram's timely death had freed her from his dominance, leaving her a pregnant but very wealthy widow.

Memories of Hiram made Cameo's old heart hammer uncomfortably. She forced her mind away from him and back to her lineage. She treasured the facts she guarded in the journals. On the inside flap of Granny Amethyst's book was a faded drawing of a necklace. Each stone represented a descendent. Amethyst. Her daughter, Pearl. Pearl's daughter, Garnet. Garnet's daughter, Opal. Then Cameo, not a gem, but the pivotal point on the chain. Cameo feared Granny Amethyst had foreseen her divine guidance might hit a snag there— Cameo's daughter, Topaz. And had Topaz produced a daughter, her name was to be Sapphire. It was a prophecy from a unique woman, and for five generations it had proved true—until now.

At fifty-two, Topaz was an old maid with what the present generation called an "attitude." A few weeks ago at breakfast, Topaz had announced she no longer wanted to live in the Beauchamp mansion. By dinnertime she'd taken up residence in the vacant caretaker's cottage, where she said she could tend her herbs in peace.

Herbs? Bah! Why cultivate herbs when the gardens lay abandoned and the fertile soil begged for the touch of a loving Beauchamp hand? Ignoring the gardens for her own self-seeking pleasure was just another way Topaz had let Cameo and the ancestors down. The gardens were the very backbone of the Beauchamp dynasty. All that had gone before, and all that was still to be, was tied to nurturing this land.

Cameo sighed morosely and closed her eyes. The weight of the mythical necklace was a burden on her shrunken bosom. Sometimes she dreamed the twinkling stones came to life. They circled her neck, and for an instant, she could feel their warmth against her skin before they squeezed—

Her eyes flew open. The sun was fading. It was time to go into the house, but Topaz was nowhere in sight. "Selfish," muttered Cameo. She glared to her left. "Topaz! I'm ready to go in." On her right the foliage rustled. "What are you doing around there?" she asked. "I thought you were gathering those blasted stems and leaves."

She peered into the shadows. The overgrown mock orange bushes dwarfed a figure. Although the weather was mild, the newcomer wore a purple jacket, red gloves, and blue jeans. A lime green stocking cap concealed the face. "Who are you?" she demanded.

"My name isn't important—yet."

"You're trespassing on my land."

"It's only your land by default."

Cameo's eyes widened. "I'll have you know this has been Beauchamp land for decades. I'm sole owner, just as my great-great-grandmother Amethyst Beauchamp was."

"Jackson Beauchamp might offer another rendition."

The sound of the name smacked Cameo with the impact of a physical blow. Her body shuddered before she regained control. Her clenched hands drove her tapered nails into her fragile skin. The stranger melted farther into the shadows, but the voice carried easily to her ears. "Shall I continue?" it asked.

She couldn't decide if the stranger was male or female. "You forced this meeting. Have your say, then go."

The stranger bowed stiffly. "It was 1857 and the eve of Jackson's wedding day. Suddenly this young man was taken ill. A doctor was called, but Jackson's symptoms resisted treatment. Jackson's devoted sister, Amethyst, nursed him day and night, but he died, leaving this estate to her."

Cameo's heart thudded painfully. Tears of frustration clogged her throat. Her life was nearly over. Why was this happening now? Behind her the terrace door hinges creaked. Inez was checking on her. How much had the housekeeper heard? Never mind, she reasoned with herself. She would deal with Inez later. Right now she had to focus all her attention on the problem at hand.

Cameo took a steadying breath. "Where did you get your information?"

"Suffice it to say, I know the entire story. My silence is golden."

"You would *dare* to blackmail me?"

"I'd rather call my plan for this house an amicable solution to a disagreeable problem."

Every vertebra of Cameo's curved spine crackled. The arthritic pain was surpassed by a blinding rage. "I won't play host to your parasitic demands. Get off *my* land!"

"Old woman, I have—"

"I don't care what you have. This is my home. If necessary, I'll burn it to the ground before I let a thief steal it from me."

"Don't be hasty, and above all, don't think I'm playing games. My plan will benefit both of us, but you're too upset to listen. I'll be in touch." There was a faint rustle, then silence.

The terrace door creaked open again. Without turning her head, Cameo said, "Inez, go to a west window and watch for my—uh—guest."

"Yes, ma'am," was the prompt reply. The door closed.

Cameo stared at the place where the stranger had stood. How was she going to rectify this new situation? What could she—a small, delicate-boned, white-haired old woman— do?

Inside this aged shell the fighting spirits of the entire Beauchamp female clan rose to the cause. Cameo squared her stooped shoulders. She might have failed to keep the Beauchamp strain intact, but she would never forfeit the estate in a blackmail scheme. Sweet angels above, how she wished she could go to Topaz and discuss everything. But that thought was as useless as the bindweed that gripped the garden in a stranglehold.

A plant sets seed to sustain life, and she had to do likewise if she was to preserve the Beauchamp estate. She mulled alternatives, nodded once, then almost smiled when the kernel of an idea found fertile soil in her mind. She poked and prodded the idea from all angles, wondering if it would germinate. What she needed was a surrogate Beauchamp.

Slowly, she raised her head and stared across the garden at the apple trees whose trunks were as bent and gnarled as her own body. Like a talisman Cameo spotted the treasure of the garden. Fortified by the sight, she finally smiled. In the time she had left, she would personally groom a candidate to watch over the Beauchamp land.

Cameo squeezed her eyes shut and willed the ghosts of her ancestors to come forth and lend her a hand. She needed the best they had to offer. From her mother, Opal, Cameo chose wisdom. From her grandmother, Garnet, she took courage. From her great-grandmother, Pearl, she borrowed the art of double-dealing.

Finally there was Amethyst Beauchamp, the grand marquise of gems. From Amethyst, Cameo carefully selected tenacity. She would approach her strategy with finesse. Implement it with determination. Before facing her kinswomen in the hereafter, she had the chance to make amends. And by damn she'd do it.

Chapter One

✿ "Deck your guests with a kissing ba-all," warbled Lois as she climbed the ladder to the arched doorway. "Fa-la-la-la-la. La-la la-la. 'Tis the way to make them—" She paused for inspiration, found it and continued, "—squ-all. Fa-la-la—"

"Cute, but not funny," I interrupted.

"Bretta, you haven't smiled all day. Relax. The house looks great."

Relax? I'd forgotten the meaning of the word. My nerves were lined up under my skin like a row of dominoes. I wondered how much of a jolt it would take to set off the chain reaction. I pictured my body collapsed in a heap, the pieces swept into a box and put away in a closet. Wearily, I closed my eyes. Perhaps then, I'd get some sleep.

Since I'd bought the Beauchamp estate and taken possession on the first of October, my life had been in turmoil. To further complicate matters, I'd decided to hold my flower shop's annual Christmas open house at the mansion—a self-imposed deadline that was moronic.

The former owner, Cameo Beauchamp-Sinclair, had secluded herself in an apartment while she decided on a permanent residence. Her temporary accommodations had lim-

7

ited space, so I'd been asked to store an abundance of personal items until her daughter, Topaz, could sort through them. Judging from events so far, that day was far away in the unforeseeable future.

The mansion had an elevator, but it went no higher than the second floor. In the past eight weeks, I'd hauled Cameo's countless possessions to the overflowing attic. I'd ordered draperies, restored woodwork, and manned a paintbrush till my fingers cramped. In my spare time, I'd haggled with plumbers, battled with carpenters, and kept a thriving flower-shop business going.

Tonight was preview night. In a weak moment, and there had been many, Cameo had talked me into inviting her and a select few for a sneak peek at the restorations. Tonight's dinner party was a prelude to what the citizens of River City, Missouri, had in store for them a week from tomorrow.

River City takes its name from the Osage River, which flows below the jagged limestone bluffs where the town is perched. We're located about twenty miles from the interstate that links St. Louis to Springfield, with Branson another forty miles beyond. When it comes to entertainment, our thirty thousand residents might not have the cultural advantage of these well-known cities, but left to our own devices we do very well.

I'd scheduled my open house for the first weekend in December, hoping to cash in on the "season of spending" before everyone's pocketbook was deflated. I didn't expect the entire River City populace to come to my soiree, but interest was high.

"Hey, Bretta, are you asleep?" whispered Lois.

I opened my eyes to find her peering worriedly down at me.

"No," I answered. "Only horses sleep standing up, which isn't too far off the mark considering—"

"Bretta," said Lois warningly.

I knew she was tired of hearing me gripe about my weight. Lois is the top designer at my flower shop. She's taller than my five feet seven, even without the benefit of the ladder, and several pounds lighter. Her age is a well-concealed secret. During our long friendship, I'd taken tidbits of information and figured her to be in her late fifties. Given the way she looked tonight, I wondered if I should deduct a few years. Her dark hair was swept back from her ears. Her blue eyes sparkled. A flame red dress draped her curvaceous body.

I smothered a jealous sigh. I'd struggled with a weight problem most of my life, and I thought I had it conquered when I lost one hundred pounds. No such luck. I was overeating again, and the weight was coming back. Fifteen pounds didn't sound like much, given the amount I'd lost, but they'd mushroomed my body to the point that my clothes were tight and uncomfortable.

I took my frustrations out on the kissing ball I was holding. Giving it a vicious jab, I said, "I guess I can be thankful this *thing* didn't clobber me."

The "thing" was a replica of a late-eighteen-hundreds floral design. I'd covered a sphere of Styrofoam with mistletoe, holly, pinecones, and cedar. Loops of red-velvet ribbon formed the hanger. I'd used a thumbtack to anchor the kissing ball at the top of the ballroom doorway, where I'd draped roping interwoven with twinkle lights. The dangling weight of the ball had been too heavy for the tack, and the globe had fallen, narrowly missing me.

Lois had sized up the problem and decided a nail was in

order. Above me she drove what appeared to be a spike into the lovely oak wood I'd worked to refinish. Her "Oh, damnation!" didn't help my frame of mind. While she muttered, I gazed around my new place of residence. The beauty calmed a few of my nerves. Lois was right. The house did look great.

I'd painted the walls a soft butternut. A magnificent horseshoe-shaped staircase blocked the view from the front entrance down the long central hall. The graceful curve of the stairs drew the eye to a balcony that circled the upper floor. The doors to all seven bedrooms were closed, and my instructions were that they remain so. I didn't want to think about the cracked plaster, samples of wallpaper, and paint-splattered drop cloths that draped the furniture. Better to concentrate on what I'd accomplished, not what lay ahead.

The library, formal dining room, ballroom, kitchen, and beyond it the servants' quarters made up the ground floor. At the end of the hall a pair of French doors led to a terrace that looked out on the gardens. Just the thought of them made me long for spring and the chance to activate my green thumb.

It was entirely too much house, too much work, and too much money. I'd sunk every cent of my savings into this Greek Revival mansion and would be making payments from now until the end of time. However, plans were already under way for recouping my investment.

What kept me awake at night was the hoped-for success of the open house. I'd gambled nearly all the flower shop's liquid assets on Christmas merchandise to sell. Numerous silk wreaths, arrangements, and tasteful baubles graced the walls, windows, and doors of this landmark house. That was my drawing card—that plus natural curiosity. River City residents would be given the chance personally to view the mansion that had never been opened to the public.

Absently, I took the hammer from Lois and handed her the kissing ball. I stared at the satiny oak parquet flooring. My knees still ached from the work that had gone into bringing the gloss back to those boards. I contemplated the heavy traffic I hoped—and feared—might tread upon this floor.

What if it snows? I asked myself. *I'll have to put down throw rugs. What if someone trips or falls? Increase liability insurance. What if it rains, and I don't have enough parking spots? Will cars get stuck in—-*

I moaned. "I can get myself into the damnedest messes."

Lois stepped down from the ladder and took the hammer out of my hands. She gazed up at the kissing ball. "I dare it to fall now," she said with satisfaction, then swung her attention to me. "Got party-night jitters?"

"Why single out tonight? I'm doomed to a lifetime of nerves." I ran my fingers through my short hair. "See? I already have more gray hair than brown. If you could look inside my head this minute and see the scrambled mess I'm calling a brain, you'd worry, too." I stopped to take a breath but gasped as another thought struck. "What happens if we get funeral orders that have to be filled during the open house?"

"Piece of cake," replied Lois. "Speaking of which—the smells coming from the kitchen are divine. I think I'll trot along and see if Inez needs any assistance."

I lowered my voice. "Don't you dare. The woman is a tyrant. She's made it clear she wants no uninvited nibblers in her kitchen."

Lois raised a finely shaped eyebrow. "*Her* kitchen? Sounds like you need to have a talk with your employee."

I plunged my hands into the pockets of my robe. "I never should've let Cameo talk me into keeping that old witch as

11

housekeeper. The only good that has come of it was her suggestion that I hire DeeDee."

My future plans include turning this mansion into a boardinghouse. Inez had insisted that she needed help and demanded that I hire the daughter of her friend. I'd complied to keep the peace, but also because once I met DeeDee I knew I had to rescue her from twenty-three years of parental sheltering.

As if my thoughts had conjured her up, DeeDee clamored down the back staircase. When she saw Lois, she skidded to a stop and lingered near the elevator, casting me quick, shy glances.

She reminds me of those ceramic figurines with the wide, innocent eyes. She goes about her duties without saying a word. An uncontrollable stutter keeps her nearly mute. Tonight a kerchief hid her brown hair. A white apron tied tight around her waist kept her black uniform from sliding off her gaunt body.

"Were you looking for me?" I asked.

After darting a swift glance at Lois, DeeDee nodded.

From past experience I knew I'd get nothing out of her while a third person was within earshot. I hurried down the hall and gave her arm an encouraging pat. "Is something wrong?" Instead of answering, DeeDee took a package from her apron pocket and thrust it at me. "What's this?" I asked, fingering the red gift. "It's too early for Christmas presents."

DeeDee gave Lois another quick look then bent toward me. With her mouth close to my ear she stammered, "G-g-g-grapef-f-f-ruit."

My lips twisted into a sour grimace. The perennial box of Christmas grapefruit had arrived from my father this afternoon. I'd directed DeeDee to unpack the fruit, eat it herself, or give it to her family. I had no use for anything sent by my father. Fact was, I had no use for *him*. He'd abandoned my mother and me thirty-seven years ago when I was eight years old. After my mother died, he'd tried to open the lines of communication by sending me a card on my birthday and grapefruit at Christmas. I'd never reciprocated. Too little and too damned late was the way I saw it, but he persisted.

"You can have the grapefruit, DeeDee, but what's this?" I asked, following the square outline of the package with inquisitive fingers.

"In the b-b-b-box."

My hands stopped their query. "This was in the box my father sent?" She nodded. I pinched a corner and held the package like you would a dead rodent. I didn't want it, didn't want to know what was inside. At forty-five I like to think I've grown past my painful childhood. That part of my life was over, but those old wounds are still sensitive. It irritates me that they have the capacity to jar my peace of mind. "Put it away," I directed.

DeeDee shook her head. "O-o-o-pen it. T t-try it, y-y-you m-m-might l-l like it."

I hate when my words of wisdom are tossed back in my face. I'd introduced DeeDee to my philosophy of life, as well as a few vices. Chocolate ice cream topped with crushed potato chips or peanut butter and mashed banana sandwiches wouldn't bring her out of her shell, but I was working on it. Soon I hoped to coax a chuckle from this solemn woman.

DeeDee made a motion to the package. "W-w-well?"

"Some things you try and you don't like."

"B-b-but you do t-t-try."

"I've created a monster," I grumbled, but I ripped off the paper, then gulped when I saw the framed photograph. It was of my father and me, taken when I was about five. My young gaze rested on his handsome face with an adoration that made me wince. I turned the picture over and saw a slip of paper taped to the back. A note. "There were good times, Bretta, and there can be again. Come to Texas and spend Christmas with me."

"How dare he?" I muttered. I forced the picture into DeeDee's hands. "Get rid of it."

"B-b-but—"

"No buts," I declared hotly.

I turned on my heel and stomped back to Lois, who took one look at my face and said, "My guess is that whatever that was about you don't want to discuss it?"

"You got it."

"I should get your mind off that business and back to the here and now?"

"That's right."

She patted her flat stomach. "I feel as if I'm putting on five pounds smelling Inez's cooking. No wonder you're having trouble with your weight."

I rolled my eyes. "Some diversion. Thanks a lot."

Lois grinned. "So what's the deal with Inez?"

"She's a fabulous cook," I said, absently. Spend Christmas with my father? Ha! There was a time when I'd have walked barefoot over an acre of wheat stubble to see him. "I can't fault Inez's work. I just wish she wasn't as prickly as a teasel plant."

A familiar burst of laughter floated out the kitchen door and down the hall to us. It was followed by an unfamiliar cackle that got my full attention. "Was that Inez?" I asked, having never heard a jolly sound from the woman.

"And Lew," confirmed Lois. "He knows how to charm the old ladies."

Lew Mouffit is my deliveryman for the flower shop. At thirty-eight, he lives with his mother, can tie a florist bow to perfection, and knows River City's streets and businesses like no other. The trouble is he knows too much about too many subjects and expounds on them *ad nauseam*.

Lois nodded to the foyer where Chris Levine, my newest designer, wandered aimlessly, waiting for the other guests to arrive. "It's the young women Lew turns off," whispered Lois. "He's ape over Chris, but so far she hasn't given him a second glance."

Lew and Chris a couple? I studied Chris thoughtfully. With so many distractions in my life I hadn't noticed a romance, even a lopsided one, developing under my nose.

In honor of tonight's dinner party, Chris had curled her long blond hair into a mass of seductive ringlets and secured them with a silver barrette. Her black dress was demure but stylish. Her stiletto heels looked treacherous. I chuckled softly when she leaned against a wall and eased one foot free to massage the arch.

She had grown up in River City but moved away several years ago. When her mother died, Chris returned for the funeral, then stayed to help her father with his cleaning-service business. Personalities had collided, and Chris approached me for a job. She didn't have any floral experience, but I needed an extra pair of hands, so I'd hired her on the spot.

Rapid footsteps from the other end of the hall made me turn. I was relieved to see DeeDee had taken the picture and gone, but now Lois's husband, Noah Duncan, stormed toward us looking efficient with a toolbox in his hand. Noah is my electrician, and he's a genius when it comes to computers and technical gadgets. He's tall and thin and combs his dark hair in the classic James Dean style. Most of the time he's quiet and easygoing, unless he has a burr up his butt—like now.

After putting the toolbox down, Noah glared a hole in me. "Bretta," he said, "last week, when we discussed the wiring in this house, you failed to mention that you planned to put lights around six doorways and both banisters of a gigantic staircase *and* decorate twelve Christmas trees, eight of which are in the ballroom." He paused for effect. "Do you know what that means?"

Hoping to lighten his mood and mine, I replied, "I'll have a place of honor with the electric company?"

He speared me with a frenzied stare. "This old house doesn't have the necessary circuits to support all that extra wattage."

A horrible thought put a kink in my feeble attempt at humor. "Not a fire," I whispered, past the lump of panic that rose in my throat.

"Could happen, but more likely a blown fuse."

"I used super-duper extension cords."

Noah sighed in exasperation. "That doesn't matter. The main part of this old house was wired for a few fixtures, not an electrical extravaganza."

"I have to light those trees, Noah. It's part of tonight's presentation." I pointed a shaky finger at him. "You're the electrician. Can't you figure something out?"

"I don't know," he mumbled. "I really think—"

"Look, I have to finish dressing before everybody gets here. Whatever needs to be done, just do it. Those trees have to be lit all at the same time." When he still looked unconvinced I pleaded, "A *River City Daily* reporter and photographer are

16

coming to this blasted dinner party. If Sylvia writes a good story—"

Lois gasped. "Not *Sylvia Whitaker*? You didn't tell me she was coming."

"I've tried to forget it, or at least put her out of my mind." When Lois started to speak, I quickly overrode her. "I know. I know. It wasn't my idea to include her. Cameo had the guest list made out."

"That Whitaker woman is ambitious and ruthless. Wonder why Cameo invited *her*?"

"Why did she invite any of these people?" I muttered.

"You never got around to telling me who was coming. I hope that was simply an oversight on your part."

"No big deal. Just your average museum curator, librarian, lawyer, and, of course, Sylvia and her photographer, Jason Thompson. You know him."

"He's okay, but the rest of them sound too highbrow for me."

"That's what Chris said. She didn't want to come—"

Noah snapped his fingers. "Hel-l-l-o-o-? Remember me? The lights."

I turned to him and blinked the relevant subject back into focus. "Oh, yeah, as I was saying, if Sylvia is impressed, I might get a great story, and people will flock to my open house. The more people, the more money they might spend on these decorations. More money means—more money," I finished lamely.

Noah unbuttoned his collar and tugged at his tie. "I don't know why I have to sit with the guests." To Lois, he added, "I'll take that hammer."

I stifled a grumpy sigh. I'd already explained tonight's situation. "Cameo presented me with her guest list, then suggested I include my staff, so they can have their pictures

17

taken with the floral designs. You round out the number to twelve. I'd have invited a date, but everyone I know was busy."

Lois snorted. "All you had to say was, 'I'm having a party,' and Bill Fenton would have come."

This was a road well traveled, and I was ready for a new route. "I told you I'm not interested in dating. It's too soon after Carl's death."

"It's been eighteen months. Seems to me you should be getting on with your life."

Lois had teased me, cajoled me, and pushed me into working on a relationship that held no interest for me. Bill Fenton is a good man—kind, thoughtful, and caring. I'd gone out with him twice, but each time I'd felt as if I was cheating on Carl. It's not my way to be deliberately cruel, but I'd had enough of Lois's good intentions.

"Have you ever put yourself in my place and wondered what it would be like?" To emphasize my message, I nodded to Noah, who was busy rummaging in his toolbox. I lowered my voice. "You've shared the good and the bad with him. You have a history. If he were to suddenly die, could you forget him and pick up another man? Some women do, but I can't. I don't think you could, either."

Lois looked at her husband. Slowly her eyes widened as a vision of living without him finally dawned bright and clear. I drove my point home. "You don't lose those feelings just because your husband isn't around. I need time. Maybe someday, but not yet."

Noah continued to grumble to himself, ignoring both of us. "I'd be more useful in the basement at that damned fuse box than making nice to a bunch of people I don't—" He broke off when Lois grabbed him and planted a moist kiss on his lips. "What was that for?" he asked.

Lois pointed up at the kissing ball. "Mistletoe," she murmured with a catch in her voice.

Noah grinned at me. "Powerful stuff. I'll need a pound of it. Go. Change. I'll figure out a way to light your trees. It may mean we'll have to—"

"Tell me later," I said as I hurried away.

Wearily, I climbed the elegant horseshoe-shaped staircase to the upper floor. Leaning against the oak railing, I stared at the crystal chandelier suspended from the second-story ceiling. The sprays of cut-glass prisms cast their lights on the foyer below, creating a dazzling pattern of miniature snowflakes.

I was beginning to care for this old house, though I had yet to think of it as home. No routine and too many problems kept me from taking pleasure in what it had to offer. After Carl, my husband of twenty four years, had passed away, I'd rattled around in my old home, alone and lonely. Buying this mansion with the intention of someday turning it into a boardinghouse seemed to be a practical solution to my solitary existence.

I heaved a sigh. Before those plans could come into being, I had to get through tonight. This dinner party was the groundwork for the open house. I sighed again. Why had my father picked this time in my life for a journey down memory lane? Didn't I have enough to contend with?

Below me, Lois and Noah strolled into view. Watching the tenderness between them made tears prick my eyelids. I opened my mouth to suck in more oxygen for yet another sigh. At this rate I was going to stress out my bronchial tubes.

What the hell? One more wouldn't hurt. I expelled a stream of air that stirred the prisms on the chandelier, making them tinkle ominously. In the foyer, Noah, Lois, and Chris looked up.

"Probably the ghost of a demented florist," I called to them, before going to my room to dress.

Chapter Two

Two hours later, all the guests had arrived except for Cameo and her daughter. I'd made everyone comfortable in the library. I'd poured drinks, and as far as I was concerned my duties were on hold until Cameo put in an appearance.

I stationed myself at the drink cart and adjusted the tight waistband of my dress. The band stubbornly rolled over the excess lump of flesh at my midriff. I pushed it down again, but it rolled back up. Across the room Lois frowned at my fidgeting. I crossed my eyes at her, but I forced my hands away from the annoying belt.

I forgot my problem as DeeDee entered the room to serve everyone hors d'oeuvres. We're not a first-class act around here, and I had thought the formality of a uniform was unnecessary. I'd lost that argument with Inez, but I'd ordered her to find something more colorful for DeeDee to wear. I was seeing Inez's choice—puke pink dress and bile green apron—for the first time.

DeeDee was embarrassed, which in her case meant she didn't have the courage to hold her head up. She shuffled from guest to guest, offering a silver platter loaded with snacks. When she approached me, her expression fairly screamed "get me the hell out of here."

I leaned close and whispered, "After tonight that outfit goes into the fireplace. *You* can strike the match." DeeDee looked hopeful. I reached for a lobster roll, but she rotated the platter, putting the celery within my reach. I pretended to give her a disgruntled once-over. "Maybe pink *is* your color," I teased. She ducked her head, but I saw her lips twitch before she scurried out of the room.

Smiling, I gave the library another quick appraisal. Reupholstering the furniture in moss green, cream, and gold had lifted the somber mood of the dark walnut paneling. An Oriental rug picked up those colors and added a bold splash of peacock blue. A blazing fire in the hearth, as well as 863 dust-free books, made this room an ideal setting for tonight's stodgy group.

My flower-shop staff—Lois, Lew, and Chris—were seated in straight chairs against the far wall. Noah shuffled restlessly at Lois's side. We hadn't discussed the lighting situation in the ballroom, but Lois had given me a thumbs-up before I opened the door to admit the first arrivals.

Cameo's guests occupied the comfortable chairs and sofa. General conversation was in progress so my two cents wasn't needed. I sorted out Cameo's "select few" by using Carl's method of observation. My husband, who'd been a deputy with the Spencer County Sheriff's Department, had taken part in many investigations. When questioning countless witnesses he'd devised a private system of mentally tagging each person for quick and easy recall.

Carl had been the light of my life. His unconditional love had shone on me with a warmth that sheltered and protected. A heart attack had extinguished that gentle radiance, and for the next fifteen months I'd stumbled through a world that had suddenly turned dark. Three more months of mourning had passed, and I was becoming accustomed to using my night sight.

I still missed him. I knew I always would, but I was beginning to function again. However, when I'm extremely nervous or when something heavy is weighing on my mind, Carl's voice speaks to me. This isn't some psychic phenomenon, but the power of love that transcends even death. I could've used some of his wry humor to put a different spin on this dull evening. Since his voice wasn't in my ear, I seized upon his private tagging system and sized up the occupants of the library.

Most of them I knew by sight or had a passing acquaintance: Everett Chandler sat in a moss green wingback chair. The curator of the River City Museum looked like Santa Claus in a charcoal gray pin-striped suit. His whiskers were white, his blue eyes merry behind a pair of wire-framed glasses. His bulging stomach lay across his lap like a pet dog.

Simon Gallagher, or Ichabod Crane, as I was tempted to call him, was perched on the edge of the companion chair to Everett's. The Spencer County librarian had a point to make. He waved bony arms sheathed in a checkered sports jacket several sizes too small. His white socks showed below the cuffs of his dark trousers.

"—circulation of books is down," he was saying. "I blame television and the electronic age. The biggest culprit is the video."

"Could be this generation needs more visible stimulus than the printed word," remarked Trevor McGuire.

All eyes shifted to him. He ducked his head like a shy, little boy—a manner incongruent with his lawyer profession. Tall, dark, and dreamy, Trevor was a visible stimulant to any female. Chris had sat up straighter when he'd been intro-

23

duced. I dubbed him Elvis, with his bashful ways and sensual overtones.

"What I mean," explained Trevor, "is that people live a fast-paced life. Watching a video takes two hours." He stopped to lift a muscular shoulder. "Reading a book takes more time. The real inducement for action-packed dramas is the need for reassurance that good does prevail over evil."

"You got all of that out of circulation being down at the local library?" drawled Sylvia Whitaker. "If that's the case, I'll be forced to add melodrama to my society coverage."

Petite and compact, Sylvia is as volatile as a vial of nitroglycerin wrapped in a deceptively pretty package. If she doesn't get her way, her expressive brown eyes can snap like a pair of castanets. Her breasts ride high on her chest and form the shelf for a red-enamel heart-shaped pin. The heart as well as the color is her trademark. She's editor of the Lifestyles section of the newspaper, and her column, *Sylvia's Snippets,* is her platform for airing River City's dirty laundry.

She drained the amber liquid in her glass, then waved red-lacquered fingers airily. "You know the stuff?" She lowered her voice menacingly. "Black clouds roiled overhead. The virgin bride lurked in the darkened hallway. Suddenly a shadow materialized on the wall." She peered across the room at me. "How about it, Bretta, can you make your designs *more* portentous?"

Before I could decide if she was taking a jab at my artistic talents, Everett said, "You're missing the point, Ms. Whitaker. Not that I'm surprised. You completely misquoted me last week in your *Snippets* column." His merry eyes hardened. "A bit of poetic license might be welcomed by some, but not when *I'm* being quoted."

Ho! Ho! Ho! I ducked my head to hide my grin. Santa has claws.

Sylvia twisted her lissome body on the floral-covered sofa so she could see Everett better. Her steady gaze surveyed him from behind a pair of red-rimmed glasses.

I shifted uneasily. This had to be the reputed "look" I'd heard about. Sylvia, "Queen of Hearts" Whitaker, was about to rip into Everett. Apparently, her colleague and photographer, Jason Thompson, recognized it, too.

Like Paul Simon, he tried to bridge the troubled waters, or at least, divert the stream of Sylvia's legendary caustic remarks. Jason is employed by the paper, but freelances in his spare time. That's how I'd gotten to know him. We'd worked several weddings together—Jason taking photos while I kept the flowers shipshape. I'd seen him in action. He's young enough, in his early thirties, and handsome enough, with a flirtatious dimple in his left cheek, to coax a smile from any neurotic bride.

He clanked his empty glass to Sylvia's and, with the hint of a Southern drawl, said, "My pipes need a bit more lubrication. How about yours?"

That was my cue. I leaped to the drink cart, but stopped in mid hustle as the doorbell rang. I flung a glance at Lois. She hopped up from her chair and hurried across the room to take over my hostess duties.

As I made my way out of the library, I checked my watch. I wasn't surprised Cameo was arriving forty minutes past the appointed hour. She would want to make sure everyone had arrived before she made an entrance.

I'd gotten to know her through the numerous meetings we'd had during the negotiations for the house. I'd learned that her fragile body belied an iron will, and that she wasn't shy about offering advice. I'd been encouraged to keep a journal, urged to wear more sapphire blue, and implored to put my past—namely my father—behind me. In her opinion, my father's desertion had been for the best. His leaving had given my mother and me a better chance at forming a solid female unit.

The doorbell chimed again, and DeeDee dashed from the kitchen like the hounds of hell were nipping at her heels. Seeing her flushed face, I asked, "Inez keeping you hopping?"

"B-b-bowing and s-s-scraping to h-h-her h-h-highn-n-ness."

From the library Sylvia's throaty chortle drove me the remaining steps across the foyer. "I'll get the door. You tell Inez I said to back off. Before this night is over, that old witch and I are gonna have words. If she doesn't like what I have to say, she can pack up and move out. *You* can be my housekeeper."

DeeDee's jaw dropped at the idea. I knew she'd never tell Inez anything of the sort, but this repressed young woman needed to be reminded that I was in her corner. She closed her mouth and nodded thoughtfully. I reached for the front doorknob, but stopped when I heard a soft hee . . . hee . . . hee from behind me. I turned. DeeDee's lips stretched in a grin that went from ear to ear. Then her shoulders hunched in their customary submissive curve, and she crept into the kitchen.

Shaking my head, I swung open the front door on the tail of a discussion. Cameo was saying, "—could have dressed in more fitting attire."

"Mother, if I'd dressed better, you'd have demanded to know who I was trying to impress."

"I wish you—Bretta," said Cameo, catching sight of me. "My dear, how lovely you look. That shade of sapphire blue is most becoming. It matches your eyes beautifully. I'm glad *someone* listens to this old woman."

Topaz puffed up, ready to blow off steam. I quickly said, "Come in, come in. It's too cold to visit out here."

"It's starting to snow," grumbled Topaz. She pushed her mother's wheelchair into the foyer. "If it gets worse, I want to leave early."

Cameo's tone was imperial. "The first snow of the season is magical, Topaz. If you'd only listened over the years, you would know that our ancestors—" She stopped. "Never mind. We've just arrived. We won't discuss our departure. I plan to enjoy this evening." Her radiant smile could've warmed a greenhouse in the dead of winter. "I'm home, again," she whispered.

While I hung their coats in the closet, I studied them as they looked over the changes I'd made to the foyer. There wasn't a wrinkle of resemblance between mother and daughter that I could see. Though she was crippled with arthritis and confined to a wheelchair, Cameo commandeered the spotlight. Traces of a past beauty lingered on her lined face. Her hair was as white as a Madonna lily, her presence ethereal, her aura majestic. She was dressed in a gown of old-fashioned lavender silk—long sleeves, full skirt, and high collar. Pinned at her throat was a lovely amethyst brooch. On her gnarled fingers were four rings—pearl, opal, garnet, and a cameo, which I took to be a signature thing.

Topaz's dress was brown, her shoes thick-soled oxfords. From the looks of her red-chapped hands, neither lotion nor rings ever graced them. Every inch of six feet, and well over two hundred pounds, she lumbered when she walked.

"See, Mother," she said with satisfaction. "I knew the credenza would look better against that wall."

Her brown hair was scraped into an untidy knot on top of her head. She poked at it with one hand, while trailing the other over the smooth wood of a side table. "This looks wonderful," she murmured. "So does the floor. You've been busy, Bretta."

Before I could speak, Cameo demanded, "Where is Granny Amethyst's rocking chair? It has always sat by that window overlooking the front veranda."

I tried to remember the piece of furniture. "Uh . . . the one with the carvings across the headrest?"

"Not just carvings, Bretta. My great-great-grandmother's skilled hands constructed the oval leaves and delicate branches into the wood of that fine chair."

"Oh. It's . . . uh . . . in the attic," I admitted.

"The attic," breathed Cameo, placing a shaky hand over her heart. "Stored away like it's a useless relic. Topaz, it will have to be rescued."

Topaz rolled her eyes. "Don't start, Mother."

"Please," I said. "Let's go into the library. The others have arrived."

"Of course they have," muttered Topaz. "It was planned that way." She whisked the wheelchair toward the doors.

I stood aside to let them pass but flashed Topaz a smile of encouragement. I knew what it was like to be her size and headed into a room full of people. It took a certain kind of person to carry that amount of weight and come across with self-confidence. Topaz didn't have it. A life of living in her mother's shadow, of being constantly nagged, had left her with a perpetual frown that took away what beauty might have shone through.

I looked at Topaz's broad back with pity. My glance dipped lower, and I nearly came unglued. The hem of her full skirt was tucked into the waistband of her panty hose. An expanse of meaty thigh was visible, as well as a hefty portion of her butt.

I swung to one side so I could see into the library. Everyone was standing. Cameo's place of honor was slated for near the fireplace. To get there Topaz would have to parade before them all. Jason had his camera ready. It was a photo opportunity.

What to do? There was only one thing for it. I took two giant steps, seized the cloth of her skirt and gave it a yank. The material unfurled, but so did several stitches. An audible rip filled the respectful silence that preceded Cameo's grand entrance.

Chapter Three

✿ Topaz took my whispered explanation and profuse apology in stride. She tucked the loose flap of material under her belt, and bitterly muttered, "It's queen for an evening, and I'm merely a peasant. The show will go on. May Mother's reign end soon."

I wasn't sure I'd heard right. Did she mean tonight's outing or—? I glanced at Topaz, but she'd turned away. I covered my confusion by offering a fresh round of drinks.

Cameo dismissed my suggestion with a wave of her hand. "Please be seated," she said. Once they were settled, she added, "I'd like an introduction to your guests, Bretta."

My guests? I blinked in confusion. Granted, I'd issued the invitations, but only at Cameo's request. I smiled uncertainly. "Excuse me, but I thought you knew everyone except, perhaps, my staff."

"Them, too. Everyone."

I felt like a pawn in some mysterious game. I looked into Cameo's kind eyes and my doubts fled. What did it matter? If it would make her happy, I was willing to indulge this aristocratic woman, if for no other reasons than friendship and curiosity. I started at the far wall. "Noah Duncan. He's standing next to—"

"Speak," commanded Cameo.

Noah's eyes widened. He darted a glare at me as if to say, "You didn't tell me I'd have to talk." I smiled encouragingly. He stammered, "Well, uh—hello. Nice to—uh—meet you."

Cameo squinted thoughtfully.

"Next to Noah is his wife, Lois, a designer from my flower shop."

Lois murmured, "Good evening."

"Speak up," demanded Cameo.

"Good evening," shouted Lois, her blue eyes twinkling merrily.

"Next is Chris Levine, another designer."

Chris sprang to her feet and teetered precariously on her heels before she righted herself. "Hello," she squeaked.

"Levine? You're Jillian's daughter?" Chris nodded. "My dear, I'm so sorry about your mother's passing. I received a Christmas card from your grandmother last week. She said you were working for Bretta."

Chris's mouth dropped open. She recovered her surprise, and asked, "Matilda Bennett wrote to you about *me*?"

"Yes, my dear, it was a lovely letter. I hope we can find time to visit later this evening." She turned to Lew, who rose graciously to his feet.

Lew has always been an enigma to me. I've never understood why he's content to drive my delivery truck. He comes from money. His family has had roots in River City soil as long as the Beauchamps. He wears suits like he was born in one and wouldn't be caught dead in a pair of sweatpants or blue jeans.

He bowed gallantly in Cameo's direction. The light made his bald head shine. "I'm Lew Mouffit," he said quietly. "I deliver for Bretta's shop."

Cameo gave him a regal nod. "I know your mother. It's a pleasure to meet you." With a flip of her hand, Cameo indicated that I was to proceed. Mystified, I introduced *her* guests. "The man on your right is Simon Gallagher."

"Well?" snapped Cameo. With that single word, the temperature in the library dropped ten degrees.

Simon's head bobbed on his scrawny neck. "I'm director of the River City Public Library."

"A historian, too," commented Cameo. "Your particular field of expertise is Spencer County." She paused then added, "A boring subject for a boring man."

Simon's eyes bulged. His bony Adam's apple quivered.

Cameo shifted her gaze. "And you, sir?"

"I'm Everett Chandler, curator of the River City Museum. It's an honor to finally meet you face-to-face. I hope that later you and I—"

Cameo stopped him cold. "You also have an interest in genealogy. You pry into other people's family histories." She gave him a haughty stare. "A snoop by any other name is still a snoop."

Everett looked as if he'd been goosed by an elf.

Trevor took possession of center stage. He leaned forward and flashed Cameo a dazzling smile. "I'm Trevor McGuire, lawyer for the firm of Collins, Rinehart, Wheeler and McGuire."

"Handsome is as handsome does. You're associated with a very prestigious law firm. Edgar Collins was solicitor for my ancestors. He was privy to many delicate conversations, but he proved to be most discreet." Cameo eyed Trevor until he squirmed. "I see," she murmured shrewdly. "I thought as much. You haven't a discreet bone in your body."

Sylvia Whitaker was next. A smirk twisted her red lips before she asked, "There's no mystery who I am. Right, your grace?"

Cameo folded her hands in her lap. "Gossipmonger."

Sylvia sucked air before she cut loose. "I'll have you know that I—"

"—live for scandal, half-truths, and innuendos," filled in Cameo. "It's a gift, I'm sure, though I can't imagine why anyone would want it."

Sylvia spluttered with outrage, but Cameo ignored her. She pointed a finger. "Jason Thompson."

He gulped. "Uh—yes, ma'am. How did you—"

"—know who you are?" finished Cameo. "I've seen you on these grounds taking pictures with your camera. Who gave you permission?" She held his gaze. "What are you seeking, young man?"

Jason numbly shook his head. I wanted to sink into the floor. Except for my employees, Cameo had insulted each and every person in the room. When she turned to me, I cringed, wondering if I, too, had a denouncement coming.

"Bretta, my dear, this is proving to be an interesting evening." She looked past me. "Here's Inez. Dinner must be ready."

The housekeeper stepped farther into the library. Slim as an icepick and with a tongue just as wicked, Inez resents my presence in this house and she makes no bones about it. Listening to her surly comments is like being pecked to death by a chicken. I hadn't suffered any serious wounds, but I was growing weary of her verbal nips. She's in her sixties with a cap of gray hair cut so short not a lock is longer than an inch. Her eyes are like bits of polished stainless steel, and for me they usually shine without a trace of courtesy.

Inez crossed the floor to Cameo and clasped her former employer's hands with heartfelt fondness. "This is where you belong," Inez said, "in *your* home. Let me get you settled in the dining room. I've made several of your favorite dishes to perk up your appetite."

Without giving the rest of us so much as a glance, Inez took the handles of the wheelchair and turned it toward the door. Over her shoulder, she said, "I haven't slaved over a hot stove all day to serve the food lukewarm. Dinner is on the table."

My cheeks burned with embarrassment. Who could refuse such a cordial invitation? It seemed everyone wanted to. I heard snatches of conversation, the gist being they wanted their hats and coats.

I didn't blame them. I would have liked to slink off to my room and lock the door. I was even willing to forgo the story on my open house. I'd buy a full-page ad. It would be less stressful.

Given Cameo's cutting remarks, I was amazed when everyone filed silently past me into the foyer and on to the dining room. My spirits lifted when I heard their collective gasps of appreciation. The table was set with ruby stemware and white china on an emerald green lace cloth. Votive candles, at five varying heights, were supported by a centerpiece of spruce, ming fern, and pristine dendrobium orchids. The soft light made the oak wainscoting shine. Place cards directed everyone to a specific seat. The burgundy carpet muted the sounds of eleven chairs being scraped into position.

Inez situated Cameo's wheelchair at the head of the table, then stepped into the shadows where I felt her eyes on me like a specter's. I was on Cameo's right. I'd mingled my staff among the other guests with instructions to keep the conversation flowing.

The food was passed and we ate in silence. I wracked my brain for an innocuous topic of conversation. Chris kept her eyes on her plate as Trevor cast her venturesome, playful looks. My gaze settled on Lew. I smiled. Good old Lew. I could count on him for easy repartee in any situation. But I couldn't get his attention. He'd seen Trevor's interest in Chris and had fastened his stony glare on the lawyer, ignoring the rest of us. I stared down the length of the table to Lois. When I finally caught her eye, I frowned.

She stopped chewing and hastily swallowed. "I—uh—understand it's supposed to snow tonight."

"It's already started," I boomed in a tone more in keeping with winning the lottery. "Maybe it'll be a white Christmas."

Cameo sipped her iced tea, then motioned for the hovering Inez to take her plate. Everyone stopped eating. "Please," said Cameo. "Finish your meal. I find my appetite has decreased as I've gotten older. I need little to maintain me."

We were a robust group, with the exception of Simon. We had a scrumptious meal before us, yet everyone except Topaz picked at the food. She was chowing down as if tomorrow was the beginning of the great American fast.

Cameo smiled at me and gestured to the dining room. "Bretta, you're living up to the expectations I had when I sold you my home. You've rejuvenated it with a spirit that only love and youth can give. For that, I thank you."

She nodded to the Christmas tree that stood in the corner. Large, creamy silk magnolias adorned the pine branches. Gilt angels and crystal ornaments caught the light and glimmered against the burgundy and gold-striped walls.

"Lovely," Cameo murmured. "But Christmas is for fools."

Heads popped up.

"Halloween, a pagan holiday to be sure, is more in keeping

with the human race. Christmas is lauded as the season for giving, yet everyone is more of a mind to take, take, take. We wear masks of deception. Some of us relish the pranks we play on others. Everyone has a skeleton in his closet."

Sylvia leaned forward so she could see Cameo clearly. "As gossipmonger of the group, it's obviously up to me to ask if you have a skeleton in your closet, Mrs. Sinclair?"

Dead silence all around.

With every eye on her, Cameo smiled graciously. "I prefer to be addressed as Mrs. *Beauchamp*-Sinclair, Mrs. Whitaker. The answer to your question is yes. My family has its share of skeletons. You see—" She paused. "I'm being blackmailed."

Forks clattered against plates.

Cameo placed her hands on the tabletop. The candlelight picked up the facets of her jewels. With the tip of one finger, she caressed the garnet stone on her other hand. "I asked Bretta to hold this dinner party, but she doesn't know that I included a blackmailer on the guest list. Thanks to her unwitting cooperation, I can now put a face and name together."

I froze, expecting an explosion of indignation, followed by an aftershock of hardy denials. Everyone remained silent.

"It took weeks of careful thought as to who might have the opportunity to uncover the facts you have in your possession. If I'd been wrong, I'd have prevailed on Bretta's hospitality with a new guest list. But that won't be necessary. You are here. You know it, and now, I know it as well."

I tried to divide my attention between Cameo, to see if she favored anyone with a look, and the others, to see if there was a hint of guilt. Everyone wore the same dumbfounded expression. I pressed my lips together and listened intently.

"In August you personally came onto this property and alluded to facts concerning my family that have been safeguarded for more than a century." Cameo switched her stroking from the garnet stone to the opal. She polished it slowly. "It was a matter of wisdom on my part. In this room we have a historian, a genealogist, a reporter, a photographer, and a lawyer. All of you have access to records that might hint at an indiscretion. Perhaps you stumbled across it. Whatever way it came to your attention, you took what you found and came to me. You wanted more than I was willing to give. I hoped to thwart your horrible scheme by selling this estate to Bretta."

Cameo took her eyes off her rings to sweep the room with an icy gaze. "But that didn't stop you. I've received three letters since August, each insistent that I give you money or you'll make your information public. When you first came to me, you said your plan would benefit us both, that we'd work out an amicable solution, but the tone of your letters was mean-spirited and cruel.

"You said you would be in touch so you could explain your plan more fully. I deliberately made myself inaccessible to everyone except Topaz, Inez, and Bretta. I wanted to see if you had the courage to continue. Your greed has made you foolish. You put your demands on paper and used the U.S. mail. Extortion through our postal service is a federal offense. I have your letters well hidden, but tomorrow I have an appointment with the postal inspector. I'll turn the letters over to him."

Topaz tossed her napkin on the table. "Mother! What in the world is the matter with you? Blackmail? You never said a word of this to me. Why didn't you—"

Cameo's voice shook with emotion. "Stop! This is my fight. It *will* be my victory." She touched each ring reverently. "This house means nothing to you, nor does your ancestry. To me it is everything."

One by one Cameo studied each person at the table. When she'd made it around, she said, "Blackmailer, I told you that I wouldn't play host to your parasitic demands. In our society a parasite goes by many different names—sponger, barnacle, freeloader, bloodsucker. All are uncomplimentary but accurate. However, none of them could exist if their host is strong of spirit and has the courage to battle your invasive tactics. You made a grave mistake when you chose me as your victim."

Cameo patted my hand, but she directed her words down the table. "Ms. Whitaker?" Sylvia froze with an odd look on her face. I tried to analyze it, but it vanished, to be replaced with her usual condescending smirk.

"Yes, your grace?"

Cameo's smile was tenuous, the look in her eyes pure loathing. "I'm sure your head is full of mental notes. After all, you have a front-row seat to some of the best gossip to hit this town in years. I'll be watching to see what kind of slant you put on your story. I also hope you'll write an article for your paper telling of Bretta's Christmas open house. She's worked hard for this event, and I'm looking forward to the people of River City viewing my home. My family has shared its wealth by contributing to many of the city's projects and organizations. For a good cause, my checkbook has always been open. For a freeloading miscreant there will be no recompense."

On that cheery note, Cameo declared, "Enough said on that distasteful topic. All of you seem to have lost your appetites." She nodded to Inez. "Which in no way reflects on your cooking. I've spoiled this part of the evening, but I understand Bretta has a lovely presentation to make in the ballroom. I'm sure *everyone* would be delighted to see it. Shall we proceed?"

Chapter Four

🌸 Expecting a stampede for the nearest exit, I stepped out of harm's way. But everyone moved with dignity through the doorway. Suspicion was in the air, but not a word was spoken.

Lois sidled up to me. "Nice floor show," she whispered. "Is the old girl batty? Do you think someone *is* blackmailing her?"

"I don't know, but Topaz doesn't seem to believe it. The part about Cameo making herself inaccessible to everyone except Topaz, Inez, and me is true. Remember when Lew asked where Cameo was going to live, and I told all of you I'd been sworn to secrecy?"

"I remember, but you didn't know the reason, right?"

"No. I wish she'd told me."

Lois nodded to the guests. "What's with them? No one's saying anything."

"What do you expect? Any remark might be misconstrued as guilt. I figure they want to blend into the woodwork, get this evening over with, and then run like hell. Not a bad idea."

"When Cameo looked around the table, taking us on one at a time, I wanted to confess to every sin I've committed. I wouldn't want to tangle with that woman. She may be old, but there was a gleam in her eye—" Lois shuddered, then asked, "Who have you set your sights on as the miscreant?"

Before I could answer, Topaz called impatiently from the hall, "Bretta, are we to go into the ballroom?"

"Yes," I replied, then hastily substituted "No" when Lois said, "Noah wants you to stall until he can get things set."

"Great," I muttered. "*Now* you tell me." My shoulders slumped from the burden of prolonging the agony of entertaining this group. "What will you be doing while I'm consorting with a suspected felon?"

Lois winked. "Setting the mood."

I didn't know what she meant, and there wasn't time to ask. I joined the others in the hall. Everett was talking a mile a minute to Cameo. She was listening and nodding. Noah disappeared into the library. One by one the lights went out. I glanced over my shoulder. In the dining room, Lois hit the switch for those lights but left the candles burning.

"Before we go into the ballroom," I quickly improvised, "I'd like for you to follow me." I led the way to the center of the foyer, and pointed to the chandelier. "This unique fixture was shipped from France to New Orleans, where it came by paddle wheeler up the Mississippi River to St. Louis, and later, here. Notice the pattern the prisms make on the oak parquet flooring."

Jason had rounded up his camera and was taking snapshots like an overzealous tourist. Chris was on the fringes of the group. Trevor was surreptitiously working his way over to her. Lew saw what the lawyer was up to and crossed the floor to Chris's side. He whispered something in her ear. She moved a step away but gave him a tiny smile.

I directed everyone's attention to the horseshoe-shaped staircase and the balcony that circled the upper floor. Out of the corner of my eye, I watched Lois. She was outside the kitchen doorway vehemently arguing with Inez. Now what? I wondered.

"At the U of the horseshoe, my designer, Lois, has created a spot of nostalgia." Behind me Jason kept clicking. The noise detracted from what little concentration I had. "The focal point is a mahogany secretary that's been in the Beauchamp family for generations. The chair's needlepoint cushion was stitched by Cameo's grandmother."

Beside me, Cameo gasped. I quickly turned to her. She was rubbing the nape of her neck and staring at the staircase above. "Is something wrong?" I asked. Cameo was clearly agitated. Her cheeks were flushed, her eyes overly bright.

She put a trembling hand to the brooch at her throat. "I—I—" She took a deep breath and offered an apologetic smile. "It's nothing. You're doing fine."

Jason clicked three more times.

I pointed again to the secretary. "The craftsmanship is superb. Notice the dovetailed drawers. See how the compartments swing aside to make room for the writing surface." I motioned to a stack of books tied together with silver ribbon. Fastened in the center of the bow was a cluster of mistletoe. "Lois used books from the Beauchamp library for this design, but it isn't for sale," I added, in case Cameo had any worries on that score.

Cameo gave the books a cursory glance, then lightly tapped the chair. "You should sit here and record your thoughts, dear." She shifted so she could gaze up the staircase again. "The twinkling lights woven into the greenery on the banister are like a string of jewels." Abruptly, she turned her head. "Let's see the ballroom."

Jason clicked on.

"It is getting late," said Everett.

"Are you in a hurry?" asked Sylvia. "If so, why don't you waddle on home? Or is something keeping you here?"

"As par for the course, you're putting words in my mouth that were never said. *It is getting late*," ground out Everett. "I was merely making an observation, but you, Madam, have to twist everything."

I hadn't seen Noah, but I'd stalled as long as I could. "Inez has coffee waiting."

"Whiskey, straight up, would be better," muttered Sylvia. "The best way to finish tonight would be in a drunken stupor."

I'd had it. With this unappreciative group, the beauty I planned to unveil would wash over them like water off a duck's back. Forget hospitality. Forget gracious smiles. "Follow me," I snapped.

I led the way to the ballroom. Simon, Everett, Sylvia, and Jason walked under the kissing ball without giving it a glance. However, Trevor paused at a strategic spot. I wasn't sure what he was up to until I saw Chris.

With Lew at her heels, she started past Trevor, but the lawyer held up a hand. He looked at the kissing ball and cocked an eyebrow at her. Chris responded with a flustered shake of her head. Lew took Chris's elbow and hurried her through the double-arched doorway framed with roping and lights.

As instructed, Inez had lit a small lamp to guide everyone to a grouping of chairs. Rather than sit, they chose to stand well apart from each other. On the sideboard were the silver coffee service and an assortment of desserts. Everything was going as planned, except, of course, the mood of the guests. Cameo's accusation had raised tension among the group to a new level.

The last to enter, Topaz abandoned her mother in the doorway under the kissing ball. Without waiting for an invitation, she crossed to the buffet and dipped a generous serving of chocolate-raspberry trifle onto a plate. After flopping into a chair, she spooned some of the rich dessert into her mouth and smacked her lips.

Cameo huddled in her wheelchair, darting swift glances around the darkened room. Her fingers fidgeted with her jewelry. She saw me watching and motioned for me to come closer. I hurried to her side.

"Bretta," she said, clutching my arm. "I shouldn't have said anything about—" She stopped to take a shaky breath. "I'd like to stay at the mansion tonight."

I covered her icy hand with my warm one. "Who do you think is—"

Cameo didn't let me finish. "I'll stay here," she repeated fervently.

"I don't have a room or a bed ready."

"Inez will take care of it," she murmured, rubbing her neck. Suddenly she leaned close, and whispered, "Time is an old woman's worst enemy, Bretta. I had so many things to share with you. I'll stay here, and we'll sit up all night. I can only hope I'll find the words to make you understand."

"Understand who the blackmailer is?" I asked, totally confused.

"No. No," said Cameo impatiently. "You have the makings for becoming a true Beauchamp, but you can't try to outthink me. You must listen. Hear only what I say. You can't put your *own* interpretation on the information I give you. The facts are the facts. You must guard them just as I have, and my ancestors before me."

I shivered at the intensity in her voice. "Tell me—"

"Mrs. Solomon?" interrupted Trevor at my elbow.

43

Irritated at his rotten timing, I turned from Cameo, and snapped, "Yes, what is it?"

"Can we get on with this?" Trevor said, flashing Chris a roguish smile. "I'm hoping for an important call later."

Never one to miss a trick or to play on it, Sylvia strolled over. "From a hot date?" she asked, then snickered when Chris flushed. "Be warned, Miss Levine, or you'll become another McGuire statistic. I've heard he notches his bedpost after each new conquest."

Chris's eyes widened at Sylvia's brazen assumption. "I would never—" She stopped, turned to flee, and stumbled on her spiked heels. To save herself from a fall, she grabbed the armrest on Cameo's wheelchair.

Cameo quickly covered Chris's hand, and murmured, "I've got you, my dear." She gave Sylvia a withering look. "You do live up to your reputation, don't you, Ms. Whitaker?"

Chris mumbled an apology and hurried from the room. Lew and Trevor started to follow, but I wasn't having that. Fisticuffs would be the last straw. "Stop!" I said. "No one move, unless you're going to take a seat."

Jason aimed his camera at me and clicked the shutter. With spots before my eyes, I said, "Pictures of the house are fine, but *I'm* off-limits."

Jason grinned. "Sorry, but I've never seen you lose your cool."

Lose my cool? Hell's bells! I was on the verge of a major meltdown. Lew was acting like a love-struck teenager. McGuire was egging him on. Chris was in tears. Sylvia was always ready for a good verbal bashing if she thought she could provoke an unwary victim into revealing a bit of gossip she could use in her column. And what in God's name had

Cameo been talking about? *Me* a Beauchamp? Was the poor old lady delusional?

"Mrs. Solomon," said Simon, squinting at the shadowy room. "It looks like a forest in here. How many trees are there?"

As I turned to answer, Noah stepped through the double doors at the far end of the room. He signaled once with his flashlight. I was ready to chuck the presentation, but too much was riding on a successful open house. "There are eight Christmas trees," I said to Simon as I crossed the floor. I clicked off the lamp, then groped behind the screen for the lever to the electrical strip that was an octopus of extension cords. Without warning, I flipped the switch.

The transformation of the dark room to dazzling light was blinding. Immense mirrors at opposite ends of the room magnificently reflected the eight ten-foot trees with dozens of strings of lights. I took malicious pleasure in the sudden too-bright glare to everyone's eyes.

"Holy solar system," breathed Sylvia. "What a sight. Get pictures of this, Jason."

"I'm out of film, I'll have to go to the library for my bag."

Noah, now in the hallway behind Cameo, said, "I'll go with you. I've turned the—uh—lights off in the rest of the house."

"I saw you doing that," said Everett. "Is there a problem?"

I waved Jason and Noah into the dark hallway before I answered Everett. "No problem. I wanted everyone to get the full effect of my presentation."

"A feat well accomplished, Mrs. Solomon," said Simon.

He ambled about, touching an ornament here, a bauble there. Sylvia wandered the length of the room, busily jotting in a notebook. Everett seemed satisfied with my answer about the lights. His interest had shifted to Carl's childhood Lionel train set I'd assembled under a tree. This afternoon I'd given the old train a test run, but the engine wanted to jump the tracks, causing sparks to fly. I'd left it silent tonight, but for the open house I hoped to have it running.

Across the room Trevor took a step toward the hall. Lew, like a cocky rooster protecting his hen, strutted into his path. Trevor eyed Lew contemptuously, snorted his disgust, then sauntered over to the mirror behind the grouping of chairs.

Topaz was serving herself seconds from the dessert buffet. Cameo sat where I'd left her. Now that the lights were on, she appeared to be more relaxed, though she was fretting with her rings again. I turned to Simon, who was speaking.

"I detect a theme among the decorated trees. Am I correct?"

"Yes. Because history plays such a large part in our daily life, I've depicted different eras." I moved to the center of the room. A brief glitter in the hall caught my eye. I turned to look, but it was gone. There was no time to wonder what it was. Simon waited expectantly, and Sylvia had her pencil poised over her notebook. I cleared my throat.

"First is a patriotic tree done in American flags and white doves of peace. Next to it is a tribute to our Native Americans. I've used feathers and beaded pieces of leather that are associated with the Osage tribe who settled near River City. The third tree is in recognition of our brave frontier men and the families of the pioneers—calico and gingham ornaments, a coonskin cap for a tree topper, and miniature covered wagons."

Sylvia nodded. "It takes something special to impress me. I have to admit this is fantastic."

Hot damn! If Sylvia was impressed, I was on a roll. Encouraged, I moved on down the room. "The Victorian age called for lace, delicately scented bags of potpourri, and frilly, fussy ornaments. The old-fashioned tree is trimmed with ginger-bread men and strings of popcorn and cranberries. Everett is by the tree representing the train age, next is the automobile. My favorite is—"

The lights flickered. The train engine began chugging its way down the rickety tracks with Everett at the controls. "No!" I said. "It's not safe, Everett. Turn it off." I was thinking fire. Instead the lights went out. We were plunged into a darkness that was thick and intense.

Across the room, Cameo called, "Bretta!"

I heard the apprehension in her voice, "Sit tight, Cameo." I raised my voice. "Noah!"

"I'm here." He turned his flashlight into the room. I glimpsed Topaz about to resume her seat. The light caught her in a picturesque squat over the chair. Behind her was Trevor. The light moved on to me. "Do you have a flashlight, Bretta?" asked Noah.

"Upstairs in my room."

"If you folks will be patient, I'll have the fuse changed in the time it would take Bretta to go upstairs."

"Do it," said Everett. "*I'm in no hurry.*"

Noah flashed his light on the screen that was hiding the extension cords. "Turn off the switch for the trees, Bretta. Lois will come with me. She'll tell you when to turn on the other lights."

"Go. I can find my way in the dark." I barely had the words out of my mouth and they'd vanished, taking with them the only source of light. Nerves made me giggle. For a sophisti-cated woman of the twenty-first century, it was an undignified sound. I swallowed another titter, and suggested, "We could sing so I'd know where everyone is, and I wouldn't step on anyone's toes."

It was an opening ripe for one of Sylvia's barbed comments. Instead, she cut loose with a rousing rendition of "Jingle Bell Rock." A few others halfheartedly joined in.

I got my bearings and crossed to the screen. I bumped into the sideboard, then felt along the wall for the snarl of wires. I found the switch and flipped it off.

"It shouldn't be long," I said to the silent room. The musical moment had petered out. "Give me a call, Cameo, and I'll come to you." No answer. "Cameo?" I repeated.

"Mother," said Topaz impatiently, "answer Bretta."

Still nothing.

"Noah!" I yelled. "Fix the damned lights. Lew, get a candle from the dining-room table."

He answered, "Got it." His hard-soled shoes beat a syncopated rhythm down the hall. I shuffled across the floor. "Where is everyone?" I demanded. My answer was a dispirited chorus of "Here." "Where else?" "Tree." "Where you left me."

Not much help, but it kept me from running into anyone. My destination was the switch to the overhead lights. It was by the door where I'd last seen Cameo sitting in her wheelchair.

Lois shouted, "Bretta! Noah says give it a try."

I hurried forward and collided with the wall. I ran my hand up the doorframe to shoulder height, then over to my left until I located the switch. I flipped it up. Soft illumination washed the room in a gentle glow.

Sighs of relief turned to gasps of horror.

There's a part of the brain that shuts down when pain looms on the horizon. I'd experienced that strange occurrence when Carl died. I felt it happening again. My movements were wooden as I turned to Cameo.

Details sprang at me. At some point during the blackout, she had tried to leave her wheelchair. Both footrests were flipped up. Her shoes touched the floor. Her hands were in her lap, but one ring, the pearl, had come off her finger and was caught against a fold of her dress.

Now that the electricity was on, the string of lights that had outlined the ballroom doorway twinkled brightly. Cameo wore them like a jeweled necklace in suffocating splendor around her neck.

My hand shook as I carefully checked for a pulse on her delicate wrist. No flutter of blood flowed through her veins. She was dead. Cameo Beauchamp-Sinclair had been murdered.

Chapter Five

🌺 Just as on the night Carl died, the paralysis to my brain didn't last. Other factors took hold. Frantically, I shuffled through the deck of emotions that were playing havoc with my breathing. I had to find something to help me through the next horrendous hours.

Sorrow? I couldn't allow it a stronghold, or I'd become a basket case.

Guilt? This wasn't the time or the place to assess my culpability.

Anger? I plucked the card out of the deck and tentatively put this emotion into play. Anger edged out the grief that was making it difficult for me to breathe. Warmth flooded my frigid limbs. Air expanded my aching lungs. Tremors still wracked my body, but I could move. I faced Cameo's guests.

Carl's investigations had proved that killers were ordinary people caught in circumstances that pushed them to the ultimate level of destruction. Cameo had given us the motive for her murder. I'd provided the means and opportunity. I stifled that unwelcome thought and let my unblinking gaze circle the group in the ballroom. Who had been desperate enough to kill?

Simon? Sylvia? Everett? Trevor? Topaz?

From the corner of my eye, I saw a flicker of movement. I

turned. Lew, Noah, Lois, Chris, Jason, DeeDee, and Inez watched from the hallway. I scanned their faces until I came to Inez. I shivered as her cold, hostile eyes met mine.

Topaz broke the silence. "Mother can't be dead." Her voice wobbled. "My God, I figured she'd outlive me." She struggled up from the chair. The plate of dessert slid off her lap, hit the floor, and broke into two neat pieces. She didn't glance down. Her broad shoulders were hunched. Her skin sagged on her large frame. She looked like a lump of dough without the leavening ingredient.

Slowly, she surveyed the group in the ballroom. "I—I—don't understand. She was considering each of your requests. Why kill her?"

All hell broke loose. I let it rage, hoping to hear something that would enlighten me to the identity of the killer. But they were too loud, too involved in being heard, and nothing they were saying made any sense.

"Silence!" I shouted. The noise fizzled like a dud fire-cracker. When a modicum of order was restored, I said, "We have to leave this room. I'll call the sheriff."

"Can't we cover Mother?" whispered Topaz. "She wouldn't want to be seen like this."

Inez said, "I'll get a blanket."

"No!" The word burst from my lips.

"But Mother wouldn't want—"

I spoke quietly, but my blunt statement made Topaz wince. "Your mother has been murdered. She would want the person responsible apprehended. A blanket would contaminate the scene."

Again bedlam broke out.

"Now see here—"

"Murdered is too—"

"I really think—"

I ignored the rest and answered the latter. "Don't bother. This is what *will* be done. Everyone will walk to the end of the ballroom where there's another door. You will go through it, up this hall to the foyer, and into the library. There you'll stay until I've called the sheriff, and he arrives."

Trevor stepped forward. "You don't have the authority to order us around, Mrs. Solomon. As a lawyer—"

"You're all suspects in Cameo's murder. Those lights didn't wrap around her throat by themselves. She said one of you was blackmailing her. Now she's dead." My voice cracked. Tears welled up. Once again I had to draw on anger to carry me through. "I'll be damned if I'll let anyone screw with this investigation. I'll preserve this crime scene to the best of my ability. If there's so much as a thread from any of your clothes or a hair from any of your heads on C-C-Cameo's b-b-body, I want it found."

"That's a bit melodramatic, Bretta," said Sylvia, "even with the stuttering."

My gaze flew to DeeDee. Distress had made me stammer, but what if she thought I was mocking her? Our eyes locked. I saw compassion, which was almost my undoing. I struggled for composure. "Perhaps. But murder is a bit dramatic, wouldn't you say? Go to the library. I have a call to make."

Topaz stumbled across the floor and reached out to her mother. I intercepted and gave her rough hand a gentle squeeze. "Don't," I murmured. "I know this is horrible for you."

Topaz pulled her hand out of mine. "You don't know. I should stay with her."

The words, "May Mother's reign end soon" echoed in my

ears. "No," I said firmly. "For your own good, you need to go with the others to the library." Topaz studied me with eyes that were dark and aggressive. I braced myself for a scene, but she drew herself up to her full height, nodded, then shuffled away.

I wasn't sure the others would follow my orders, but to my relief they moved to the far end of the ballroom and out the door. "Noah," I said, as they filed silently past, "stay in the foyer. Lois, make sure *everyone* goes into the library."

Lew took Chris's arm, and they followed the others. Jason and DeeDee trudged along behind. Inez hadn't moved. She stood in the doorway by Cameo. I was the width of the wheelchair away from her.

"Well," I said wearily, "get it over with. Have your say, then you can join the others."

Inez crossed her arms over her thin chest and raised her sharp chin. "You've appointed yourself watchdog over us. I'm volunteering my services to watch you. The closest phone is in the kitchen." She backed into the hall, keeping her eyes on me.

I couldn't figure this woman out. In the weeks after I'd bought the estate, I'd bent over backward being nice to her. I complimented her work. I ate her cooking, though I'd known my diet would be shot to hell. Nothing I did or said seemed to make a difference in her attitude toward me.

Averting my eyes from Cameo, I made a very elaborate circle around the wheelchair. Once I was in the hall, Inez nodded in the direction of the kitchen. "After you," she muttered.

I wanted to say, "No, please, after you," just to see how far she would take this, but I wasn't in the mood for games. I strode ahead of her but stopped at the kitchen doorway. "Oh," I gasped in dismay.

The room was a disaster. Stacks of pans. Greasy dishes.

Leftover food uncovered and sitting on the counters. At this angle I could look through the butler's pantry into the dining room. The lights were on, the candles out. The table hadn't been cleared.

Behind me, Inez said sarcastically, "I was told I couldn't clean up. Couldn't use the dishwasher. Couldn't use the garbage disposal. Couldn't even make myself a cup of coffee. There were big doings in the ballroom. Anything electric had to be shut off."

I ignored her and went to the telephone. I could have dialed 911, but I wanted to speak to the sheriff, Sid Hancock, personally. Sid had been my husband's friend as well as his commanding officer. He's strong and dependable, if you don't ask for his help too frequently. Tonight's call to him would stretch the limits of our shaky friendship.

The problem between Sid and me had cropped up out of an innocent game of armchair detective that Carl and I used to play. We'd discuss his cases, and I'd poke holes in his theories, pointing out other possibilities.

Not long ago, I'd left the security of my armchair and taken my detective skills on the road. The results had put a criminal behind bars, but I'd almost lost my life in the process. My success hadn't changed a thing in Sid's mind. I was an amateur, pure and simple. I was also his best friend's widow, a complication Sid resented. If anyone other than me had messed in his investigation, he'd have tossed her butt in jail. I'd gotten a severe warning not to try any more asinine stunts.

My finger trembled as I slowly punched in the familiar numbers for his home phone. While the number rang, I turned so I could see Inez. It gave me a moment of pleasure to see her surprise at my use of a full-digit number. Under different circumstances, I might have laughed out loud at her amazement when I addressed the sheriff as Sid and identified myself simply as Bretta. Any amusement I felt vanished as I gave Sid the bare, grim fact.

"Sid, I was having a dinner party, and one of the guests has been—uh—murdered."

"Murdered?" he blustered. "Holy shit, Bretta, what kind of people are you fraternizing with?"

Conscious of Inez, I kept the defiant note out of my voice that always wants to creep in when I'm confronted with an irate Sid. "River City residents," I answered vaguely. I dropped the bomb. "The victim is Cameo Beauchamp-Sinclair."

He sucked in his breath then expelled it with a whoosh. "Crap, Bretta. Crap. Crap. Crap. I don't need this."

"And I do?"

"Call the city police."

"I can't do that, Sid. My new home, the Beauchamp mansion, is outside the city limits. This murder is in your jurisdiction. I'll expect you and your professional entourage shortly."

"Keep everyone away from the body," he ordered.

"I am."

"Don't go meddling."

"Of course not."

"Don't let anyone leave."

"They won't."

"See that—"

"Just get here as fast as you can, Sid." Quickly, I replaced the receiver and gave Inez a cool smile. "The sheriff has been notified." I indicated the hall. "After you. Let's join the others."

Chapter Six

✿ The air in the library was thick with a blue haze. Sylvia and Everett were graciously sharing a bowl for their cigarette ashes but had spitefully turned their backs to each other. The white, unfiltered cylinder dangling from Everett's lower lip brought me up short. My image of him as Santa Claus crashed and burned. What had Carl done when one of his "tags" jumped character?

Sylvia crushed her cigarette into the bowl. I took another look at what they were using for an ashtray and identified my mother's lead crystal candy dish. I wasn't pleased at the smoking in my house, but a vice is a vice, and I knew what that was like. What galled me was their use of my mother's dish. I crossed the room, snatched the treasure and gestured to the fireplace. "Use that, if you have to smoke," I said. Miffed, I put the dish behind a silk bouquet on the mantel.

Lois was at the drink cart. "They wanted liquor, but I told them the bar was closed."

"That's right. I've called the sheriff. He'll be here shortly." I checked to make sure everyone was present.

Simon stood at the bookshelves studying titles. Chris sat white-faced next to Lew. Trevor watched them coolly. Topaz had parted the heavy drapes and was staring outside. I contemplated her stiff back. Were her thoughts filled with happy memories, regrets for harsh words, or unspoken sentiments?

Cameo had dominated Topaz, and yet, after living under her mother's thumb for fifty-two years, Topaz had moved out of the mansion. Cameo had told me the decision had come as a surprise to her. Why, at this late date, had Topaz decided to distance herself from her mother?

Since I didn't have the answer, I continued with my canvass of the group. Jason was kneeling on the floor, fiddling with his camera. He glanced up, caught my eye, and gave me an encouraging smile. His dimple was charming, and I responded with a weak twist of my lips. DeeDee had tucked herself into an obscure corner. Her brown hair was limp, her eyes stretched wide. The bile green apron was wrinkled and grimy. The hem of her puke pink dress was hiked up. All she lacked was a smudge of dirt on her face to complete the picture of a street urchin.

I felt a rush of affection and wished I could give her a prescription for poise and a major injection of self-confidence. Speaking of which, Sylvia had an overdose of both. Briskly, she clapped her hands for our attention.

"We could settle this here and now. Someone in this room killed Cameo. Did anyone see anything?"

"Whoa," I said. "We can't discuss this until Sid gets here. He'll want to interrogate each of us separately."

Sylvia raised her eyebrows. "I think we can solve this case, and the sheriff won't have to do a thing."

Everett chuckled snidely. "Stepping out of your league, aren't you, Ms. Whitaker? Mrs. Beauchamp-Sinclair was strangled. She wasn't *gossiped* to death, which is your bailiwick."

Trevor smoothed the lapels of his suit jacket. "Let me

advise all of you not to say a word without council present." He flashed that slick smile I was beginning to dislike. "I'd do the honors, but there could be a conflict of interest."

"Meaning you'll protect your ass, but will leave the rest of us to flop in the breeze?" said Sylvia.

"I'll tell my story."

I didn't like his attitude, and I didn't like him. Against my better judgment, I asked, "And what will that be?"

"That someone hurried past me in the dark."

"Who?"

"I can't say."

"Can't or won't?" I demanded.

Trevor shook his head. "Don't try to pin a lawyer down, Mrs. Solomon. It's a waste of your time."

Sylvia drummed her fingers on a small table. "Simon?" she called sharply. "You're very quiet. Did you see or hear anything?"

With a blank expression, he looked up from the book in his hands. He lifted a scrawny shoulder. "I was at the far end of the ballroom. I was nowhere near Mrs. Beauchamp-Sinclair."

Sylvia gave Simon's lean frame a speculating stare. "You could have left by the end door, slipped down the hall, and choked her. With those long, skinny legs you could've done the deed and been back in place before the lights came on."

"Yes," he nodded slowly. "I see what you mean. I could have done that," he admitted, "but I didn't. However, Ms. Whitaker, that same hypothesis could be applied to you, to any of us. As I recollect, you, Mr. Chandler, and I were near the far doors." He pointed to Trevor. "That young man was closest to Mrs. Beauchamp-Sinclair, other than the people who were in the hallway."

"That reminds me," I said. "When we were in the ballroom

I saw something glitter in the hallway. Did anyone else see it and know what it was?"

For a moment there was silence, then Jason said, "I think I know what you saw, Bretta. It was Miss Levine's hair barrette." Everyone looked at Chris. Her cheeks turned a deep crimson at the unwanted attention. Jason continued, "Turn your head, Miss Levine, so the light—"

Chris's chin shot up. "I don't know what you're implying, Mr. Thompson, but I was—"

"See?" said Jason, as the light glinted off the silver finish. "I thought that might be it. I saw it, too, when I was in the library."

Everyone was waiting for an explanation. I could have stepped in, but figured Chris needed to clear the air. Apparently, she reached the same conclusion. She was obviously upset. Her voice wobbled as she spoke.

"After I left the ballroom, I was going to get my coat and leave, but I had to use the powder room. As I passed the ballroom doors, I heard you, Bretta, describing the Christmas trees. We've worked hard for this open house. I couldn't abandon you, but I wasn't going back into the ballroom. After I left the powder room, I went to the front staircase and sat on the steps. I didn't move again until I heard the commotion in the ballroom."

"Did you see Jason in the library?" I asked.

Chris glared at the photographer. "Yes, though why I should give him an alibi, especially after he—"

The dimple in Jason's cheek deepened. "I wasn't trying to cause you trouble."

Chris sniffed. "It sounded like it to me."

"No, really, I was just—"

"Okay. Okay," I said sharply. Their "did not" "did too" argument was wearing thin. "We get the picture."

Sylvia smirked at me. "Testy, testy," she murmured, then turned to Inez, "What about you? What were you and"—she waved a hand to include DeeDee—"doing while we were in the ballroom?"

"We should have been cleaning up the dinner dishes, but I'd been told I couldn't touch anything electric." Inez launched into the same spiel she'd given me. She finished by sliding a sly glance my way. "We were watching television in our rooms."

"Television?" I repeated. "But I thought you said everything electric had to be shut off."

Inez answered, but in such a way that it sounded like someone other than me had made the inquiry. "In her eagerness to make everything fresh and new in the main house, Mrs. Solomon hasn't been to the servants' quarters. She wouldn't know if we used flashlights for illumination."

"That's not fair, Inez. Your rooms are private. I've left them alone."

Topaz turned from the window. I expected to see traces of tears, but her eyes were dry. "That's enough, Inez," she said quietly. "There's a simple explanation. This house was built in two stages." She waved a hand. "The main house—kitchen, library, ballroom, foyer, hall, and the upstairs—were built first. The east and west wings were added later. The east wing is the three-car garage. The west wing was built for the employees' living quarters, so the attic rooms could be used as storage to accommodate my ancestors' penchant for never getting rid of anything."

"Attic?" said Everett. "I've heard—"

"Not now," snapped Sylvia. "So when the lights went out in the ballroom," she pointed to Inez, "you didn't notice because the wings have separate circuits?"

"That's right," said Inez.

Sylvia, still prying for information, continued, "And the kitchen is on the main fuse box?"

Topaz answered. "Yes. It's part of the original floor plan. Only the two wings have modern wiring on circuit breakers, not fuses."

Noah had come to stand in the doorway. He'd loosened his tie and unbuttoned his shirt collar. "There's something bothering me," he said, giving me an apologetic nod.

I knew Sid would have a coronary if he found out we'd openly discussed the case, but we'd come too far to stop now. I waved for Noah to say what he wanted.

"I can't figure out why the fuse blew. All the other lights in the main house were off. There should have been plenty of power to take care of the ballroom."

DeeDee happened to be in my line of vision. She opened her mouth, gave the crowded room a quick glance, then clamped her lips shut. I took a step in her direction, but stopped when Everett said, "Before anyone points a finger, I'll admit I turned on the electric train."

"Electric train?" said Noah. "Was it in the ballroom, too?"

I explained about Carl's Lionel train. Before I finished, Noah was shaking his head. "I don't see how a train set could have pushed the wattage over the top. It took more juice than that." He stepped back into the foyer. "A car has pulled up. Red lights are flashing."

"This is it, folks," said Trevor, rubbing his hands together. "It's show time."

I tossed him a dirty look and hurried out of the library with Inez on my heels. This time I wasn't having any of her smart mouth. "Relax, Inez," I said, "the cops are here. An expert will watch over me. You can wait with the others." She backed away but went only as far as the library doorway. "Old rip," I muttered.

The doorbell rang. Sid pushed the door open before the chimes had finished their melodious song. Behind him was one of his female deputies, Donna Meyer. Donna had been on staff with Carl. In her early fifties, she has a round face, florid complexion, and eyes that are sharp and intelligent. I was glad to see her and smiled a warm greeting before I turned to the sheriff.

Sid is a fair and just man, if you can get past his crabby disposition. He's my height, about five-foot-seven with light red hair, ginger freckles, and a touchy temper. I once overheard him tell Carl that he considers himself a confirmed bachelor, that way he never has to worry about being charming.

He stomped past me and into the foyer. I hadn't seen Sid for several weeks, but received no courteous "hello" or "how are you" from this man. He was all business.

"It's snowing. It's cold. Where's the stiff?"

I treated him to a disgusted glare. "Mrs. *Beauchamp-Sinclair* is this way." I was going to take them to her, but Sid put a restraining hand on my arm.

"We'll find her," he said. "Point us in the right direction."

I jerked a thumb down the hall. "You can't miss her," I said dryly. "She's the one in the wheelchair with the Christmas lights wrapped around her neck."

"Don't cop an attitude with me, Bretta. If this is homicide, the shit's gonna hit the fan."

"What do you mean *if*?" I demanded. "I know a murder when I see it."

I turned on my heel and stalked toward the library. I stopped before I got to the door. I'd had all I could stomach of that group. I detoured to the staircase and sank down on a step. I closed my eyes, but they immediately popped open. I'd had a mental image of Cameo sitting alone and defenseless in the dark. The string of lights wrapped around her throat, her air passage blocked.

The tears I'd worked to suppress filled my eyes. Why hadn't I taken her aside and demanded answers about the black-mailer? Obvious. I hadn't been sure if her tale was true. Topaz had pooh-poohed the idea. She hadn't taken her mother seri-ously. Why should the rest of us?

I tried to recall Cameo's exact words when she'd told us about the blackmail, but she'd overloaded us with information. I'd been amazed to learn that she'd been hiding from a black-mailer in the weeks since she'd left this house. I'd been shocked that she'd methodically set him up for exposure. If only she'd taken me into her confidence, we might have discovered the identity of the blackmailer without her getting—killed.

I swallowed the lump of grief that swelled in my throat. Why hadn't I demanded answers? I was right back where I'd started. "Around and around I go," I murmured.

"Talking to yourself?" asked Sid, coming to stand by the newel post.

I wiped my tears away before I looked up. "Just thinking out loud," I mumbled.

He scowled. "That doesn't bode well for me or my investi-gation."

"Ha, ha." I gestured to the empty foyer. "Where are all your people? I thought this place would be crawling with cops."

"They're on their way." He jerked his head toward the library. "Before I go in there, I want to hear your version of what went on tonight."

I swept my dress tail out of the way. "Have a seat," I invited.

"In a house the size of a hotel, you can surely do better than a step." He looked around, saw the straight chair that matched the mahogany secretary, and carried it over. He plopped his rear on the cushion Cameo's grandmother had stitched, then twisted sidewise to pull a miniature tape recorder from his pocket. His action made the chair's wooden joints creak.

"You're sitting on an antique," I cautioned.

Sid eyed me narrowly. "Today's my birthday. I feel like an antique, too." He wiggled his bony butt on the cushion. "What's in this damned thing?"

"Probably horsehair. That's what they used for stuffing in the olden days."

"Never did like horses," he grumbled. "So, who snuffed the old broad?"

Chapter Seven

🌸 My spine grew ramrod stiff at his offensive words. "I'm not going to answer your questions until you show some respect. I liked Cameo. She was my friend, and if you think I'm going to sit here and listen to your warped brand of humor, you can just—" I stopped because my throat had filled with tears. They worked themselves up to my eyes, ran unchecked down my face.

"All right. All right," grumbled Sid. "Stop bawling. Won't do the old—uh—Mrs. Sinclair any good."

"Mrs. *Beauchamp*-Sinclair," I corrected, sniffing noisily.

"Whatever."

"Do you have a tissue?"

"A tissue? Lord, no." He reached in his pocket and pulled out a handkerchief. "I've got this. Take it with my compliments. Now get on with your story. Holy shit, we're wasting time."

Nothing ticks Sid off more than personal observations and rambling accounts of nothingness. In honor of his birthday, and because I'd already pushed him to his limit, I forced myself to stick to the facts. I gave him everything in chronological order, but I was in no rush to give him the guest list. As I recounted all that had happened, I omitted names, using a bunch of we's them's, and us's in my awkward statement.

When I came to a stumbling halt, Sid rumbled, "What the hell kind of rigmarole was that? And what about this hosts, parasites, and parasitic demands?" He jerked his head toward the library. "Who've you got in there? The River City Horticultural Society?"

I took a deep breath, then braced myself before giving him the names of Cameo's guests. Just as I'd expected, he overreacted. His face paled dramatically. The freckles on his skin stood out in stark relief like a dot-to-dot puzzle gone haywire. His eyes widened, then closed to slits.

He switched off the recorder and leaned closer. "Damn it, Bretta, that Whitaker woman is a barracuda. She'd roast her own mother if the feast would get her a tasty story. McGuire is an ambulance chaser always looking for someone to bring suit against. Chandler wants to run for mayor in the next election, and now he's a suspect in a murder investigation. Not just any murder, either, but a high-profile murder." He cracked his knuckles and muttered, "What a mess. What a goddamned mess, and I'm smack-dab in the middle of it."

The doorbell rang. Sid leaped from the chair like his legs were spring-loaded and hustled across the foyer. From my seat on the staircase I watched men with wet shoes enter and cross my polished floor. Sid took them to the ballroom and gave them terse instructions before coming back to me.

"Let's go into the library," was all he said.

When we stepped through the doorway all eyes were on Sid. He faced the group with his shoulders squared. "Cameo Beauchamp-Sinclair was murdered tonight. Like it or not, you are all witnesses to the crime. As witnesses you are commanded by law to step forward with any information you may have seen, heard, or have in your possession."

Everett had taken a seat in the wingback chair he'd occupied earlier in the evening. He made a steep pitch of his fingers like a doghouse over his rounded belly. "Sheriff," he said, "are we to assume Mrs. Solomon has filled you in on events before Mrs. Beauchamp-Sinclair died, as well as those that transpired afterward?"

"I have Bretta's account, but I want to hear all of yours."

"Looking for discrepancies," drawled Sylvia. She tossed her cigarette into the fireplace, then gave me a tight smile. "I'm sure Bretta covered all the important points. She has an eye for detail."

"I want to hear from each of you," said Sid sharply. "Leave your name, phone number, home address, and place of employment with my deputy. He's waiting for you at the front door. Other officers will take brief statements and set up appointments for each of you to come to my office tomorrow for an in-depth interview. As you leave, you'll be asked to open your purses, briefcases, or whatever you brought with you this evening, as well as volunteer to a pat down."

"A pat down?" asked Lew. "You're going to search us?" His voice rose in outrage. "Whatever for?"

"The blackmail letters," snapped Sylvia. "The sheriff wants to make sure we aren't absconding with the motive for the murder." She raised her hands above her head. "Pat away, Sheriff. I've always had a thing for a man in a uniform."

She was baiting Sid. I waited for him to explode, but he took it in stride. "For the ladies I've assigned Deputy Meyer to that task, Ms. Whitaker. I'd appreciate your cooperation." He surveyed the room once again. His look left no doubt as to who was in charge. "Don't discuss this case with each other, or with anyone outside this room." He leveled a glare at Sylvia. "I can't ask you not to print this story, but I can ask that you be circumspect in your reporting." He stepped aside and gestured for them to leave.

Sylvia waited around until there were only the three of us in the room. She didn't waste time letting us know her intentions. "I'll be watching this investigation, Sheriff. I've got a hunch—" She came to a halt and gave him an enigmatic smile. "I'd better stop there."

"If you have information, I'd suggest you dump it here and now," said Sid.

"Oh, it's nothing specific, at least not yet, but I'm working on it."

"Stay out of this," warned Sid.

"You can't keep me from thinking." Sylvia looked from Sid to me. "And what I'm thinking shouldn't be too hard to prove. The right questions put to the right people should net me a whale of a story, and I'll be—"

"—jerked off your feet and into deep water," finished Sid. "Playing Ms. Sherlock Holmes in a murder investigation can get you into serious trouble." He gave me a knowing look before he swung his sharp gaze back to Sylvia. "The right questions asked of the wrong people can get you killed."

Sid was warning me, too. I had a hundred questions about Cameo's murder, but Sid didn't have to worry about me getting involved. I had plenty to keep me occupied—the flower shop and the open house. But as Sylvia left the library, with a spark of conviction in her eyes, I grouched, "I don't like this."

"What don't you like?" Sid asked, eyeing the rows of books.

"You called for brief statements when this group needs a thorough grilling. By the time you talk to them tomorrow, they'll have their stories nailed down. Just because you told them not to discuss the murder doesn't mean they won't. What if they get together, or call each other and hatch some fabricated tale that lets them off the hook?"

"My dear, Bretta," said Sid sarcastically, "when we entered this room you could have taken a bite out of the tension in the air. They won't be making any effort to help each other."

I persisted, "You're giving them time to think things over and get their stories straight."

"Maybe, but the way I see it, the more they think about things, the more elaborate their stories, the harder it'll be to keep all the facts straight. Every sheriff has his own way of conducting an investigation. Circumstances and the people involved dictate what procedure is used. This wasn't some back-street killing, Bretta. These are prominent River City people. None of them are going on the lam. I'll have to treat them with kid gloves."

"But one of them killed Cameo."

"But the others *did not*. Before I drag out the rubber hose to beat them into submission, I want more information." Sid glanced at his watch. "My men should be arriving at Mrs. Beauchamp-Sinclair's apartment to search for those blackmail letters. Other men have started searching here. I'm covering all the bases, Bretta." Satisfied, he nodded. "Before the hour's up, I'll have those letters in my hands. She was an eighty-year-old woman in a wheelchair. How hard can they be to find?"

"Still, I think—" I began.

Sid cut me off. "You don't have time to think. You have to go to your room and pack a bag."

"A bag?"

Inez stomped into the library. Her mouth was pursed in an

expression I knew only too well. She was pissed. "That man keeps following me. He says I have to leave."

"That's right," said Sid. "This house is being closed down. I'm taking charge of the scene."

I gasped. "For how long?"

"Until we've collected the evidence, searched the house for the letters—until I decide to release it."

"When will that be?"

"Depends." When I would have jumped in with more questions, Sid held up his hands. "Enough!" he thundered. "Pack what you'll need for a couple of nights. A deputy will accompany you to your room. That's it. Done." He strode out of the library and into the foyer.

"Well," snapped Inez. "This is a fine kettle of fish, and it stinks to high heaven." Her voice cracked. "Miss Cameo killed in her own home. I'm being tossed out." She stuck her sharp chin in the air. "I'll leave, but I doubt that I'll be back."

"Suit yourself," I muttered as I walked past her. "Don't forget to tell your whereabouts to the deputy."

In the foyer I found what appeared to be controlled chaos. The front door was wide open. Outside, red lights flashed from the roofs of several patrol cars. Men were entering, while others were going out. Conversations, conducted in low tones, made the air hum. An empty gurney waited in the hall outside the ballroom doorway.

Cameo's guests were leaving. My staff was in the line to speak to the deputy at the door. Lois and Chris had their coats on and their purses open. A deputy had just finished giving Lew a pat down. My decorous deliveryman looked as if he'd inhaled a bug and couldn't find a polite way to hawk it up. His throat muscles constricted as he swallowed, but from the look on his red face, the taste of humiliation lingered.

I checked the foyer for DeeDee but didn't see her. Concerned, I asked Lois if she knew where she was.

"From what I gathered, her parents heard on their police scanner that officers had been sent to the Beauchamp mansion. When DeeDee finished her statement, which must be the shortest one on record, her father whisked her away."

I nodded, and told my staff I'd see them in the morning at the flower shop, then walked across to the staircase. A deputy barred my way.

"Sorry, ma'am," he said, "but no one goes upstairs without the sheriff's okay."

I spun on my heel, looking for Sid. He was in the middle of a huddle. I approached him with trepidation. The man had earned my respect, but that didn't mean I had to like him. He was arrogant, opinionated, and sometimes, completely insufferable. I tapped him on the arm. When he turned, I told him I'd be spending the night at the flower shop on the sofa in my office, but needed clothes from my room.

His only comment was a brittle snap of his fingers. Three deputies looked up. Sid pointed to me, to one of the officers, then to the second floor.

With the deputy at my heels, I climbed the staircase. I didn't know the young man accompanying me, but his adolescent appearance made me think he ought to be in junior high school, not dressed in a uniform with a gun strapped to his hip.

At the top of the staircase, I paused to look over the railing to the scene below. I ached in every joint. Pain throbbed behind my eyes with each beat of my heart. It seemed like an eternity had passed since I'd stood in this spot and lamented my troubles with a series of gusty sighs. What a difference a few hours can make. I moaned and gripped the oak railing tighter.

The deputy stepped forward and took my elbow in a firm grasp. I looked at him and caught the uneasiness on his face. "We'd better move along," he said in a pubescent squawk.

Poor kid. Did he think I was going to jump? I chuckled weakly. His hand tightened on my arm.

I sobered. Cameo was dead—murdered. I was being put out of my home, and it was being closed for an undetermined length of time. The Christmas open house was a week from tomorrow. My father wanted me to spend the holidays with him. I gave one last look over the railing to the muddy floor below.

Hmmm? Maybe jumping wasn't such a bad idea.

Chapter Eight

✿ An uncomfortable sofa bed and memories of an evening that had gone beyond bad should have kept me from sleeping, but when I woke up it was morning. Before I got out of bed I knew River City had been blanketed by a heavy snowfall during the night. There's a special kind of hush to the world when several inches of new-fallen snow cover the ground. The white powder would disguise shapes, blur boundaries, but it couldn't mask last night's tragedy.

I crept out of bed. My back was stiff from sleeping on the foldout sofa. My jaws ached. I figured that came from grinding my teeth in frustration. I made a trip to the bathroom, where I washed my face and brushed my teeth. In the workroom I started coffee brewing. I was irritated to feel hunger pangs gnawing at my stomach. Some people lose their appetites in the face of disaster, but not me. It seems even murder had me looking for a tasty treat.

I keep a few food items in a minifridge near the workroom. I opened the door to check on my choices for breakfast. Diet Coke. A can of Sprite. A moldy package of string cheese. Some salami, curled and dried around the edges. I shut the door. It was a waste of electricity to have the thing hooked up.

Electricity? I shuddered as my mind backpedaled to last

night. What had caused the ballroom lights to go out? Simon and Sylvia had been behind me as I talked about the Christmas trees. To look at Simon you wouldn't think he had a brain in his head, but he must surely be knowledgeable to be the director of the library. Could he have done some clever maneuvering to short-circuit a connection? Everett had asked about the house lights being switched off. Had he surmised the problem and decided to take advantage of it? Who had hurried past Trevor in the dark?

With more questions than answers, I went to my office and rummaged in my suitcase. I sat on the edge of the sofa bed and struggled into a pair of panty hose. I hate the damned things. Skintight to my calves. Tighter yet to my thighs. A royal pain across my broad butt.

Last night, with the deputy watching my every move, I'd hastily grabbed the first things I'd come to in my closet. I groaned as I surveyed the chosen results. The gray skirt I'd packed was too tight. The last time I'd worn the green slacks, a maverick meatball had escaped my fork and had left a stain on the left pant leg.

I picked up the skirt and squeezed into it. It wouldn't button. Even zipping it was an exercise in futility. I tucked the loose flaps into the waistband of my panty hose, which brought Topaz to mind. I wondered what she was feeling today. Did she mourn her mother's death?

My burgundy sweater was big and bulky, so it covered the three-inch gap at the waistband of my skirt. I slipped my feet into a pair of low-heeled shoes, combed my hair, then applied a light dash of makeup. After a spritz of cologne, I was ready to face the day, until I caught a glimpse of my reflection in a mirror I had hanging above my desk.

Lumpy. Bumpy. Curves in all the wrong places. I've been working hard, getting plenty of exercise. There was no mystery here. I was eating too much of the wrong things. I wake up with good intentions of getting back to my healthy way of eating. I come downstairs, armed with a firm determination, only to find Inez has whipped up some fabulous dish—breakfast pizza heaped with scrambled eggs, bacon, and sausage, or fluffy omelets stuffed with cheese, onions, and peppers.

My stomach growled with longing for Inez's flaky biscuits and cream gravy. I tugged at the tight material across my hips and sighed. I was going to have to take control over my eating, or I'd gain back all the weight I'd lost. This thought struck terror in my heart.

Dejected, I packed my nightclothes and other paraphernalia into my suitcase and folded the sofa bed away. I left the office and went to the back room, where I filled a watering can. This was going to be one of those days when I needed to finish the early-morning chores before I opened the shop and the phones started ringing. I left the main lights off in the front showroom so I could enjoy the peace and quiet.

Cameo's murder was uppermost in my mind. I examined all the clues until they were tattered fragments without a speck of glue to hold them together. As I checked the potted plants to see which ones needed a drink, I forced myself to concentrate on other things.

I loved the old house and the plans I had for making it into a boardinghouse, but this flower shop is my anchor in a turbulent world. I looked around me for a moment with fondness. When Carl died I'd been grateful to have my own business. It's as demanding as any family. Sometimes, I feel as if it needs my attention twenty-four hours a day. If I'm not arranging flowers, I'm doing bookwork, placing orders for supplies, looking ahead to the next holiday, and always, thinking of ways to keep the account figures black.

So far my hard work had paid off, but the purchase of all the Christmas merchandise had drained my bank account to an all-time low. I needed the open house to be successful so I could recoup some of my expenses. Granted, most of the stock was nonperishable, and I could pack it away until next year, but that wouldn't put money in the bank.

I paused at the front windows and looked out. Traffic was picking up. Four inches of snow covered the sidewalk. Lew could shovel it away when he arrived. Across the street Kelsay's Bar and Grill was coming to life. It would be so easy to hop across the street for a fried egg sandwich. I squared my shoulders, sucked in my stomach, and turned my back on temptation. To get my mind off of food, I gave the shop a once-over.

The building is long and narrow and divided into thirds. The front third is the showroom, with a counter separating it from the middle third—the design area. My employees and I each have workstations—tables with the tools of our trade within easy reach. When we're busy we aren't particularly concerned with hitting the trash cans under our tables. Most of the time the floor around us is littered with stems, broken flower heads, and leaf debris. I'd thought about building a partition so the customers couldn't see what a mess we make, but people seem mesmerized by our talents.

The back third of the building has a bathroom, the big walk-in cooler, a utility sink, and storage space for the floral supplies. Deliveries come and go from the back door, and my employees and I park in the alley.

The stateliness of the mansion had called for holiday decorations to follow a nostalgia theme. At the shop, I'd kept the displays high-tech and contemporary. I'd bought three mechanical elves, replaced their green-and-red costumes with stonewashed jeans, T-shirts, cowboy hats, and boots. Noah had rigged the elves so they would bebop to the Christmas music of Garth Brooks or Clint Black.

Silver and gold tinsel caught the light and glittered. Cinnamon and spruce potpourri in baskets released a spicy aroma. Fluffy snowflakes hung from the ceiling, and a string of bells tacked to the front door tinkled a welcome when anyone walked in. The final touch would be a shipment of poinsettias scheduled to arrive in a few days.

I sighed softly. Now, all I needed were paying customers.

I got my wish, or at least part of it: the customers placed orders. But not for Christmas merchandise. The news of Cameo's death spread through town like a hayfield on fire.

River City has always been a people's kind of town, with home-owned businesses, a sharing of the good and bad, and a general air of cooperation between the bureaucracy and the citizenship. Ordinarily, River City has a low crime rate, so murder was the hot topic of the day. Gossip sizzled since the victim had been a Beauchamp.

Sylvia had ignored Sid's request to use discretion when she reported her account of Cameo's death. A special edition of the *River City Daily* hit the streets at noon. Rumor had it that the staff had stayed up all night compiling information on the Beauchamp family. I wondered if Sylvia had used this article as an excuse to scrape back the flesh of Cameo's life so she could look for that skeleton in the closet. Or had the gossip columnist already made the discovery?

According to Lois, who'd taken the time to read the lengthy story, there wasn't any mention of a scandal, unless having that much money was against the law. I didn't have time to read the piece and draw my own conclusions. Between the floral orders coming into the shop and my staff and I having to leave one at a time to go to the sheriff's office to give our formal statements, we were kept busy.

During my turn I'd tried to get some information from Sid, but he'd been annoyingly tight-lipped. He wouldn't even tell me if he'd found the blackmail letters. I wanted to quiz my staff on their return, but Sid had stressed "no discussion." Though it pained me, I felt I had to set an example.

My flower shop has three phone lines. At two o'clock, I had to put one of them on hold. My part-time designers were either out of town or sick, so it was just Lois, Chris, and me filling today's orders while Lew braved the slick streets making deliveries.

Since I'd bought Cameo's house, was present at her murder, and owned a flower shop, customers asked for me when they called. It wasn't that I was so incredibly popular, but that they hoped to pick up a savory tidbit for the price of a bouquet. Eight times straight I had to stop what I was doing to take calls and field questions about a topic I'd been warned not to discuss.

After I hung up from the last call, I faced my staff, and declared, "If another person asks for me, get a name and a number, and tell them I'll call back later."

The phone immediately rang. Chris was closest. She answered, "The Flower Shop. Bretta?" She looked at me. I held up my hands and shook my head. "She's busy right now. May I ask who's calling?" Chris replaced the receiver. "She wouldn't give a name. She just hung up."

I shrugged. "No name. No return call."

The bells on the front door jingled. Lois had sat down to type a card. Lew was in back loading the delivery van. Chris said, "I'll go," and hurried up front. I was in a position to see what happened. If I could have saved Chris the humiliation, I'd have done it. But by the time the identity of the customer sank in, it was too late. Chris's grandmother, Matilda Bennett, had walked to the front counter, bypassing Chris like she was a piece of trash on the floor.

Mrs. Bennett has been a customer for years, but I can't say I know her. We don't travel in the same social circles. I do know she favors vanilla candles, red roses, and black towels in her guest bathroom. I'd been to her home on several occasions to oversee the flowers for some affair or another. A garden party in July wouldn't produce a bead of sweat on her genteel brow.

My calculations put Matilda in her seventies, but the woman looks fifty. Her hair is blond and appeared to be freshly done. She was dressed in a green-tweed suit with a cream-silk blouse. Her winter coat was fake fur, though she could well afford the real stuff, but one of her many, many causes was the protection of defenseless animals.

In a strangled voice, Chris said, "May I help you?"

Matilda didn't glance her way. She stared across the workroom at me, and said, "I prefer to have the owner, Mrs. Solomon, help me. She understands my taste in sympathy bouquets."

Chris's eyes welled with tears. Lois's head snapped up. I bit my lip and wondered how to handle the situation. I moved from my workstation and went to the front counter. I took an order form from the basket and picked up a pen. With the point poised above the paper, I said, "I'd be happy to help you, Mrs. Bennett, but Chris has excellent taste." I indicated an

arrangement of red gladiolas, white carnations, and blue stat-
ice she'd just designed. "In fact, she made this—"

Mrs. Bennett said, "In all my business transactions I'm
accustomed to the owner helping me, not one of the employees."

Chris gave her grandmother a mocking bow. "Of course,
you are. I'll go wash a few flower containers. Bleach and deter-
gent are what's in my blood. Your daughter—*my mother*—
taught me how to use a scrub brush. I wonder who taught
her?" she added, before hurrying away.

Not a hair of Matilda Bennett's sleek coiffure twitched, but
two tiny spots of color tinted her cheeks. "Mrs. Solomon, I
wish to order a floral tribute for my old friend, Cameo," she
said crisply.

I took the order and remained polite, but it was a struggle. I
wanted to rail at the woman for her treatment of her own
granddaughter. Chris never spoke of the troubles in her family. She didn't need to. Flower shops are notorious for being
gossip central. We know who's having a birthday, who's having a baby, and who's having an illicit affair if the sender is
careless enough to leave the envelope for the enclosure card
unsealed.

When Jillian Levine, Chris's mother, had passed away, the
old gossip had been resurrected. I'd heard the tale from all the
elderly matrons coming into the store. Jillian Bennett, debu-
tante, had gone against her mother's wishes and married
Hank Levine, a common workingman. It might have been a
juicy piece of gossip thirty years ago, but time had sucked the
tasty morsel dry. I knew Hank Levine as a conscientious businessman. His cleaning service is successful, and from what I
understand, his marriage had been filled with love.

I finished with Matilda Bennett, wished her a happy holiday, then waited until she'd left the shop before I went to find Chris. She was at the sink, up to her elbows in soapy water. "Are you okay?"

Chris shrugged. "I'm great." Her thin shoulders stiffened. "No, I'm not. I'm mad because I didn't tell the old hag what I think of her. She is such a snob. She can't see beyond the fact that my father cleans other people's messes. When I worked for him I was amazed at his list of clients—some of River City's best families and businesses. He might have to enter by the back door, but they trust him enough to give him a key."

Chris stopped to take a breath. "Did you know *she* didn't even come to her own daughter's funeral service? She couldn't forgive Mom for loving Dad, or for proving to the whole town that Matilda Bennett was wrong because she didn't agree to their marriage."

"What does your dad say?"

Chris chuckled weakly. "What he always says, 'Sticks and stones might break my bones, but Tilly can kiss my squeaky-clean ass.' "

I grinned. "I don't think she bends at the waist."

Chris took a quivery breath. "Thanks, Bretta. I—uh—I—"

I touched her shoulder. "We all have family problems. I have my own, and someday, when we aren't busy, I'll match you pain for pain." I left Chris and went to my workstation. Lois caught my eye and silently asked if Chris was okay. I wobbled my hands in a gesture that meant she was upset.

The phones finally slowed in their incessant ringing, and we were able to design in peace. I left Lois and Chris to finish the day's work while I took the basket of orders for Cameo's funeral to my office. I had to put together a supply list for all the flowers we would need. After separating the orders into two stacks—cut-flower bouquets into one, potted plants into another—I leaned back in my chair and rubbed my eyes.

Timing is everything—in life, death, and business. My bank balance could use the boost Cameo's passing had generated, but we would be hard-pressed to get the work done.

Absently, I reached for the mail and thumbed through the pile. Near the bottom was a slim envelope addressed in my father's familiar handwriting. I swallowed hard as I slit the seal, then skimmed the letter, reading only the words not the sentiment behind them. I shrugged my shoulders nonchalantly. Just a more involved invitation to visit him in Texas. No big deal.

I crumpled the letter and tossed it in the trash. I picked up my flower list, but found myself casting furtive glances at the trash. Dammit! Why couldn't I let it go? I rolled my chair over to the wastebasket and pulled the letter out. I didn't bother smoothing out wrinkles, but stuffed the ball of paper into my purse.

For the next hour I was on the phone dealing with suppliers. I studied my list a second and a third time, wondering if I should include another bunch of Sonia roses. The coral blossoms had been Cameo's favorite. I sighed and made another mark on the sheet of paper. It was only money, which was in short supply. If my father continued to press me to come to Texas, perhaps I could use my lack of finances as an excuse. Keep my reasons mundane not personal.

Lois called from the workroom. "Bretta? Telephone."

I needed a break, but I was thinking bathroom, not phone. I went into the workroom. "I don't want to talk to anyone. See if you can handle it."

"No choice," she said, holding the receiver out to me. "It's Sid."

"Oh." I took the phone from her, and said, "Hi, Sid."

Without any preliminary small talk, he asked, "When do you want your guest?"

"My what?"

"The coroner has released the body. Cameo is at Delaney's Funeral Home. Even as we speak, the old man, Bernard Delaney is working his magic on her. Bernard says he'll have the body ready to travel about two o'clock tomorrow afternoon. Does that suit you?"

I answered, "Why should it have to suit me?" but I knew what Sid meant. I'd forgotten. My world crumbled. My legs gave way, and I flopped into a nearby chair.

Sid's voice filled my ear. "I know you're having that wingding in a few days so I asked the coroner to speed things up as a personal favor to me. By two o'clock tomorrow, I'll have released the scene." He was silent a second before he asked, "Whatever possessed you to agree to her lying in state at the house?"

Before I could tell him Cameo's request had come weeks ago, he said, "I can see it now. The cash register'll be ringing. Right next to it'll be the old lady, lying stiff as starch in her casket, making a joyous addition to your Christmas open house."

Chapter Nine

🌿 I massaged my temples in a taut, circular motion. I hadn't actually forgotten my promise to Cameo. I'd simply neglected to think about it. A hundred other details had demanded my concentration.

Rapidly, I reviewed my time frame. Today was Friday. Cameo's body would be delivered tomorrow, Saturday. We could begin the lying in state on Sunday. I'd promised her two or three days depending on the turnout of mourners. I decided two days would have to be enough. Tuesday would be the private service. That would leave Wednesday and Thursday to get ready for the open house, which would begin at 10 A.M. on Friday. It could work—if Topaz would agree.

I looked up. Lois, Lew, and Chris watched me warily. I gave them a weak smile. "Another small glitch in the scheme of things."

"How small?" asked Lois, knowing me all too well. When I minimize, it usually means maximum trouble.

Seeing the glint in her eyes, I tried to smooth the rough terrain ahead. "When I bought the mansion, Cameo included several stipulations in the contract. Inez was to stay as housekeeper. Topaz's herb garden and caretaker's cottage were to be sectioned off from the sale of the main property. Cameo was to be buried in the family mausoleum located on what is now my land."

"There's a family cemetery?" asked Chris. "Where is it?"

"Behind the house," I said.

Lew pompously corrected me. "It's actually west of the house, Bretta. You can see part of it from the Jackson Memorial Cemetery."

Chris had finished sweeping the floor. She hung the dustpan on a nail. "I've always wondered why people refer to the River City Cemetery as Jackson. Where does that name come from? We're in Spencer County. The town's founder was Horton."

Seeing Chris's interest, Lew used his knowledge to try to impress. "As I understand it," he began in a tone Lois and I despise, "land was donated to the city by the Beauchamp family to honor the only male offspring, Jackson Beauchamp. Poor man developed a malady on the eve of his wedding and succumbed a few days later."

Under her breath, Lois said to me, "Malady? Succumbed? Why can't he simply say the man got sick and died?"

I elbowed Lois when Lew turned to me. "Bretta," he said, "you should look into getting a gardener or a landscaper to scope out your property. Behind the house is a small pond framed with weeping willow trees. There are lots of redbud and dogwood trees and a gigantic hard maple. The gardens, with their brick paths and that huge flagstone terrace, would make an ideal setting for receptions or even a wedding."

I didn't need Lew to point out the obvious to me. I'd already been doing some preliminary sketches, but I had no plans to hire a gardener. I'd reserved the pleasure of working in the gardens for myself. I longed to feel the sun on my shoulders, and the earth caked under my fingernails. What was that line?

"You can take the girl out of the country, but you can't take the country out of the girl." Then something Lew said registered. I didn't know there was a pond. It must be beyond the orchard.

"When were you at the back of my property?" I asked.

"I haven't been, but Jason showed me pictures. They were fantastic."

"Let's get back to these stipulations," said Lois. "I haven't heard anything that sounds like a small glitch."

"The last stipulation was that I allow Cameo to lie in state for a public viewing in the—uh—ballroom."

"Oh, brother," muttered Lew.

"I hope you mean the ballroom at the Cedar Crest Hotel?" said Lois.

"Nope. I mean *my ballroom*, the one with the eight Christmas trees."

Lois's jaw dropped in amazement, and then she burst out laughing. "Lord, Bretta, working for you is like chasing a butterfly in a minefield."

"The way I see it," said Lew, "is we'll have to remove the decorations and—"

"No way!" I interrupted. "We will not undo one thing."

Lew ran his hand over his shiny head. "Everyone in town will come. Morbid curiosity will bring them to see the house, the body, and the scene of the crime. The line of viewers could stretch a mile long."

I jumped up and paced the floor. "They can come in the front door, form a line in the foyer, file in the first door of the ballroom, go out the other door to the terrace and on to their cars."

"There's no sidewalk around there," said Lew.

Lois's blue eyes danced with mischief. "Forget that. I want to know where you're going to put the casket?"

"Don't even start," I groused. "Sid's already had a good laugh. I haven't had time to think everything through."

"If we take out the sideboard," mused Lew, "it's about the length of a casket. Move the patriotic tree farther down the room. There might be space."

"What about all the flower orders? Where are you going to put them?" asked Chris.

"She's right," said Lois. "We may pretend we're the only flower shop in town, but there'll be five other shops with orders to deliver, too."

I threw up my hands. "I don't know all the answers, but we'll have to work out something." I looked at the clock. "It's after five. You all go on home and rest up. I know we usually close at noon on Saturdays, but forget that. Tomorrow we'll have to fill the orders for Cameo's service. I'll call my suppliers and have them deliver the flowers first thing in the morning."

"Are you sleeping here again tonight?" asked Lois.

"Probably, but first I have some errands to run."

Chris and Lew got their coats and headed for the alley. I heard Lew telling Chris about a new restaurant that had opened on the south side of town. Chris said, "I have plans. Sorry." She hurried out the door. Lew sighed forlornly and followed, with his feet dragging.

Once the door had closed behind them, I said to Lois, "Lew isn't getting to first base with Chris, is he?"

"He isn't even on the team. What errands are you doing?"

I shrugged. "A bite to eat, then perhaps I'll buy a new dress or maybe go to a movie to take my mind off—"

Lois snorted. "This is me you're talking to. You've got something planned, and it isn't a movie or shopping."

My tone was droll. "But you will buy the idea that I'm going to eat, right?"

Lois gave me a long, hard look. "If I didn't have Erin's Christmas pageant tonight, I'd go with you to make sure you aren't up to something."

I looked at her innocently. "What could I be up to?"

After I made my phone calls and locked the shop, I stopped at an outlet mall to buy two new skirts and a sweater, all a size larger than what I'd been wearing. When I saw my reflection in the dressing room's triple mirror, I resorted to old habits. I drove to a fast-food restaurant and quickly parked. Inside I sought solace in my favorite comfort food—a double cheese-burger and a chocolate milk shake.

Once again in my car, I reached in my purse for my keys and touched my father's letter. Anger filled my stomach and went to war with the food. I grabbed the keys, started the engine, and roared out of the parking lot. I pressed hard on the accelerator, hoping to leave my thoughts behind, but they rode snipping and snarling at my side.

I might have been more charitable toward my father if I didn't carry a daily reminder of what his leaving had done to me. I laid the blame of my weight problem squarely at his feet. I'd been a scrawny child when he crept away in the dead of night. His farewell note had been simple: "Lillie," he'd written to my mother, "farming isn't the life for me. When I'm settled I'll send you an address, and you can divorce me. The truck is at the River City bus depot."

At eight years old, I couldn't comprehend the radical change my life was taking. When Mom had asked a neighbor to take her into River City to retrieve the pickup, I'd thrown a fit, not speaking to her for days. I knew if Mom brought that truck home, I'd never see Daddy again. How would he get back to us?

I'd kept a vigil at the end of our driveway, trusting that soon I'd catch sight of him hurrying down the road. Tears burned my eyes as I pictured that heartbroken little girl waiting hopefully, helplessly in the sun. Finally, I'd turned to Mom, begging her to make me understand why my father had left. If she had answers, she hadn't shared them with me. Instead she'd funneled my grief to food.

She had soothed and cajoled me with cakes and pies, cookies and treats. At first I ate to please her. Later, it became a habit to grab a snack when I was confused or needed consoling. My thirty-seven years of compulsive eating are as integral a part of me as the blue eyes and dark hair that I'd inherited from my father.

I made the five-mile drive to Topaz's home in record time. The caretaker's cottage sat east of the mansion and was a charming structure, painted white with shutters a pale robin's-egg blue. Window boxes were filled with cut pine boughs. A dried herbal wreath, tied with a red-velvet ribbon, hung on the door. The porch light was on.

While I waited for Topaz to answer my knock, I turned in the direction of the mansion. From Topaz's front stoop, trees shielded the bottom half of the house, but lights shone from the second floor and attic. Sid and his men were still there. With a sigh, I turned to knock again, but the door opened.

"You're earl—" said Topaz. "Oh, Bretta. Hello."

"If you have time, I'd like to talk to you."

She glanced past me to the drive. "Sure. Come on in. I was fixing supper." She swung the door wider, releasing a rush of tantalizing aromas.

When Topaz stepped back so I could enter, I saw she was carefully groomed. She wore a denim shirtwaist dress, hose, and flat-heeled dress shoes. Her hair was neatly combed into the knot on her head, but she'd allowed little curls to escape. They softened the severity of the style and framed her face becomingly. Her lips were the color of cranberries, her cheeks dusted with peach blush. She was attractive and well-groomed, a description that was out of character for the woman I'd come to know.

"If this is a bad time—" I began. It was evident she was expecting company.

"No, not at all. We probably need to talk."

I stepped across the threshold into one big room that was an immaculate arrangement of polished wood, vaulted ceiling, braided rugs on a hardwood floor, and a toasty crackling fire in a limestone fireplace. The kitchen was on my right, and a pot steamed on the stove. A staircase at the far end of the room led to an open loft, where I could see the corner of a quilt-covered bed. Beams overhead held bundles of dried herbs. Their musty odor filled the room with an earthiness that blended with woodsmoke and the contents of the simmering pot.

"How lovely," I said. "What a beautiful, cozy place."

"I like it. I never felt at home at the mansion. Too much space, yet nowhere for me to work on my herbal remedies." She gestured to a doorway. I stepped closer and saw the opening led to a ten-foot-by twelve-foot greenhouse attached to the back of the house.

"This time of year I grow culinary herbs—chives, oregano, rosemary, and such in the greenhouse. My medicinal herbs do better outside, but now they're winter dormant." She pointed to the beams. "I've collected plenty over their growing season to make my decoctions and tinctures."

"My knowledge of this branch of horticulture is pretty limited. What do those terms mean?"

"Decoction is extraction by boiling herbs with water and saving the liquid. Tincture is extraction by soaking the herbs in an alcohol solution."

"Herbs are a hot commodity these days. At the flower shop I've been asked if I have pots of herbs to send to someone in the hospital, but frankly, I'm leery of picking and eating something when I'm not sure what it's supposed to do."

"I've played with herbal remedies all my life. They're wonderful restoratives. Using nature's way to heal is as old as man. I cultivate all my herbs, but I agree, you have to know what you're doing."

Topaz pointed to a collection of bottles sitting on wooden shelves near the fireplace. Their colors—cobalt blue, emerald green, and amber—glowed with the firelight behind them.

"Some dosages have to be restricted. I label everything, but sometimes the paper becomes loose or the writing fades. As a precaution, I use those special bottles, which are more valuable than anything I can put in them. They date back to the early eighteen hundreds when candles or kerosene lamps were used for illumination. In poor light or even in the dark those ridges molded into the glass alerted the user to beware of the contents."

I nodded to show Topaz I was listening, but my attention was on a portrait hanging above the mantel. The man was handsome, dignified, and elegantly dressed. From the angle where I was standing, his eyes seemed to pierce mine. His hair was dark, his jaws covered with a heavy beard. A whimsical smile softened what could have been a very stern face.

Topaz had warmed to a subject that was close to her heart. "—found the bottles in the attic. Mother threw a fit when she learned I'd dumped the contents down the drain and was using the antique bottles for my medicinal herbal remedies. I don't actively practice healing anyone but myself. However, some of my remedies have to be guarded against overdose. I wanted those ridged bottles as a precaution. Anyone who picks one up would know that she's holding a dangerous potion in her hand."

Since I rarely crave stems and leaves, and anything I ingest comes with a secure label on the outside, I solemnly nodded before gesturing to the portrait. "He's a handsome man. His eyes are riveting."

"That's my father," said Topaz proudly. "Hiram Sinclair."

"Cameo said he died before you were born. I'm sorry."

"So am I. My life might have been different if I'd had a father around. I needed someone in my corner, and I like to think that he'd have been in mine." She studied me. "Mother said your father left when you were eight. I know that must have been rough for you, but at least you had a few years with him. I understand he lives in Texas—a phone call away."

I rubbed my hands briskly together. "The fire feels good this evening. It's getting colder."

Topaz smiled sympathetically. "Forgiveness doesn't come cheap, does it? The price is usually the cost of our pride. I was raised on pride and force-fed family obligations until I wanted to choke." She waved a hand. "You don't want to talk about it. I can appreciate that." She nodded to a table set for two. "Have a seat. I'll just give this pot a quick stir."

I sat down and said, "I won't stay long. I don't want to interrupt your evening." It was an opening I hoped she'd fill with information. Was Topaz involved with a man? Did he account for the way she looked tonight? Or was she expecting a friend to help while away the evening after her mother's death? I waited in vain for an explanation. Topaz stirred the pot but was silent.

"It sure smells great," I said, then afraid she might think I was angling for an invitation, I added, "even on a full stomach."

"Red beans cooked with Polish sausage and ham, and seasoned with rosemary, coriander, and a sprinkling of parsley. I'll serve the beans over a bed of rice. It's a recipe a special friend taught me." She leaned against the counter and stared at me. "I guess we'd better get down to business. I know why you're here," she said quietly. "It's about Mother."

I nodded, assuming she meant the funeral service.

Topaz sighed softly. "Mother died prematurely, and I contributed to her death. I'm guilty as hell, and it's eating me alive."

Chapter Ten

I'd told myself I wasn't going to get involved with solving Cameo's murder. I could speculate to myself all I wanted, but I wasn't going to question any of the suspects. Sid's face flashed in my mind, and I quickly asked Topaz, "Is this something you need to tell the sheriff?"

"I did not wrap the Christmas lights around Mother's neck," she declared. "There are other ways of shortening someone's life without physically attacking her. I disappointed Mother hundreds of times. You heard what she said about my ancestry not mattering to me?"

"I heard, but that hardly—"

"Maybe not, but I'll carry my guilt until I die." Topaz gestured to her heavy frame. "My size was a disappointment to Mother. I take after my great-great-great-grandmother Amethyst, who was a large woman. Mother could have accepted my portliness if I'd made an attempt to dress with style, or if I'd been the least bit congenial. No matter what request she made, I wanted the opposite. What hurt her most was my total lack of interest in social or family obligations.

"I never married, though she all but put a price tag on my head so I'd attract some would-be suitor. Years ago, she forced me to leave River City, hoping I'd find a mate." Topaz's eyes softened at a memory. I waited to see if she was going to share it. Again, she stayed silent, keeping her thoughts to herself.

"It's difficult living up to other people's expectations," I said. "Sometimes you have to forget what they want and do what's best for you."

"I look back and wonder what I should have changed. At the time everything I did seemed right for me. My own company suits me. I've never needed a man to complete my life. I once read that parents and families are at the root of more psychological pain than any other aspect in our lives. I remember seizing that knowledge and placing blame on Mother. It took some of the burden off of me, and I could go ahead with what I wanted. Most of the time I didn't give her needs a thought."

This kind of discussion would accomplish nothing. I'd already skirted the issue of my father with Topaz. But I couldn't keep the words in his letter from flitting through my mind. "Forgive me." "Time to make amends." "Get to know my little girl." "Spend Christmas with me in Texas."

A mature woman of forty-five should be able to assess the situation and make a decision. I blamed the holidays for putting a crimp in my judgment. This was the time of year for sharing, giving, and being with people you love, none of which I could apply to my father.

Topaz murmured, "My grandmother, Opal, used to say I was a stubborn weed in the family garden." A tiny smile tugged the corners of her lips. "In my garden, a weed is only a misplaced flower. Even weeds have a purpose in the scheme of things."

Was I being stubborn in regard to my father? Didn't he deserve the opportunity to tell me his side of the story? I hardened my heart. No. He'd had thirty-seven years to talk, but he'd chosen to remain silent until now.

In my present frame of mind, the topic of murder was safer than exploring family connections. My good intentions to leave this investigation in the hands of the proper authorities flew out the window. I asked, "How much do you know about Cameo being blackmailed?"

"Nothing. She never said a word about it to me."

"Do you have any idea what it could have been about?"

Topaz didn't pause to think. "No, I have no idea."

"At the dinner table Cameo said the information had been safeguarded for more than a century. Do you remember stories she might have told you that would give us a clue?"

"Mother lived for her heritage. She doted on the lives of past generations. If there had been a scandal, she'd gloss it over. She'd mull it to the point that whatever was done would've been the honorable thing. In Mother's mind, recounting the facts to anyone would be unfair to her ancestors because unfavorable conclusions could be drawn."

What information had Cameo been willing to share with me that her own daughter didn't have? "Somewhere there's an account of what happened, or the blackmailer wouldn't have gotten hold of it."

"I'm sure you're right. Mother was cunning. As she pointed out, all the guests have access to records, or she wouldn't have invited them." She took a deep breath, and said, "I suppose we'll have to look in the ancestral mini-bibles."

My interest perked up. "Ancestral mini-bibles?"

Topaz grimaced. "Palm-sized journals kept by all the Beauchamp women. I call them the bibles because Mother worshiped them."

Cameo had urged me to keep a journal. I thrust that thought away, and asked, "Do you have them?"

Topaz laughed bitterly. "Are you kidding? Mother

wouldn't have trusted those precious books to anyone, especially me. I didn't have the right attitude. Outside of the blood in my veins, I have little to connect me with my ancestors, other than my name—Topaz Beauchamp-Sinclair."

Scornfully, she singsonged, "Amethyst. Pearl. Garnet. Opal. Cameo. Topaz. The Beauchamp *gems*. Mother never wore all those rings. She usually kept them in special boxes in her cedar chest. But that last evening, while she was dressing, I heard her talking to herself, like she was performing some ritual. Amethyst/tenacity. Pearl/duplicity. Garnet/courage. Opal/wisdom." Topaz rolled her eyes. "If Mother had showed half as much interest in the living as she did in the dead, maybe things would have been different."

"Back to these journals. Where are they?"

"I haven't a clue."

"Would Inez know?"

Topaz shook her head emphatically. "No. Mother appreciated Inez's devotion, but Inez was a paid employee. Mother would never have divulged anything so personal. Most assuredly, she would never trust her with something as sacred as the journals."

"If Cameo felt that strongly about them, she must have taken them with her when she moved out of the mansion."

"I haven't found them. Today, after the sheriff interrogated me, two deputies escorted me to Mother's safety-deposit box and later to her apartment. The bank box held insurance papers, a few pieces of jewelry, a copy of her will and burial information. At the apartment, I got Mother's clothes together to take to the funeral home. The deputies did another search for the blackmail letters. They found nothing. I looked for the journals. They weren't there."

"Did you tell the sheriff about the journals?"

Her chin shot up. "I'm not volunteering any information. He's made it clear that I'm the number one suspect because family is always at the top of the list in a murder. I'm the only one left," she said, then grew still.

"What is it?" I asked. "Have you thought of something?"

Topaz swallowed. "No—no. It's nothing. I was just thinking about Mother. She wanted me to have a girl so badly to carry on tradition. I was to name her Sapphire."

Sapphire? The hairs on my arms tingled. Cameo had told me, "You should wear more sapphire blue, Bretta." Another time, "Bretta, that shade of sapphire blue is most becoming."

I wanted to pursue this, but Topaz was sneaking a peek at her watch. I was running out of time and had questions concerning other matters. Quickly, I asked, "If Cameo received three blackmail letters, but the blackmailer didn't know where she'd moved, how did she get them?"

"I probably took them to her. Her mail was delivered to me here, and I passed it on to her."

"I don't suppose you remember seeing them?"

"It's not a matter of remembering. I simply didn't pay any attention. Mother rarely left the house, and she disliked talking on the phone. She received lots of mail, mostly requests for money or organizations asking permission to use her name to help raise funds for some project or other."

"That night at the house, you said, 'May Mother's reign end soon.' What did you mean?"

Topaz turned and switched one of the knobs on the stove. "I saw the look on your face. And no, I wasn't wishing her dead. I just got so tired of her dictatorial ways. I was errand runner, nursemaid, taxi driver, and message taker. Mother and I didn't have a typical mother/daughter relationship. We never sipped tea or reminisced. She knew I wasn't interested in her stories about the ancestral gems, and I knew she could care less that the parsley had worms or the rue wasn't growing as well as it should."

Topaz gave me a quizzical look. "Didn't you wonder why everyone stayed for dinner after Mother insulted them in the library?"

"I have to admit I was surprised."

Topaz chuckled. "I enjoyed it. They had it coming. She had them over a barrel because they didn't dare anger the *queen*. Each had a private stake in keeping her happy."

"You said something along those lines after Cameo was— uh—"

"Murdered," supplied Topaz. "You can say it. One of them killed her. I'm just not sure which one."

"What were these private stakes?"

"Everett Chandler has been begging Mother for artifacts from the Beauchamp estate for the museum. Simon Gallagher wants a new wing for the library. The man is obsessed with giving River City an intellectual standing. A few weeks ago, that Whitaker woman wrote something in the paper that infuriated Mother. She took her complaint directly to the publisher, and Sylvia was severely reprimanded. I imagine Sylvia stayed for spite. As for that lawyer, McGuire, he'd proposed that Mother set up some sort of trust fund or endowment for the city. Of course, he'd volunteered to do the paperwork if she'd name him as executor."

"And Jason? Why did he stay?"

Topaz's face softened. "He's a good boy—talented with his camera. His family should be very proud of him. I'm sure he stayed merely out of curiosity. History intrigues him." She darted a quick glance at me. "I gave him permission to photograph the grounds. I should have told Mother, but knew she'd never agree. I had no idea she'd seen him." She licked her lips. "I wonder why she never said anything to me?"

Abruptly, Topaz turned and looked at the clock on the stove. I took the hint and stood up. "I'd better go. I only came by to ask you about Cameo's funeral arrangements." I outlined the timetable that would work for me.

Topaz nodded. "If that suits you, it suits me, too. Would you fix the spray of flowers for her casket and send me the bill? You know better than I do what she would have wanted." She gave me a tight smile. "Mother liked you very much. Had she lived longer, I think you would have become to her what I never could be."

Tears sprang to my eyes. I didn't miss the fact that of the two of us, I was the emotional one. "That's a nice thing to say," I murmured.

Topaz ruined it by adding, "Mother was ingenious when it came to finagling people to do her bidding."

I had no trouble believing that statement. "I keep thinking about those journals. If you don't have them, and Cameo wouldn't have trusted them to Inez for safekeeping, then where are they? They must be in the mansion. But if they were that important to her, why didn't she take them with her when she moved out?"

"Make no mistake about it. Those journals were very important to Mother. I'm sure she carried them back and forth——" Topaz broke off and turned away to busily check the temperature of the burner under the pot of beans.

"Carried them back and forth? From where? Her apartment to your cottage? From her apartment to——" Now it was my turn to stop. There was only one place on earth that meant anything to Cameo. I hazarded a guess. "Last night wasn't Cameo's first trip back to the mansion, was it?"

Reluctantly, Topaz faced me, but she didn't meet my gaze. "She's been back a few times," she admitted.

"When?"

"During the day, when you were at the flower shop."

"What did she do?"

"I never stayed. I'd get her in the front door, and Inez would take over." Topaz sighed. "Didn't you think it odd that my mother left so many personal items behind?"

"Not really. Cameo said you would go through everything in due time. I could store what was in my way in the attic."

Topaz shook her head. "Mother left things because she was coming back."

The pulse at the base of my throat picked up its rhythm. "Coming back?" I echoed.

"Her plans were to offer you the rent money for *all the rooms* when you completed the renovations for your boarding-house." Topaz flashed me a smile of pity. "On paper you might have owned the mansion, but Cameo Beauchamp-Sinclair was returning to be queen of the estate. There was no way she would abandon her home while there was breath in her body."

Chapter Eleven

❀ I made my excuses and left the cottage. I sat in my car, warming the engine before I started back to town. Discovering Cameo's hidden agenda regarding the mansion had knocked the props out from under me. I thought she'd trusted me with her most prized possession—the mansion. It hurt to learn that she expected to waltz back in and oversee my care-taking skills.

How would I have handled Cameo's plan, once the time came and there were rooms to rent? Would I have gone along with her, just as I'd gone along with all the stipulations she'd asked for when I bought the house? At the time none of them seemed out of line. She had looked at me with kind eyes, had smiled a gentle smile, and I'd been charmed. She was the grandmother I'd never known.

There it was again. Family. I couldn't get away from it. I put the car into reverse and backed down the lane to the main highway. A car popped over the hill from the direction of River City. I waited for the vehicle to pass, but it slowed. The driver put on his turn signal for Topaz's driveway. I maneuvered out onto the road, giving the other car plenty of space. As my lights flashed across the windshield, I saw Jason behind the wheel. If he recognized me, he didn't give a sign. He pulled up the lane.

I welcomed new thoughts to fill my brain on the trip to town. A table set for two. Topaz's tender smile at the mention of Jason. Her praise of his talents. Giving him permission to take photos of the property without telling Cameo. It was a strange deal. Idly, I wondered if they were having an affair.

In my ear, Carl's voice admonished, "No facts, Babe, all supposition."

A smile teased my lips. "I miss you, sweetheart." If I couldn't have Carl with me in body, I loved having his spirit close to me. It had been weeks since he'd "spoken" to me, or maybe I'd been too busy to hear his voice.

"I wish it was spring, Carl," I said aloud.

"Why's that?"

I waved a hand at the darkness outside the car window. "In winter there's such a desolation to the leafless trees and stark landscape. I want sun and tons of flowers blooming their heads off."

"You're thinking of the Beauchamp gardens?"

My tone held a light rebuke. "Carl, they're the *Solomon* gardens. That place is mine—ours—because I used your life insurance money to make the down payment."

"Don't take offense, Babe, but you've hardly spent time looking over *our* investment."

"Yeah. I hate it that Lew knows more about the land beyond the gardens than I do. Even Jason knows more. Wonder why he wants pictures of overgrown gardens?" I chuckled suggestively. "He sure wasn't there to take pictures of the grounds tonight."

I waited for a touch of Carl's innate wisdom, but he was silent. I shrugged and concentrated on my driving. I'd passed the city limits, and traffic had picked up. I entered River City on Chestnut, traveled about eight blocks, and then made a right onto Millstone Road. The main thoroughfares had been plowed, and the pavement was damp. I gave scant thought to checking into a motel. As if my car knew no other route, it took me down Hawthorn to the flower shop.

I parked in front and had my key out to open the door when I heard my name called. I turned and was surprised to see Sylvia Whitaker beckoning to me from across the street.

"I'm busy, Sylvia," I called.

"I want to talk to you."

I waited until a car had passed. "Will tomorrow be soon enough?" I asked hopefully.

She flashed me a friendly smile. "I'd rather take care of this tonight, if you don't mind?"

I muttered a word that normally isn't in my vocabulary. I crammed the flower-shop key back in my purse, then picked my way around the hills of snow in the gutters and leaped a slushy puddle. I waited for two cars to pass before I crossed the street.

Sylvia was dressed to the teeth—red boots, red coat, red-leather gloves, and a red beret on her curly dark hair. Eyes, wide and alert, watched me from behind her red-frame glasses. I pointed to her outfit. "All dressed up and nowhere to go?"

"Been there, done that. I'm ready for a drink." She nodded to the bar and grill behind her. "Join me?"

I wasn't much of a drinker, but Kelsay's served a great hot chocolate. I agreed, and we went inside. The décor is dedicated to fifties memorabilia. Framed photos of the Coasters, Perry Como, Fats Domino, The Platters, Frank Sinatra, and Johnny Mathis lined the walls. Forty-fives played on the old-time jukebox that flashed neon pink, green, and blue. The only concession to the holiday season was an aluminum Christmas tree sitting on the end of the bar. The branches had been decorated with miniature beer cans and candy canes. Tables were strewn down the middle of the room. High-backed booths hugged the walls.

Sylvia headed for an empty alcove, making eye contact with a waitress as we sailed past. We shrugged out of our coats, then slid onto the bench seats across from each other. Pat Boone was crooning "April Love." Sylvia's eyes were closed, her shoulders swayed to the dreamy beat. The waitress stood at my elbow.

"What'llyouhave?" she asked, running her question together so that it sounded like one word. When Sylvia didn't answer, I said, "A cup of hot chocolate and forget the whipped cream."

With her eyes still closed, Sylvia murmured, "The usual, Maureen, but add a slice of orange. I need some vitamin C to combat this weather."

Pat finished his song, and Elvis rocked his way into the room. Sylvia's eyes flew open. She waved her hand toward the jukebox. "I never cared for that guy. After last night, I like him even less."

I raised my eyebrows, but shifted uneasily. Surely, Sylvia and I hadn't made the same comparison. "Last night? Elvis?"

Sylvia grinned, revealing teeth dingy from nicotine. "McGuire," she said, digging in her purse. She brought out a pack of Salems. "Don't tell me you didn't notice the resemblance? He's a good-looking man, but I wouldn't trust him to help my grandmother across the street." She snapped her lighter into a flame and applied it to the cigarette. Inhaling deeply, she talked, puffing smoke out the corner of her mouth. "He may look shy and innocent, but I'd give you odds, he'd pinch Granny's butt before she'd taken more than a dozen steps."

"Maybe, but I think Trevor McGuire is more interested in someone younger than your granny."

"Like your designer? What's her name?"

"I don't think Chris was impressed."

"Chris Levine," murmured Sylvia. "The newspaper could use her father's cleaning service. I work with a bunch of slobs. Empty soda cans leaving marks on the tables. Candy wrappers littering the floor. Coffee cups creating a mess if you turn one over."

She's stalling, I thought. There are three topics of conversation that crop up when someone is wasting time—weather, work, or health problems. I knew I was right when Sylvia said, "—never liked driving in it, but snow is better than ice. I remember the time I drove from KC to St. Louis. I-70 was a sheet of ice. I got behind a highway truck that was spreading salt. My car was a mess, but at least I—"

Sylvia stopped as Maureen approached with our order. The waitress set our drinks on napkins, then waved the ticket. "Whogetsit?

"Mine," said Sylvia, tucking the piece of paper under her purse. "This is my treat." Maureen moved off. Sylvia swallowed a quarter of her drink, then crushed out her cigarette. "I've been watching for you," she said. "I parked out front and waited to see if you'd come back to your shop. From what I hear your shop is getting a bunch of orders for Cameo's funeral."

I picked up my spoon and stirred the chocolate. "No surprise there. It's called commerce, Sylvia."

"Big money in death," she commented. Before I could reply,

she hurried on. "I also understand you agreed to Cameo lying in state at the mansion. Is the service going to be on Tuesday?"

"Is that why you called me over? To find out when Cameo's funeral is going to be? You can forget coming. It's going to be a private service."

"I wondered if *her grace* would be buried by the time of your open house. Tuesday should work. It gets your butt out of a sling."

I tapped the spoon sharply on the cup before I laid it carefully on the napkin. "Don't lose any sleep over my affairs, Sylvia. Everything's under control."

"Like the lights in the ballroom?" she asked. "I checked into that Duncan man's reputation. He's a top-notch electrician. If he says the train didn't blow the fuse, I'm for taking his word."

"I never doubted it."

"So," she drawled, "what blew it? Or better yet, who? Who knew what to turn on to suck enough juice to blow the fuse to set up the opportunity for murder?"

Apparently that was a rhetorical question since she didn't give me the chance to respond. She tapped her red-tipped fingernails on her glass. "I've been doing some speculating based on facts. It was your house. You knew the lights could go. You staged the presentation in the ballroom. You were—"

I stopped her cold. "I was in the ballroom. My whereabouts were known to everyone."

Sylvia lifted a red-clad shoulder. "I didn't say you pulled it off by yourself. The house was crawling with your employees."

" 'Pulled it off?' " I repeated the words, then froze as the full realization of what she wasn't saying sank in. I stared her in the eye. "Do you think I'm involved in Cameo's death?"

Sylvia's eyebrows arched inquiringly above the red-rimmed glasses, but she didn't say a word.

I could have poked a hundred holes in her theory, as well as punched her lights out. But I wasn't going to waste my breath or energy. "Why are you telling me this?"

"I'm doing an investigative report."

"Bull! You're a society gossip. Who else have you told this ridiculous story to?"

"The sheriff was interested. So were several other people I've interviewed."

I mentioned slander, but Sylvia laughed. "Bretta, get real. I've been a journalist for years. I know what I can and can't say." She leaned closer. "I have information that will put you at the top of the sheriff's list of suspects. I want your side of events. Tell me, and I'll keep quiet, at least for now."

Scathing words burned my tongue, but I choked them back. "Let me get this straight. You think I know something, and if I confide in you, you're willing to stay quiet about this other fantastic bit of information?" When she nodded, I said, "Damn, Sylvia, correct me if I'm wrong, but that sounds like blackmail. You do it very well. It must come with practice." I pulled three dollars out of my purse and flung them on the table. "I'll pay for my own drink. I want nothing from you, and you'll get nothing from me."

When I made a move to leave, she grabbed my arm. Her eyes narrowed, her mouth was taut with anger. "I'm sick to death of dealing with River City's social fiddle-faddle. This story is mine, and I'm not going to let some pissant florist, who thinks she's the great detective, screw me out of it. Don't get in my way, Bretta."

I shook off Sylvia's hand. "You'll do or say anything to get a story, won't you? All this garbage was a bid to get me to talk, to blab away, and later, you'll sort it all out and put together some fabricated tale. Topaz said Cameo complained to your publisher about one of your columns. What upset her, Sylvia? What did you write?"

"Don't mess with me, Bretta," she warned again. "I've got my eye on a syndicated column, and solving this murder could cinch it."

"Your brand of journalism is as yellow as pee in the snow, Sylvia. I wish you luck, especially if it means you'll be leaving town. River City would be better off without you."

"I'm going to solve this murder, Bretta."

As I slid out of the booth, a Conway Twitty song came on the jukebox. I cocked my head toward the music. "Listen to what's playing, Sylvia, 'It's Only Make Believe.' I couldn't have said it better myself."

Chapter Twelve

❀ I found a motel room downtown. I checked in with the clothes on my back and my mall purchases in a sack. I showered, then washed my undies, giving them a good wringing before I hung them across the towel bar. After leaving Sylvia in Kelsay's, I'd wanted to put as much distance between us as possible. The flower shop was out because Sylvia would know where I was.

Since I couldn't circle the city streets all night, I'd gone to the motel. Fifty bucks for a few gallons of water and a place to lay my head was a rip-off, but I'd made that decision. Sleep was impossible. Food was an alternative, but that meant getting dressed again and going out into the cold.

At 5 A.M., I gave up all attempts at trying to sleep. I put on my damp underwear and one of my new skirts and a sweater and checked out.

I bought two jelly doughnuts from a local bakery. The cashier's comment, "We haven't seen you for a while, Mrs. Solomon," didn't help my disposition. My mood was dangerous to my diet, to anyone who crossed my path. My head throbbed. My eyes burned from lack of sleep, and I had a helluva day to get through.

I stepped out of the doughnut shop, glanced across the street, and thought I was seeing things. Sylvia had been on my mind constantly since the night before. To look up and see her walking along the sidewalk fueled my fury. I'd whiled away the long night composing numerous clever, but cutting, remarks that I should've made to her. Now was my chance. I opened my mouth to call to her but stopped. Something about her looked off kilter, or in this case off-color.

It felt like the middle of the night. The sun was still snoozing. The streetlights were the only illumination. On my side of the street, I lagged behind, giving Sylvia the evil eye. She wore a taupe coat, brown scarf and boots. There wasn't a speck of red anywhere on her person. Dark gloves covered her red fingernail polish. She kept her head down, but her quick, decisive gait was a dead giveaway to her identity.

I was more than curious as to where Sylvia was going before six in the morning on this street. We were on Oak, one of the four main arteries that led straight to the heart of River City's governmental district. The quadrangle covered four city blocks. The five structures were situated like the dots on a die. Four buildings—post office, city hall, the sheriff's department, and the public library— encircled the three-story limestone county courthouse. In between were slots for parking, planters, trees, and ornate wrought-iron lampposts capped with white globes that glowed like full moons in the frosty morning air.

It was too early for any of the offices to be open, unless she was headed for the sheriff's department. I hurried to keep up with her, clutching my sack of doughnuts in one hand, my purse in the other. Tailing someone was a new experience. All my astute knowledge came from watching television. I darted from tree trunk to tree trunk, lamppost to lamppost. I crouched behind banks of piled snow and leafless bushes, peering at my quarry like I knew what I was doing. Sylvia never looked back. She crossed the parking lot, then walked around the public library to a side entrance and went in.

I scurried after her, but hesitated at the door. What to do, what to do? Was Sylvia having a rendezvous with Simon? Or did she have something else on her devious mind? I was too curious to let it go. I eased the door open and stepped inside. Sylvia was nowhere in sight, but I heard voices coming from down the hall.

I skulked along the shadowy corridor, skirting a puddle of light that shone from one of the open office doors. The middle of the corridor gave me excellent eavesdropping advantage, but it was too vulnerable a position to maintain. I slithered into the recessed alcove next to the drinking fountain. I'd be up shit creek if someone decided he needed to wet his whistle. I twisted my neck around the corner and strained my ears. Sylvia was speaking, but she must have been pacing because her words came to me disjointed and muddled.

"—rid of file. Might—look bad—won't know I was—"

"I can't do that," said Simon.

"—have to but—remind you—owe me."

"It will look suspicious."

"—fish has it, too. Office—link is all—check—done."

"I don't like this."

"—help or I'll—next column."

Sylvia's heels clunked across the floor. At the door, she paused to say, "Don't waste any time. Solomon is persistent, as well as a pain in the ass. She might come snooping today. I want it done, Simon."

He must have nodded his agreement because she sounded triumphant. "I'll talk to you later." She started to leave, then added, "And the next time the phone rings, pick the damned thing up, or at least get an answering machine. I don't like getting up early, and this anonymous shade of brown makes me feel like a bran muffin."

Sylvia's heels clattered down the corridor and out the door. I followed her, casting a quick peek at Simon as I crept past. He sat at his desk, his head in his hands, his shoulders sloped dejectedly. What did Sylvia have on him? I wondered as I let myself out the door.

Sylvia was gone, but I took my time getting back to my car. I wanted her to have plenty of opportunity to leave the neighborhood. Why was Simon cooperating with Sylvia? What file did Sylvia want him to get rid of? And who the hell was Fish? What did he or she have to do with anything? Somehow this tied in with Cameo's death because Sylvia figured I'd be snooping.

I wasn't going to disappoint her.

At the flower shop, I made a pot of coffee. When it was done, I poured a cup and took it to my office. I turned on the small desk lamp, leaving the shop lights off. I pulled the River City directory from under a stack of magazines. I thumbed to the F's and found five Fish families' phone numbers. I chuckled dryly. Sleep deprivation brought out the worst in me. None of the Fish listed stirred my memory.

I flipped to the S's and dialed Topaz's phone number. Gardeners have an "early rising" gene so I didn't think twice about calling her. She answered on the second ring. Her evening spent with Jason must have been pleasant. Her hello sounded chipper.

"Topaz, this is Bretta."

"Good morning."

"When we talked last night you mentioned Sylvia had written something that upset your mother. What was it? Do you remember?"

"Not at all. I don't read *that* woman's *Snippets* column."

"Do you remember the date?"

Topaz mused, "Hmmm. I assume this has to do with Mother's death."

"I can't be sure. I hope I'll know more after I read whatever it was that upset Cameo."

"I can't give you an exact date, Bretta. But if I remember right, Mother was making the move from the mansion to her temporary apartment. That would make it the last week of September or perhaps the first week of October."

"Good enough," I said. "I'll see what I come up with. Oh, yes, I have one more question. Do you know anyone by the name of Fish?"

"Not offhand, though I think the manager of the east Piggly Wiggly is Aaron Fish, or is it Fisk?"

"Would Cameo have known him?"

Topaz laughed. "Good heavens, no. I doubt if Mother would have known that a Piggly Wiggly is a grocery-store chain."

"Thanks, Topaz. Will I see you later at the house?"

Reluctantly, she said, "Yes. I'll be there at two o'clock."

Thoughtfully, I took a smashed jelly doughnut from the crumpled sack. Munching and sipping my coffee, I looked over the orders for Cameo's funeral. This time I paid close attention to who they were from. Over the years I'd gleaned information about "the honored guest" from the people who were compelled, by whatever reason, to send flowers.

Numbered among Cameo's admirers were bankers; the mayor; city council members; the *River City Daily* publisher,

Milo Sorkinsen; and an assortment of civic organizations—a hospice, a shelter for unwed mothers, Veterans of Foreign Wars, River City Historical Society, and Daughters of the American Revolution.

My hand lingered over the order from the shelter for unwed mothers. I stared at it, wondering why the shelter would send flowers to Cameo's funeral. I knew the shelter's director, Susie Graham, more by reputation than personally. Did I dare call her for a few subtle questions? On what pretext? I had it in my hand: her order.

I glanced at my watch. It wasn't yet seven, but Susie is a dynamo. She'd be up and going strong. The unlisted number was on the order form as was our shop policy. I wiped my sticky fingers on a napkin and dialed. It rang twice, three times.

"Susie, here."

"Susie, this is Bretta Solomon from The Flower Shop."

"Yes, Bretta. You're up early for a Saturday."

"Big day ahead getting the flowers ready for Cameo's lying in state tomorrow."

"I heard it's to be Sunday and Monday."

"That's right. I'm calling to check your order. You wanted a potted plant sent?"

"Yes. Something blooming. Maybe an azalea if they're in season."

"We're getting fresh ones delivered today." I took a breath, then asked, "I was wondering if Cameo played an active part in your shelter?"

Susie chuckled. "She never stepped a foot inside the door, but she was always there with the money. That's the kind of active cooperation I like."

"You contacted Cameo when you wanted a donation?"

Susie had been forthright, but now a note of wariness crept into her voice. "What's this about?"

I laughed easily. "No big deal. I'm not sure if you're aware of this, but I've bought the Beauchamp estate. I'd gotten to know Cameo rather well, but I'm amazed at the number of different organizations she helped. Yours is just one of many."

"Oh," said Susie, "I'd forgotten you have that connection with the family. Yes. Cameo was a fine woman. She's helped see us through some difficult times by being a financial contributor. However, it's the volunteer work that makes a difference. Topaz helps regularly. She talks to the girls, brings them gifts, and gives them moral support. The azalea is for her after the service. She's a dandy."

"That she is," I agreed. "Well, thanks for the order." My conscience nagged me. "I'll pick out a nice plant and give you a discount."

"Thanks. Every little bit helps."

"No problem," I said, and hung up.

My mind was making quantum leaps. Jason. "He's a good boy," Topaz had said. Jason Thompson is hardly a boy, but a *mother* might see him as such.

"Investigating is tiny steps, Bretta," said Carl's voice in my head. "You're skipping and jumping like an amateur."

His disapproval hurt, and I felt I had to justify myself. "But, Carl, you should have heard Topaz talking about Jason. When she spoke of him there was a special note in her voice. I never heard it a single time when she talked about her mother."

"A 'special note' hardly warrants this rash conclusion, Babe."

"Maybe not, but Topaz doesn't strike me as the type to run all over town doing good deeds. Yet she's an active volunteer at the shelter for unwed mothers. Perhaps because she feels a special bond with these girls."

"I see your point. It's possible, but how are you going to prove it?"

"If Topaz had a child out of wedlock, and that child is Jason, there might be more here than the question of maternity. This could be the motive for Cameo's murder."

Carl's exasperated sigh whistled in my ear. "Step by step, Bretta," he cautioned. "Back up and think. Get your facts in order, then move on to the next level of the investigation."

"You're right, Carl." I flipped through my personal card file, found Jason's home number, and dialed. When he answered I told him Cameo's body was being delivered to the house at two o'clock. "I thought you might like to get some pictures of her coming home a final time."

"That'd be great," he said, "but the sheriff might not like the press being on the scene."

"I'm not telling the press, Jason. I'm only inviting you. Sid is releasing the house, so I don't think he'll mind." As the words left my lips, I cringed. Sid minded everything and everyone when it came to his investigations.

Jason didn't need any further encouraging. He agreed to be at the mansion at two. Casually, I asked, "Do you have time to do me a favor?"

"Sure, if I can," was his prompt reply.

"I need a copy of one of *Sylvia's Snippets*. I'd come to the newspaper office, but I don't want to run into her."

Jason chuckled. "You and about forty other people I could mention."

"I don't have any specific dates, but the one I'm interested in would have been printed during the last week of September or the first week of October. Whatever Sylvia wrote upset Cameo, and she went directly to the publisher with her complaint. From what I understand, Milo came down pretty hard on Sylvia."

"Say no more," said Jason. "I know exactly what you're talking about. I don't remember the article per se, but the blowup came the day I got back from my vacation. I'll hunt it down and bring it with me this afternoon."

As I hung up the phone I made a mental list of what I knew about him. Quick wit. Happy smile. Ready to help when necessary. He'd come to River City about a year and a half ago. I hadn't a clue as to where he'd lived before he came to town, but there was a hint of a Southern accent in his voice. A vague thought touched my brain, but before I could get a handle on it, a floorboard creaked in the workroom.

I whirled from my desk. Was someone in the shop? Noiselessly, I stood up and tiptoed to the doorway. Peering around the corner I came nose to nose with Lois. We both screamed.

When I could breathe, I asked, "What are you doing here so early?"

"I thought I'd fill the buckets with warm water so they'd be ready when the shipment of fresh flowers arrives. I didn't want to make any noise in case you were still sleeping."

"Why are you always so efficient?" I grumbled.

Lois grinned. "It impresses the boss."

I patted my chest where my heart was resuming its normal pace. "The boss about had a heart attack."

"Sorry. You don't look like you slept very well."

"I didn't, and don't even start about the fact that I'm gaining weight."

Lois leaned past me and pulled a Kleenex from a box on my desk. "Here," she said, holding the tissue out to me. "Wipe off that powdered-sugar mustache, then you might get some sympathy."

I grabbed the tissue and scrubbed my upper lip. "I've made coffee," I said.

"We'll need it. This is going to be a long day." Lois flipped the switch for the lights in the workroom. "Why don't you rest for a while? I'll get things going."

"I'm too wired for that." I grabbed a sheaf of papers off my desk. "I've already separated the orders for Cameo's funeral service. Here's the list of flowers that are coming in this morning."

Lois took the paper and went to the back room, where she began filling plastic buckets with warm water. I needed to get to work, too, but I trailed along behind her.

"So," she said, raising her voice above the running water, "what did you do last night?"

"Bought this outfit."

Lois looked over her shoulder. "Blue's your color."

I grimaced. Blue again. Should've bought the lavender. "I talked to Topaz. She agreed to a two-day visitation, with the funeral set for Tuesday. That will give us Wednesday and Thursday to finish the last-minute details for the open house."

"Sounds good." Lois carried the buckets closer to the alley door, where the boxes of flowers would be delivered. When she came back, she said, "That Matilda Bennett is one self-righteous, well-dressed old toad. I felt sorry for Chris yesterday."

"I did, too, but I think Chris handled herself very well."

Lois put a scoop of powdered flower preservative into another empty bucket. "I wonder how she's going to handle Lew's infatuation. She's got someone else."

"Really? Did she tell you that?"

"No. But about a week ago a man called asking for her."

Lois grinned. "You should have seen Chris's eyes light up when she heard his voice. Mark my words, Lew is in for a fall because Chris's heart is already taken."

Ready for a good gossip, I asked, "Do you know who it is?"

"Chris didn't say, but his voice sounded familiar."

"I bet its Phil from over at RadioShack. He's been giving her the eye."

Lois snorted. "I'd know his voice even if my ears were plugged with a head cold. That man irritates me like a hemorrhoid. He was seventy-five cents short on his order last week, and you know what he had the nerve to say? 'Let the flower shop absorb the loss.' Can you believe that? And from another businessman, too."

She slammed the bucket in the sink and turned on the water. She faced me with her hands on her hips. "Well," she declared, "I'm all fired up now. Phil has that effect on me. So we might as well get to the good part."

"What good part?"

"I've been making idle chitchat, waiting for you to tell me what you did last night, besides the shopping. Have you figured out who the killer is?"

I teased her. "I haven't given it a thought."

"Yeah, right. I know you better than that."

I leaned against the doorframe. "I did have an interesting conversation with Sylvia Whitaker last night."

"Knowing that woman, you listened more than you conversed."

"True, but I did get in a couple of good digs."

"What's on her puny brain?"

"She thinks I'm the mastermind behind Cameo's murder."

Lois stopped the flow of water with an angry twist of the faucet. "Did I hear you right?"

Before Lois blew a gasket, I told her about Sylvia's under-handed tactics for getting me to talk. I finished with, "She said she has something that would put me at the top of Sid's list of suspects."

"Got any ideas?"

"Not a clue. It's probably another of her sick ploys. Be warned. She'll be calling you next."

"She already has, but we were gone to Erin's Christmas pageant. There was a message on our answering machine, asking me to call her. I need my beauty sleep, so I didn't return the call. I knew a conversation with Sylvia would've kept me wide-awake."

The phone rang. Lois picked it up and said, "The Flower Shop." She promptly put down the phone. "Another hang up. This is getting old. There were three calls yesterday afternoon. I wonder whose number closely resembles this one."

I went up front to wait on an early-bird customer who was trying to peck a hole in the door. While I was gone, Lew and Chris arrived, as did the shipment of flowers. I could hear a low buzz of conversation taking place in the back room as they cut the stems and put the flowers in the containers Lois had prepared.

Finally, I finished with my difficult customer and went back to my workstation, where I found my three employees standing idle, looking glum. If we were going to get any work done, I knew I'd better clear the air. "Staff meeting," I said. "I take it Lois has told you about my conversation with Sylvia."

"That woman has some nerve," said Chris.

"A lawsuit would be in order," declared Lew. "Lois says Sylvia practically accused one of us. 'The house was crawling with your employees.'" He snatched a pair of clippers off the table and clicked them sharply. "I say we nip this nonsense in the bud."

I grinned weakly. "Cute. How do you propose we do that? Sylvia admits she knows what to say and when to say it so slander won't be easily proved. If she keeps talking, she might just hang herself."

"I'd gladly provide the rope," muttered Lois.

"What if people believe her?" worried Chris.

"She can't name names. Slander. She can't print her asinine theory. Libel. Let's wait and see what Sid comes up with."

"What if she tells him?" asked Lois.

"She says she has."

They gasped like a trio of deflating balloons.

"Relax," I said. "There's nothing to worry about. Outside of your initial statement yesterday, Sid hasn't hauled us in for questioning. He's busy following up real leads, not some flaky tale told by Sylvia Whitaker."

The phone rang. I streaked across the floor and grabbed it up. "The Flower Shop," I said.

"May I speak to Mrs. Solomon?"

"This is she."

"Everett Chandler. I've looked at my daily planner, Mrs. Solomon, and I'll be free to come to the mansion at ten o'clock tomorrow morning."

"Why?"

"To look at the Beauchamp memorabilia. I feel it would be a travesty not to immediately let the rest of River City see what wonderful treasures this family has bestowed on our fair city."

"Bestowed?" I repeated. "I don't know anything about—"

"My dear woman, I was having a correspondence with Mrs. Beauchamp-Sinclair on this very subject. On the night of her—uh—passing, she divulged a sentimental yearning to see her families' possessions showcased at the museum."

"I don't—"

"I'll be at the mansion at ten," he said and hung up.

I hung up, too, but before I could take a step, the phone rang again. I heaved a sigh and picked it up. This time the caller was Trevor McGuire. His voice was smooth and sweet as syrup. "Bretta, I'd like to take you out to dinner."

Forever blunt, I asked, "Why?"

"I thought we might discuss a specific detail of the case."

I wouldn't discuss the weather with Trevor, let alone Cameo's murder. He was the type of lawyer to use anything I might say against me. "Sorry, Trevor, if you need to discuss Cameo's murder, I suggest you call Sid. Offer him dinner. I'm sure he'd jump at a free meal." I replaced the receiver, then moved away from the damned thing. "First Everett, now Trevor. I wonder what 'specific detail of the case' Trevor wanted to discuss? Why did he pick me?"

Lew sniffed righteously. "The man is obviously desperate." Under my narrowed gaze, he quickly explained, "What I meant was that he's obviously desperate because he's worried—under suspicion. But getting back to Sylvia. She's a loose cannon. She doesn't care who or what she says to implicate anyone. My mother will be devastated if I'm classed as a murder suspect."

I felt only a mild twinge of regret when I said, "We're all suspects because we were there. If you don't have anything to hide, it'll work out."

The phone rang. Lew was closest. He answered, then slammed it back into place. "Another hang up. Someone needs to learn some manners."

Lois was nervously twisting a piece of floral wire around and around her finger. "How far do the police look when they do a background check?"

"Why?" I asked.

She tried to smile, but it was a feeble effort. "I was arrested once."

We gasped.

In a rush, Lois explained, "It was during the sixties. A bunch of us rallied against town hall to oppose the closing of a nightspot where we hung out. I got caught up in the moment," she ducked her head, "and I burned my—uh—"

"Bra?" I supplied with a snicker.

"No, my sweatshirt. It was a disaster. The damned thing wouldn't flame, but it smoked to high heaven." Even haughty Lew laughed. Lois made a face. "It's not funny. They arrested me for indecent exposure and polluting the air."

I cackled. "What a hoot! And just when you think you know someone."

The bell on the front door jingled. We were still chuckling when we turned. Our amusement faded like a week-old bouquet. Sid Hancock, every inch the county sheriff, strode toward us.

He stopped at the front counter and put his hands on his gun belt. "You're a jolly group," he said. "Don't let me keep you from your play. I have just one question. It's for you, Bretta. Where the hell have you been? Are you hiding from the law?"

Chapter Thirteen

✿ "That's two questions," I muttered.

"What's that?" snapped Sid. He proceeded to read me the riot act. "I've been looking everywhere for you. You told me you'd be here. I had officers cruise by all night, but you didn't show up. Where the hell were you?"

That wasn't the time to tell him about my meeting with Sylvia. I didn't want to drag her name into the conversation with my employees already on edge. "I decided to stay at a motel."

"Why didn't you tell me?"

"It was a spur-of-the-moment decision."

"Spur of the moment, huh? I was ready to put out an APB for you." He glared at me. "I know how you like to poke your nose into things that don't concern you."

My mouth turned down at the corners. I didn't need this. "I haven't done—"

"Yeah. Yeah. Right. I'll believe that when Christmas trees sprout legs and waltz around the room." He jerked his head toward the front door. "Come on. We need to chat."

"I can't leave," I said stiffly. I gestured to the stack of orders waiting to be done. "Before I meet you at two this afternoon at the mansion, I've got work to do."

Sid's tone was ominous. "And I don't?"

"Of course you do. I'm not saying that. Can't we talk here?"

He gave my group of supporters a curt look. "Nope."

I don't get easily riled, but Sid was pushing all the wrong buttons. I crossed my arms over my chest. "I'm not going to your office unless you're arresting me." Those in the room I sign a paycheck for gasped.

Sid scowled. "It's tempting. Damned tempting."

Might as well try to get along with him. "Where?" I asked.

"In my car—"

I snorted. "Parked on a busy street in this town? I'm not sitting in your patrol car where everyone can see me and speculate on what we're discussing."

"Damn it, Bretta, you can be the most frustrating female. Carl always said—" He stopped and swiped a hand across his brow. "All right. I'll pull around to the alley. Be there, and no talking among you." He stomped out, slamming the door with such force that the string of bells came loose and crashed to the floor.

"Gosh, Bretta," said Lois, "whatever possessed you to talk to him like—"

I shook my head at her. "Lew, fix the bells. Chris, make bows for the plants that will be arriving shortly. Lois, since the part-time designers are unavailable, why don't you give June and Vicki a call? See if they're willing to come in to take orders, wait on customers, type cards, or whatever else needs to be done."

With my head held high, I grabbed my jacket and marched out of the workroom. I was on the loading dock when Sid pulled around in back. He left the engine running. I climbed in and closed the door. The radio crackled as the dispatcher directed officers to calls. I stared straight ahead. I could feel Sid studying me, but I refused to meet his gaze.

"Worked yourself into a real snit, haven't you?" he asked. "Your face is as purple as your jacket." I gave him my best you're-skating-on-thin-ice stare. He shrugged. "I'm not the enemy."

"You're not acting like a friend."

"I don't have to. I'm the sheriff of this county, and you're up to your eyeballs in a murder investigation that's getting screwier by the minute." Sid fingered the sharp crease on his khaki trousers. "A piece of information has been brought to my attention, and it sticks out like a whore in church."

I rolled my eyes.

"I talked to the real estate agent who handled the sale of the mansion. He said it was the dangest thing. Cameo had interviewed several buyers but wouldn't sell. You came along, had an hour's private chat with her, and boom. It was a done deal. He says Mrs. Beauchamp-Sinclair even dropped the asking price by ten grand."

"That's right. Cameo and I got along very well. I explained to her what I had in mind for the house. She liked my ideas."

Of course now I knew she'd planned on renting those rooms from me. She'd had that in mind from the start. Duplicity popped into my mind. It was a fleeting thought, but I couldn't track it with Sid staring a hole in me.

"Bretta, did you have something on Cameo Beau—"

I didn't give him a chance to finish. "Stop right there," I said. I twisted on the seat so I faced him. "Sylvia called you and dropped this theory into your lap, didn't she?" Reluctantly, he nodded. "I thought as much. She told me she had some information that would put me at the top of your list of suspects. To answer your question, Sid, no, I didn't have anything on Cameo. I liked her. I respected her."

Tears blurred my vision. My voice trembled. "I'm sorry she's dead. I've been gypped out of a friendship that could've been good for both of us. I'm sorry she didn't trust me enough to tell me who was blackmailing her. I feel as if I've let her down. I should have protected her. I should have cleared the house that night instead of going on with my presentation of the ballroom." I gulped. "I should have done something."

"Like call me?" He flicked a glance at me and grumbled, "Most people would've called the authorities at the first mention of blackmail."

"How was I to know if it was true?"

"We still don't know. The blackmail letters haven't surfaced. Mrs. Beauchamp-Sinclair was a sharp woman. She may have been in a wheelchair, but she had the run of the mansion."

"Except the attic. The elevator doesn't go to that floor. But the upper story can't be discounted as a hiding place for those letters. When I moved in I carted loads of Cameo's possessions up there from the bottom floors."

Sid shuddered. "I don't want to think about that attic. It's what nightmares are made of. But speaking of the elevator, I had Noah come to the mansion yesterday. He and I did some experimenting with the lights. By a process of elimination, we figure it was the elevator that blew the fuse."

I was glad to have this question answered, but it raised another. "The elevator is at the far end of the hall. Who pushed the button?"

"You tell me."

"I don't know."

"We have to go over your story again, Bretta. I want to

know where everyone was before the lights went out and afterward."

"I told you—"

"No. I mean exactly."

"But I can't say exactly. I wasn't in the hall. I can only assume Lois, Chris, Jason, and Noah were. According to Inez, she and DeeDee were in their rooms. I was in the ballroom. So were Topaz, Simon, Everett, Trevor, Lew, and Sylvia."

"Sylvia." Sid breathed the word like a curse. "No wonder the woman wears red. It's to warn the rest of us of approaching danger." He lowered his chin and gave me an intense stare. "I want to know where you are at all times." When I spluttered my indignation, he held up a hand. "It's for your own good. For some reason, Sylvia is trying to drag you further into this mess than you already are."

"Sid, you don't think I—"

"No. You're capable of some pretty stupid tricks, but murder isn't among them."

"Gee, thanks," I muttered.

"Without those letters this investigation is going nowhere. None of the postal inspectors in Kansas City, St. Louis, or Springfield knew anything about an appointment with Cameo Beauchamp-Sinclair." His voice dropped. "We've got a murder, but was the motive to cover up blackmail?" He shook his head. "I don't like it. Why would the old lady lie about the appointment? Did she lie about everything?"

"She didn't lie about the blackmail," I said firmly.

"How do you know that? Where are the letters? We turned your house and her apartment upside down, but we came up empty-handed. In a case of extortion, it's the blackmailer who gets snuffed, not the proposed victim. You don't kill the goose that could lay you a golden egg." He tipped his cap back on his head and sighed. "There are too many loose ends, and I can't get a firm grasp on any of them."

"What can I do, besides tell you where I am?"

"This afternoon we're going to walk through the entire evening of the murder. I want to know everything. What was said? Who said it? Where everyone was?" He paused to see if I was listening.

"Sure, Sid, if you think it will help."

"How do I know? Just get the facts straight in your head." He sighed morosely. "Eyewitnesses have been known to be unreliable when it comes to pertinent information." He sighed again. "But I guess you're better than most."

It was a back-ass compliment, if ever I heard one.

Having June and Vicki come into the shop was a last resort, but I was desperate for help. In between taking orders, waiting on customers, and answering the telephone, these Martha Stewart "wanna-bes" annoyed us by talking nonstop about the wonderful finds they were salvaging from our discards. Scraps of ribbon would be sewn into a "darling" garland, which would be an asset on any Christmas tree. Bruised flower petals would be used as a natural potpourri. As for the stems and leaves that littered the floor, the women swept up the fodder and put it in plastic garbage bags for use on their compost piles.

Sid's unannounced visit to the flower shop this morning had put a crimp in my schedule. I started my workday by making Cameo's casketpiece—a traditional spray of flowers that would cover the closed half of the casket. As I tucked coral roses among the leather leaf fern, I thought about the murder investigation. My mind hopped and skipped from one notion to the next.

I needed to see DeeDee. I was sure she'd been about to say something the night of the murder, but her stuttering had kept her lips sealed. I wondered who Fish was? What were Sylvia's exact words? "Fish has it, too." Who was Fish, and what did he have? Why was Topaz a volunteer at a home for unwed mothers? What did Sylvia have on Simon? Why had I let Everett talk me into seeing him tomorrow morning? Maybe I should have taken Trevor up on his dinner date. What "specific detail" of the case had he wanted to discuss with me? What exactly did Sid mean when he said he'd turned my house upside down? I skimmed over that thought.

I finished with the casketpiece and went on to my next order, and the next, and the next. By noon, we were making headway. By one o'clock, I was assured that Lois and Chris could finish up with June and Vicki's help. I put on my coat, grabbed my purse, and hurried out the back door. Lew was just pulling the delivery van into the alley. I waved to him and got in my car.

The River City Public Library was out of my way, but a sudden whim made me drive the eight blocks to Oak Street. I turned into the crowded parking lot, where I circled like a bird looking for a place to roost. A truck backed out, and I eased my car into place. I grabbed my purse and hurried inside, this time using the front door.

My footsteps echoed on the marble floor. Two people looked up and frowned. I tiptoed toward the reference desk, where a woman watched my approach with a helpful smile.

Her hair was dark, and her body pear-shaped. A bell the size you'd hang on a Doberman dangled from around her neck.

"May I help you?" she asked, leaning forward. The bell plinked.

I whispered my request to see copies of the *River City Daily* newspaper for the last week in September and the first week in October. She nodded and moved into the room behind her. I waited. Every few minutes I glanced at my watch. I would have to hurry if I was going to make my appointment with Sid.

Five minutes later, she came back, her face a perplexity. "I'm sorry, but for some reason that microfilm reel isn't available."

"It's been checked out?" I asked. Was this the file Sylvia had asked Simon to get rid of?

"No, we don't check out our microfilm or microfiche files. If you want to view any of them, you have to do so here at the library." She gestured to another room. "The projectors are in there."

"Microfiche?" I murmured. "I see." Fish—fiche?

"Apparently, the file has been misplaced," she went on in a worried tone. "If you'll leave your name and phone number, I'll do a search and call you when it's located."

"That's not necessary. I'll go to the newspaper office."

"Yes. Fine." She turned and hurried back into the storage room. Her muttering was punctuated by the bell's hearty clanking.

I headed down the corridor marked OFFICES. This time I didn't soften my steps. My heels clicked decisively. I stopped at Simon's open door. He'd heard my noisy approach and eyed the doorway with a disapproving frown. The wrinkles in his forehead deepened when he saw me.

"Good afternoon, Simon," I said. He was wearing the same checkered sports jacket he'd had on the night of the murder. Above his crooked red bow tie, his throat muscles convulsed, making the protruding cartilage flutter like a leaf caught in a breeze.

In a friendly, chatty tone, I said, "I needed to see a microfilm file, but your employee couldn't locate it. I'm interested in one of Sylvia's columns. I've been told the one I need was printed the last week of September or the first week in October." I waved a hand airily. "Oh, well, I'll run by the newspaper office. I'm sure they'll have a copy."

"Was this—uh—file important?"

"I can't be sure until I see it, Simon. From what I understand, Cameo read something in Sylvia's column that was upsetting. It might or might not tie in to the murder. I guess I'll let Sid be the judge of that."

"Sid?" Simon gulped. "The sheriff?"

"Of course. Any information has to be passed on to him. He'll decide if it's relevant."

"Yes. Yes, absolutely. The right thing to do."

"I don't suppose you remember what the subject of her column happened to be around that time?"

His eyes widened. "Oh, no. My lands, no. I don't keep track of what Ms. Whitaker writes. I have too many responsibilities here."

"I'm sure you do," I said quietly. "Don't come down too hard on the woman at the reference desk. She seems very competent. I can't believe it was her fault that the microfilm reel is missing."

"Quite right," he said, then added piously, "but I can't abide shoddy work habits."

"We all have our little pet peeves, don't we? You don't like shoddy work habits, and I can't abide deceit." I gave him a cheery wave and hurried to my car.

Chapter Fourteen

❧ I nearly skidded into the ditch when I turned off the dry blacktop road onto my icy graveled driveway. Heavy traffic up and down the lane had packed the snow into a glaze. The quarter mile approach to the mansion was enclosed with tall pine trees. The thick branches had shaded the road, keeping the sun from melting the ice. I gripped the steering wheel and navigated the slick surface, wondering how I was going to remedy this new problem before the open house.

I parked next to Sid's patrol car. After climbing out, I stood looking at the house. I loved the clean architectural lines, the six Corinthian columns, the wide gracious veranda that stretched the entire width of the mansion, but I dreaded going through those beautiful oak doors.

What kind of disarray had the deputies left behind in their efforts to find the letters? Sid said they'd turned the house upside down. I hoped that wasn't one of his literal statements. Frustration often leads to mayhem, and Sid was very frustrated.

Sid hadn't come to the door, so I stayed where I was, leaning against the warm hood of my car. Missouri weather is said to be some of the most changeable around. If you don't like today, there's always tomorrow, but usually you don't have to wait for another day. I've seen the weather conditions vary by the hour.

The afternoon sun shone with such radiance on the white-covered landscape it hurt my eyes. Clouds were building in the north—thick, gray clouds that would soon collide with the sun and cover it as effectively as a damask curtain.

I pushed off from my car and headed up the walk. The mansion needed some exterior work. In my mind's eye the snow and ice melted away. I saw fresh white paint, mowed grass, and a kaleidoscope of annuals in the circular flower beds near the veranda, water spraying from the fountain near the front walk.

In its present state the brick fountain was an eyesore, but I'd run out of time and money for repairs. I'd done what I could to make the fountain presentable. I'd picked up the loose bricks and aligned them with the others, but as soon as possible, I wanted them cemented into place.

I skirted the front steps and walked around the garage. I was the proud owner of sixty acres of land, but it was the gardens that piqued my interest.

I'd done some research and discovered that an estate garden is an extension of the family. The skill and creativity of the plantings reflects the quality and refinement of the owners. I liked that idea—quality and refinement. The area immediately off the terrace had been formal—reflection pool, brick paths, meticulously trimmed bushes. I wanted to restore this tangled jungle back to its original beauty.

It would take lots of work and plenty of muscle. Common junipers had spread unchecked to twenty feet wide. Alberta spruce trees looked like upside-down ice-cream cones. I spied a pussy willow bush. I should cut some twigs and take them into the house. The warm temperature would make the tiny buds pop open and give me hope that spring would be here soon.

My biggest problem was figuring out what to do with the decrepit apple orchard. Some of the trees might still be alive, but even mantled with snow, they were a deplorable sight. I squinted. What was the patch of green up in that apple tree? Wanting to investigate this oddity, I took a couple of steps closer. Strange. There wasn't a speck of green anywhere else in this winter wonderland, yet in the crotch of that one tree, I could see—

"Bretta!"

I turned and saw Topaz crossing the crusty snow with mincing steps. Her gait was halting, but it was obvious I was her target. I gave the spot of green another glance before hurrying toward Topaz. We met at the front porch steps.

"I want to—have—a word—with you," she puffed. After she'd collected herself, she asked, "Why did you call Susie Graham?"

"I asked her about an order the shelter is sending to Cameo's funeral service."

"Leave it alone," was all Topaz said, but it was enough. I was onto something.

"What?" I asked innocently.

Before Topaz could reply, a car pulled into the drive. She caught her breath when she saw Jason at the wheel. "Oh, good," I said. "I hoped he'd make it." Topaz frowned. "I called him. I thought he should get pictures of Cameo coming home a final time."

Jason got out of his car and hurried to us. He didn't have a hat on. His jacket was unbuttoned, his trusty camera in hand. The dimple in his cheek deepened as he smiled at us.

"Hi, ladies," he said. "Thanks for the call, Bretta" He nodded to Topaz. "Hello, Miss Sinclair. I was hoping to see you. I wanted to thank you again for that great supper last night. Red beans and rice reminds me of home. Dad says nobody outside of Louisiana knows how to cook beans. I'll have to tell him I've found someone in Missouri who knows her legumes." He held up his camera. "I haven't developed the pictures I took last night, but as soon as I do, I'll get you copies."

Topaz nodded politely, almost impersonally. Jason's casual dropping of information as to why he'd been at Topaz's last night came across as an elaborate camouflage that only made me more suspicious.

He turned to me. "Something weird is going on concerning that newspaper clipping you wanted," he said. "I went to the morgue, but the spool of microfilm with that particular column has vanished. I talked to Albert, who's in charge of keeping track of back issues of the paper, and he's mystified."

"Thanks for looking, Jason. I appreciate it."

"You might check the public library. They keep files of the paper on film."

I murmured that I'd give it a try, and we went up the steps to the veranda. Jason hustled ahead, searching for the best place to take his photos. "So," I said to Topaz, "Jason's from Louisiana. I thought I detected a hint of a Southern accent. He's a long way from home. It must get lonely for him without family close by." Fishing, I added, "He'd make anyone proud to have him as a son, wouldn't he?"

My answer was a cold, broody stare that had the power to crumble stone. I met that gaze unflinching, letting Topaz know that I wasn't fooled. The front door opened, and Sid stepped out of the house just as the hearse came up the drive.

Jason had his camera ready. He began clicking as the vehicle came to a stop. Three men from the funeral home got out and went around to the back to unload Cameo's eternal home onto a handcart. As the mortuary attendants rolled their burden up the walk, Topaz sidled over to Jason, and murmured, "She knows."

Jason jerked in surprise and looked at me. He tried to smile, but it was a failed effort. Slowly, he looked from me to Sid, then back to me. He mouthed, "Not yet." Briefly, he gave Topaz's hand a squeeze. She added her own unspoken plea when her eyes brimmed with tears.

My brain buzzed with indecision. How could I not tell Sid? This might be the motive for Cameo's murder. I looked away from Jason and Topaz, sneaking a peek at Sid. He was skimming the pages of his notebook, oblivious to what was going on under his nose. I bit my lip, then reluctantly nodded. I'd keep their secret—for the moment. Like a bad omen, the wind picked up and blew the clouds across the sun.

Sid took a final slurp of his coffee, then banged the mug on the table. "Well," he grumbled, "this was a waste of time. I still don't know any more than I did."

I'd apologized over and over for not knowing the answers to his questions until I didn't have an ounce of regret left in me. As for the amount of time he'd spent at the mansion, he couldn't blame that on me. He'd offered to help move things around in the ballroom to accommodate Cameo's casket.

Stiffly, I said, "Thanks for letting me back into my house and for helping get everything into place for the lying in state."

"At least something got accomplished," he said as he came wearily to his feet. "I'm gonna take off."

The phone rang as we started out of the kitchen. I grabbed

it and said, "Hello." Sid paused to see if the call was for him. When I said, "Hi, Lois, be right with you," Sid waved and walked out. I waited until I heard the front door slam before I turned to the phone.

"Sid's just now leaving," I said. "He's been hounding me with questions."

"Like what?"

"Where was this one or that before the murder. I didn't have the answers. I could surmise, but I couldn't be factual, and you know how he gets when I offer my opinion on anything that has to do with his investigations."

Lois chuckled. "I called to tell you the funeral orders are finished. Noah came by and helped sweep and clean up. Chris went home with a sick headache. Her first major flower shop event just about blew her away. I thought the pressure was going to get to her, but she stuck with it."

"I remember when she applied for the job, she said she thought it would be peaceful to work with flowers. I tried to explain that sometimes you forget you're working with flowers. They become only a commodity to get the work done."

"I think she's well aware of that tonight." Lois changed the subject. "Are you sleeping at the flower shop or a motel room?"

"Neither. Sid said I could stay here.

"Good for you. I'm ready to relax, but a hamper of dirty clothes is screaming for attention. Can you sit down and call it a day?"

I looked around the kitchen. The food, dirty dishes, pots, and pans were exactly where they'd been when I walked out of my house on Thursday night. Time had dried the food beyond recognition. I uttered the world's biggest understatement. "I have a few chores to do, too. I'll see you tomorrow," and hung up.

The dishes and pans were too crusty for the dishwasher to clean. I filled the sink with hot, soapy water. Washing up by hand was therapeutic and it gave me time to think. I could easily relate to Chris's headache. My time with Sid had tried my patience as well as his. He'd wanted me to remember things I never knew in the first place. He wanted me to contradict alibis and statements made to him. He'd even tested the floorboards in the ballroom and the hall, hoping some telltale squeak might jog my memory.

A couple of times I'd hazarded a guess as to what might have happened, but he'd reiterated that he deals in facts, not supposition. If I didn't know it to be God's truth, he didn't want to hear it.

Sid's attitude made it easier to keep my mouth shut about several things. Since I'd entered the mansion, the "ancestral mini-bibles" had been on my mind. As Sid and I walked through the house, I'd kept my eyes peeled for a hiding place. I hadn't mentioned those journals. I was afraid he would close the house again to make another search.

I also hadn't mentioned the microfilm file that was missing from both the library and the newspaper office. I had no proof that the file was important to his investigation. I also didn't know for a fact that Sylvia's hold over Simon had anything to do with Cameo's murder. I was, however, more than a bit uneasy about keeping Jason and Topaz's relationship quiet.

Poor Topaz. Gobbling dessert when her mother was being murdered. I stopped swooshing the dishwater. Topaz had just gotten a refill and was about to sit down when the fuse blew.

The extension cords were next to the sideboard. Had Topaz done some finagling?

I didn't like playing a part in this subterfuge. If Cameo's murder was involved, I wanted out. I pulled my hands from the dishwater, ready to call Sid. I took two steps toward the phone, then stopped. Again, I couldn't be sure of my facts. Topaz had told me to "leave it alone." She'd told Jason, "she knows." But what did I know for sure? I suspected plenty, but given Sid's stuffy disposition, he'd never listen to me. Better to wait and see what developed before I brought in *the law*.

Relieved to have reached a decision, I scraped plates, rinsed glasses, and flushed smelly garbage down the disposal. I picked up a stack of plates and plunged them into the hot water. I hadn't known what to expect when I'd entered the house. A search for the letters could have resulted in a mess, but for the most part, everything looked good.

The police had taken the roping and Christmas lights—murder weapon—from the ballroom doorway, but had left the kissing ball hanging forlornly in the arch. The mistletoe was dropping little white berries all over the floor, so Sid had taken the decoration down.

I had finished washing the glassware and plates and was scouring a crusty pan when I heard footsteps coming from the servants' quarters. There was no mistaking the familiar tread. It was Inez. I'd come to recognize her even gait and avoid it whenever possible.

She came into the kitchen but didn't speak. I didn't, either. She moved past me, out of the kitchen, and into the hall. From the sound of her steps, she entered the ballroom. After a time, she came back into the kitchen. I glanced at her. Her cheeks were wet with tears. I opened my mouth to offer her sympathy, but she was ahead of me.

"Why aren't you using the dishwasher? And besides, you don't use steel wool on an aluminum pan. It scratches the metal." She nudged me out of her way. "I'd best get this cleaned up so I can fix you supper." I blinked my surprise and stepped away from the sink. "It's snowing again," she continued. "Soup will taste good. I've got vegetable in the freezer. I'll heat it up and make some biscuits. I'll bring you a tray in the library."

It was a cool dismissal. I wiped my hands on a towel. "How did you know the house had been released?"

"Called the sheriff's department."

"Does DeeDee know?"

"Figured you told her."

"I haven't seen her since Thursday when the house was closed."

"Her mother, Darlene, told me DeeDee was meeting you at six."

I frowned. "Meeting me?" I looked at the clock hanging above the refrigerator. It was six-fifty. "Where?"

Inez lifted a shoulder. "I don't know. Darlene didn't say."

"Well, that's odd. Did she say *why* I was meeting DeeDee?"

"Darlene said you wanted to discuss something that happened the night Cameo died. She asked me if I knew what it was. I told her it wasn't any of my business."

I felt a prickle of consternation. I did want to talk to DeeDee, and I should have done it earlier. "DeeDee doesn't talk on the phone, so how did I make this arrangement to meet her?"

Inez shrugged.

Frowning, I went to the telephone and looked up the number for Darlene and David Henry, DeeDee's parents. I found the number and dialed. Mr. Henry answered and our conversation was short and disturbing. A note with my name had been left in his mailbox for DeeDee. He let me know in no uncertain terms that he didn't approve of his daughter meeting me in a *bar*, even if it was conveniently located across from my flower shop.

I hung up the phone and dialed Kelsay's. My questions were met with negative results. DeeDee wasn't there.

On the night of the murder, I had gotten the impression that DeeDee was going to say something, but with so many people in the room she didn't have the nerve. Or maybe she saw something and with the murderer present she was afraid to say it out loud. Had someone else noticed that DeeDee had been about to speak?

"I'm going into town to check on DeeDee," I said to Inez. "Her father said she got a note from me. I never sent it."

"But Darlene said—"

Impatiently, I interrupted, "I don't care what Darlene said. That note wasn't from me."

I didn't take time to explain further. I grabbed my coat and purse and rushed out the front door of the mansion into a snowstorm. I started the car, got out, and scraped the windshield. My teeth were chattering from the cold and apprehension.

Surely, DeeDee would know if I wanted to get a message to her, I'd drop by personally. Why hadn't she taken the time to verify that I was the sender? A thought nudged my brain, but I was in too much of a rush to give it a closer analysis.

I jumped into my car and headed down the hazardous drive. Hunched over the steering wheel, I peered into a swirling maze of white. The snow fell in clusters; the flakes caked with ice. They hit my car with a soft, ticking sound.

As I approached the end of the drive, I tapped the brakes. A patrol car suddenly turned in front of me. I pushed harder on the brake pedal, and the rear of my car swerved before I brought it to a sliding stop. The other car drew alongside of me, and I lowered my window.

The driver was Sid. A curtain of snow fell between us, but it didn't mask his grim expression. "Go back to the house, Bretta," he said. "There's nothing you can do."

"Do? About what?" I had no idea what he was talking about, unless—

I gasped. "DeeDee?"

Sid jerked in surprise. "Who the hell is Dee—" He broke off. "Oh, yeah, the maid. No. Trevor McGuire. I haven't got all the details except that he's dead."

Chapter Fifteen

🌿 The words "Trevor's dead" played over and over in my mind as I drove up the lane to the mansion. I'd asked Sid how Trevor had died, but I'd gotten no answer. I'd told him about DeeDee and the bogus note I'd supposedly sent. He'd ordered me back to the house. I'd explained that I wanted to go into town to make sure she was all right. He'd told me to use the telephone. At the end of our conversation, he'd threatened me with obstruction of justice if I set foot off my property. When he used that tone, I knew he meant it.

This time I parked my car in the garage. I went into the house and down the hall. Passing the ballroom doorway, I saw Inez had turned on a couple of lamps. In my frame of mind the last thing I needed to set eyes on was Cameo tucked into her casket.

I hurried on by and into the kitchen. Inez was sitting at the table calmly sipping soup. I ignored her, just as she ignored me. I went to the phone and dialed the Henry household. While the number rang I shrugged out of my coat and flopped it over a chair.

DeeDee's mother answered. "David?"

"No, Mrs. Henry . . . uh . . . Darlene," I said, "This is Bretta Solomon. I'm calling to check on DeeDee."

"Mrs. Solomon, your earlier phone call upset us. We

assumed DeeDee was with you. My husband is out driving the streets looking for her." She stopped to take a quivery breath. "We haven't seen DeeDee since four o'clock this afternoon when she left the house to meet you at some bar. I'm holding you personally responsible if something has happened to my . . . my . . . baby."

I tried for reassurance. "I'm sure she's fine. DeeDee is a very smart and resourceful *twenty-three-year-old* young woman."

"I never should have allowed her to work for you—for anyone. She's safest here at home with her father and me. I feel faint at the thought of what she might be going through out in public. People can be cruel—making fun of her stutter. That's why I home-schooled her. DeeDee is so naive. So easily hurt."

"If she needs you, I'm sure she'll get word to you."

Darlene sniffed wetly. "She has been practicing using the telephone."

"Oh, really? In what way?"

"She'd dial a number, listen for a minute, and then hang up."

The shop had been having a rash of phone hang ups. "Did DeeDee dial this number repeatedly? Or wait for time to pass?"

"What does it matter? My daughter should be here with me. She needs to be with people who can look out for her."

I mumbled something meant to comfort, then quickly broke the connection. I dialed Lois. When she answered, I asked, "You know those phone hang ups we've been getting at the flower shop?"

"How could I forget? We took six more after you left today."

"Did anyone speak?"

"Not to me," was her answer. Lew echoed Lois's response when I called him next. I dialed Chris, but her answering machine picked up. I was in the middle of leaving her a message to call me, when she broke in breathlessly.

"Here I am, Bretta," she said.

"Are you feeling better?"

"My headache is gone. I decided I needed some fresh air, so I was outside sweeping the snow off my porch, which is a waste of time. It's snowing again."

I asked Chris the same question I'd asked Lew and Lois. I got the same reply. The caller hadn't said a word.

"What's this about?" asked Chris.

I didn't want to outline the entire scenario. Briefly, I said, "DeeDee isn't home, and her parents are concerned, and so am I. I got to thinking about the phone hang ups and wondered if it might've been her."

"I couldn't tell you. No one said anything."

I told her I'd see her the following day at Cameo's lying in state, and we hung up.

Inez said, "Your soup is getting cold."

"I'm not hungry," I muttered, searching in the telephone book for yet another number. I felt her eyes drilling into my back. I turned. "What?"

She put her nose in the air. "I never said anything."

"But you were thinking something. Spit it out."

"It's not my place."

"Whatever," I mumbled. I found the number I wanted. As I dialed I tried to compose my thoughts. I was still working on what I wanted to say when Deputy Donna Meyer picked up the phone.

"Hello," she said cautiously.

I chuckled. "It's me, Bretta, not a call to come back to work."

"Thank God. I don't think I could take another shift. All I want is a hot bath and a warm bed."

"I'll let you get to both in just a second. I was wondering if you had any news on Trevor McGuire's death?"

The cautious note was back in Donna's voice, but it was there for a different reason. "Bretta, I'm not at liberty to discuss an ongoing case."

"I don't want to discuss it." God, I hate wheedling information from a friend, especially when I know she could get into trouble if she came across. "Please, Donna, give me something. Did he fall in the bathtub? Have a heart attack? Choke on a chicken bone?"

"None of the above."

"Car accident?"

Donna didn't say anything.

"So a car was involved, huh?" I mused out loud. "Slick roads come to mind, but a cut-and-dried traffic accident isn't normally considered so hush-hush. Since you won't talk about it, there must be something fishy going on. If there's something fishy, that means Trevor's death is being questioned. If it's being investigated that means—"

Donna broke in with a tired laugh. "You've missed your calling, Bretta. Carl used to say that you should've been the deputy, not him."

I felt a rush of gratitude for Carl's confidence in me. "Look, Donna, I'm not being nosy. As you well know, Trevor was a guest in my house the night Cameo was murdered. Now Trevor's dead. If it was a simple car crash that killed him, tell me so I can sleep tonight. If it was something . . . uh . . . sinister, I want to be forewarned."

Donna's voice dropped to a whisper. "It was a sloppy attempt to make it look like an accident." She hung up.

Slowly I replaced the receiver. I leaned against the cabinet, feeling sick to my stomach. A sloppy attempt? Had fear of discovery made the killer careless? Or had the killer been pushed into committing murder before a solid plan could be made?

"Are you going to eat now?" asked Inez. "Or can I clean off the table?"

I waved a limp hand. "Clean."

"Are you on a new diet since the old one isn't working?"

Peck, peck, peck. The old chicken is back at her game. I faced Inez. "I've got a few questions."

"I'm getting ready to bake a triple-layer fudge cake."

A picture of the proposed dessert flashed before my eyes. I swallowed and told myself to remain focused. "On the night of the murder you said you and DeeDee were watching television? Was she with you?"

"We don't have the same taste in television shows. I was in my room, she was in hers."

"Did you notice if she left her room?"

"She went into the kitchen. I heard the cookie-jar lid rattle." Inez cast me a cagey look. "Since you've come here, I've heard that sound often enough to recognize it."

I chose to overlook Inez's snide poke at my overeating. I went to the doorway that led into the hall, then looked behind me. The cookie jar sat on a shelf near the sink. DeeDee could have come into the kitchen to get a cookie, seen someone in the hall, thought about it, and later realized the episode might be important.

Inez was rattling pots and pans, muttering to herself. I raised my voice. "I want to talk about Cameo."

Inez stiffened. "What about her? She was a fine lady."

"I won't argue that. She was fine, but she was also murdered. I want to know what she did here at the mansion when I was at work."

If Inez was surprised that I knew about Cameo's visits, she didn't let on. "Miss Cameo would sit in her rocker and read her special books."

"Special books?" I murmured, thinking "journals." "Did Cameo take these books with her each time she left the mansion?"

"I don't know. Wasn't none of my business." Her tone implied that it wasn't any of mine, either.

"What did these books look like?" I asked.

"Just books," said Inez. "Miss Cameo had her own taste in literature. Your employee's choice of books for the secretary wasn't to her liking. Miss Cameo made her own selections, and I helped her retie the silver bow."

I nearly busted my butt in my rush to get to the secretary. I untied the silver ribbon, tossed the cluster of mistletoe aside. Were these books the keys to the hidden journals? I spread the tomes across the top of the secretary and read the titles: *Christmas Poems. Norse Mythology. Compost Made Easy.*

I picked up each book and shook it, looking for a note, a scrap of information. Nothing. I flipped the pages. Maybe she'd written something in a margin.

Inez had followed me into the foyer. She broke into my thoughts. "When are you going to bring Miss Cameo's rocking chair back down here?"

"The one in the attic?" I asked, absently.

"The day she saw it up there, I thought I was going to have to call an ambulance. She was so upset."

Saw it up there? I turned to the housekeeper. "Cameo was in the attic? But I thought she had to use the wheelchair." A flash of the murder scene came to mind. The footrests on Cameo's wheelchair had been flipped up out of her way. "How did she get up there?"

"She could walk," Inez said, "but she had to have help. She trusted me to steady her, and we took the steps slowly."

"Did she go to the attic often?"

"Usually every visit."

"Why?" I wondered out loud.

"She didn't *need* a reason," Inez said sharply. "The rooms are chock-full of personal items. Lots of things for Miss Cameo to look at and reminisce over."

I mumbled good night, then hightailed it out of there. I headed straight for the attic, where Cameo had visited, where Sid had said nightmares were made.

Chapter Sixteen

🌸 "Cameo's mission up this staircase must have been extremely important," I muttered under my breath. I pictured her taking one painful step at a time while Inez braced her from behind. I was amazed that I hadn't come home from work to discover the two of them lying at the bottom of the flight of stairs with their necks broken.

At the top of the staircase I fumbled for the light switch. I flipped it on, prepared for the usual dismal illumination. What I got was a dazzling burst of light that momentarily blinded me. I staggered back and nearly plunged down the staircase. I grabbed the railing, quickly righted myself, and scurried to safety. I shaded my eyes and looked up. Sid had replaced all the low-watt bulbs with megawatts to give his men plenty of power to make their search.

When my heart stopped racing, I took stock of my surroundings. The staircase opened into one huge antechamber with four smaller rooms off of it. Thanks to Sid, there weren't any dark, spooky corners. The ceilings were low, the floor made of pine planking. The walls were covered with a faded paper from an era when dinner-plate cabbage roses were in vogue. The air was musty but warm. A nearby furnace vent spewed heat. I'd have to check into getting the louvers closed off. I couldn't afford to heat the attic.

The room on my right held dishes, knickknacks, and other bric-a-brac. I shook my head at the amassed teapots, plates, cups and saucers, and what looked like an extensive collection of porcelain figurines.

Next door I found rack after rack of vintage clothing haphazardly covered with plastic drop cloths. Lace, as fine as cobwebs, edged fine silks, satins, and velvets. Antique clothes often sparked my interest, but this time all I noticed were the many hems, pockets, and linings that should be meticulously explored for the blackmail letters and the mini-sized journals.

The other two rooms were filled with trunks. I opened the lid of one and saw it contained sentimental birthday, anniversary, and sympathy cards, programs from dances, theater ticket stubs, and invitations to cotillions and Christmas or New Year's Eve parties.

I sifted though the litter of memorabilia, in awe that people would keep such sentimental fluff. Could the blackmail letters be stashed among this folderol? I supposed it was possible, but I didn't think so. The contents had been tossed haphazardly into the trunk. Bits of ribbons, that had probably tied bundles together, were scattered on the floor. Sid and his men had already done some serious checking.

In the farthest corner of the last room were humongous stacks of *River City Daily* newspapers. The papers were tied together by year, except the ones on top, which were current. I picked through them until I came to the last week of September. I had to go through several issues before I found what I was looking for. The date was September 30. The topic of *Sylvia's Snippets* was privacy.

In my work I'm often privy to information that lends itself to a blockbuster of a story. Do I tell all or keep silent? Fair warning, River City citizens, I write what I know. If you are foolish enough to commit an indiscretion, and I discover it, be prepared to read it in my column. I'm on the trail of a hot piece of gossip, and as soon as I have it verified, you will read some of my best work. This is big, folks. BIG!

What a bunch of ambiguous nonsense. I could see why Cameo had been upset. I was willing to bet that Sylvia didn't have one speck of scandalous information on the Beauchamp family. The society gossip had been on a hunting expedition for her *Snippets* column.

Exasperated, I flung the newspaper on the towering pile and went back into the main room, where I did a slow 360-degree turn. Furniture was piled around the walls and stacked like a fortress in the center of the room. My mind was boggled by the sheer magnitude of it all. Nothing had been tossed out. Everything had been kept, stored away, but for what purpose? I was looking at more than a century of one family's accumulation.

In a far corner I spied a gilded sheen. The spot of gold stood out like a beacon in this mahogany forest. Curious, I walked closer and removed the heavy drape that had slipped aside to reveal the tantalizing bit of ornamentation that had caught my eye.

Five oil paintings leaned against an old china hutch. Highlighted with gilt, the wooden frames were intricately carved with delicate branches bearing small oval leaves interspersed with tiny round berries.

There was no question as to the identity of these portraits. My heart thumped with excitement. I was looking at the ancestral gems, as Topaz had called them. Each woman was easily recognized by the jewelry—brooch, necklace, bracelet, and ring—that adorned her. Amethyst. Pearl. Garnet. Opal. Cameo. All were painted at the same age, about fifty to sixty, with white hair, blue eyes, translucent skin, and mouths tipped up in smiles. Each wore a dress that would've been the height of fashion during that period of her life, but all the gowns were the same shade of deep rose pink.

I stood before them in my faded jeans and sweatshirt. I looked into their eyes, and felt as if they were laughing at me. How could I, a mere woman of the twenty-first century, hope to uncover a secret these women had shared and protected for over a hundred years?

I concentrated on each woman's mouth, comparing and contrasting, trying to gauge her personality. Amethyst's smile was tight at the corners. It was as if she couldn't let herself relax. Pearl's portrait made me chuckle. She shared the same stiff pose as the others, but the glint in her eyes was pure enjoyment, her lips spread in a devilish grin. Garnet appeared to be concentrating on making the best of a questionable situation. Whatever the outcome, she was willing to meet it head-on. Opal was the daintiest of the lot, pale and delicate-looking. Her tiny bowlike mouth was pursed as if she were in deep thought, calculating her next move.

I stared at Cameo's portrait, looked deep into the eyes, and willed her to send me a message. I like to think we have guardian angels watching out for us, keeping us on that straight and narrow path. But just as we have bad people in the world, there are bad spirits looming close by to tempt and titillate us with wrong choices.

Once more I studied each portrait. What wrong choice had these women made that had left them open to blackmail?

What I saw—what I fantasized—as their natures intrigued me. I wanted their journals. I wanted to know more about these women.

I reined in my scattered thoughts and got back to the business at hand. Namely, why had Cameo come to the attic? Was it as Inez had said? To reminisce about a time that was long gone? For one thing Cameo wouldn't have been standing. She'd have hunted for a place to sit down.

I circled a bureau, a dressing table with a wavy mirror, and found the rocking chair I'd carried up from the foyer. The one Cameo had asked about the night of her murder. The one she already knew was in the attic.

The word "duplicity" came to mind. I shifted so I could see the portraits again. Topaz had used that word when she'd described one of the gems. Which one had it been? Amethyst for tenacity. Opal for courage. Wisdom was Pearl, or was it Garnet? I couldn't remember, but something was tickling my depleted brain.

I returned to the rocker and gave it a careful inspection. Solid oak. Nothing taped to the bottom of the caned seat, but the headrest sported the same carvings as the frames holding the portraits of the gems.

I sat down in the chair and rested my feet on a three-legged stool. "Why did you come up here, Cameo?" I wondered aloud. "Was it to think and scheme? Or did you feel close to your family? Did you find comfort in being surrounded by the material things your ancestors possessed?" Tears gathered in my eyes as I pictured her sitting alone, staring at—what?

I dashed a hand across my eyes. The rocking chair faced a west window. There wasn't a shade, but the night was like a navy drape across the glass. On my left was a box full of sewing notions. On my right was a table without any drawers.

I needed to go to bed. The next day would be horrendous. Everett was coming to the house at ten o'clock. Now that I'd given the attic a closer inspection, I could see why he was interested. There was an entire museum right here. At noon the other River City florists would be delivering their orders for Cameo. In the afternoon was the lying in state. I sighed. All those people tramping through the house. When I added in another day for Cameo's lying in state, the funeral, two days to clean up for the open house and an ongoing murder investigation, I decided I would be Looney Tunes by this time next week.

Always at the back of my mind was DeeDee. Where was she? Had she come home? Did I dare call her house again? I couldn't just sit here. I had to do something. I jumped up from the rocking chair and my foot tipped over the footstool. I grabbed it before it hit the floor and saw a small hinge.

I righted the stool and lifted the lid. Inside were six loose photos of six different men. The backgrounds were identical. I recognized the fireplace in the library. I scanned the faces. All were posed stiff and pompous for the camera. I flipped the pictures over and found what I assumed were their names: Douglas Lindquist. Taylor McNeally. Leonard Ikenberry. Steven Murdock. Hiriam Sinclair. Jackson Beauchamp.

There weren't any accompanying dates, but I could tell from the age of the prints and the clothing the men wore that years had passed between the taking of each photo. The oldest seemed to be a daguerreotype of Jackson Beauchamp. The most recent was Hiram Sinclair. I studied his picture the longest. It was the eyes. The first time I'd seen his picture had been at Topaz's house, but he'd been sporting a full beard. Here he was clean-shaven; a dimple winked provocatively at me—an indentation with the same shape and location as Jason's.

"Jason's grandfather," I murmured. If I could spot the resemblance, wasn't it a fair assumption that Cameo had, too? Had she died knowing Topaz had delivered a child, just not of the gender she'd hoped for?

I decided to keep the pictures of the men. I suspected they were the gems' husbands, but I wanted that confirmed. I bent to close the footstool lid but saw something nestled in a corner.

I reached in and brought out a beautiful cobalt blue bottle that looked just like the ones Topaz had at her cottage. The bottle fit easily into the palm of my hand. I cupped it and felt the thick heavy ridges molded into the glass. I held the bottle up to the light. A quarter of an inch of liquid sloshed when I jiggled it.

Topaz had said, "Ridges were molded into the glass as a warning to the user to beware of the contents." She'd also said, "that anyone who picked one up would know that they were holding a dangerous potion in their hand."

What was in this bottle? I pulled out the stopper and carefully sniffed. Whew! I made a face. It smelled like two hundred proof grain alcohol. A tincture is extraction by soaking herbs in an alcohol solution. Was this one of Topaz's herbal remedies? Why was it in a footstool in the attic?

Everywhere I turned it seemed I had more questions than answers. My biggest question right now was DeeDee's safety. I hoped it wouldn't be too late for another call to her house. I gathered up the pictures and the bottle, and once I was back in my room, I dumped them in the top drawer of my dresser. I sat on the bed and picked up the phone.

PLOP! PLOP! Something hit my window.

"What in the world?" I put the phone down and hurried across the room. When I moved the curtain aside, I found snow splattered on the window screen. I peeked around it and saw a figure, aiming a flashlight at my window.

I raised the sash and shivered as a rush of cold air flowed into the room. "Who's there?" I called, squinting at the light. I got the impression of a dark coat and a scarf tied over the head. No answer. "What do you want?" I demanded. No answer. "DeeDee?" I guessed.

The light blinked once.

I pressed closer to the screen. "Does that mean yes?" I asked.

One blink.

I breathed a sigh of relief. "Oh, thank God. Come around to the front door," I said. "I'll let you in. Your parents are frantic with worry about you. You have to call them immediately."

Slowly she turned and walked away.

"DeeDee! What's wrong? Don't go. Come—" But she kept walking. I slammed the window down. "Hell and damnation," I grumbled under my breath. I pulled on a pair of sweatpants and a heavy sweater. I tugged on boots, jammed on a stocking cap, and grabbed a flashlight before I ran down the stairs.

I opened the foyer-closet door, passed over my good purple jacket, and took an old green coat off its hanger. I pulled on gloves and was headed for the front door when I remembered my promise to Sid. I wasted precious seconds calling his house and getting his answering machine.

"Sid," I said in a rush, "DeeDee is outside the mansion. I'm going to try to persuade her to come inside so you can question her."

As I stepped out into the biting cold, I told myself I'd followed Sid's order. I'd let him know where I was. It was a major case of nit-picking. I shut the door on warmth and security and headed after the light.

Chapter Seventeen

❧ I took the sidewalk to the garage, then hesitated on the concrete apron watching DeeDee's light. The mansion faces north. The back of the property faces south. Topaz lives to the east. River City is to the west. Given these four choices I thought DeeDee would turn toward town. Instead she headed for the back of the estate.

The wild flurry of snow was gone, but the storm had left an inch of ice pellets that rolled under my feet like ball bearings. The crescent moon was a pale sliver of light. Evening had brought a rapid fall in the temperature. A bone-chilling wind nipped my nose and made it drip. I dashed a gloved hand across my upper lip, then buttoned the gap at the top of my coat.

Approximately two hundred feet in front of me, DeeDee motioned frantically with the light. I did as it directed. I waved my flashlight and hurried forward, trying to gain ground on her. As I slipped and slid across the snow, I wondered why she wanted to talk to me away from the house. Hopefully she'd stop at the grove of trees straight ahead. Nope. She detoured around the trees and kept walking. I picked up my pace, and called, "DeeDee, don't be afraid. I've phoned the sheriff. He'll be here shortly."

My words were meant to comfort, but they had the opposite

affect. She ran as if I'd threatened her with dire consequences. "Wait!" I shouted. Suddenly her light went out. I swung my flashlight in a wide arc, but I didn't see her.

"DeeDee, honey" I called, "if it'll make you feel better, I'll stay with you while you talk to the sheriff."

After a few minutes, the light came back on and blinked once. I lost sight of her, but followed her footprints up a slight incline. Twenty feet away she huddled, the flashlight aimed at the sky. I took half a dozen steps then stopped. The surface under my feet felt strange. I played my light over my surroundings and saw only smooth, virgin snow without a ripple caused by a concealed log or fallen branches. I moved the light higher and saw the embankment framed by the slender limbs of the winter-denuded weeping willow trees.

I caught my breath. I stood on the frozen pond. Swiftly I turned my light on DeeDee. She hadn't moved. I panned my light more slowly. The scarf was gone. In its place was a lime green stocking cap. She was sitting on a bright red toboggan.

"Please, DeeDee, come with me." I took a tentative step toward her. The ice creaked—a deep, grating sound that meant stress and strain. I held my breath and slid my left foot forward. "I know you saw something the night Cameo was murdered. It's all right, DeeDee. I know you're afraid." Twice more I moved my feet before I touched her shoulder. "Let's go back to the house, honey," I said, giving her an encouraging pat.

The flashlight toppled. She didn't stir.

With my heart in my throat, I grasped the collar. The body was featherweight. I ripped off the stocking cap. A huge teddy bear leered up at me. I was too shocked to move.

Now that I was closer, I saw that a rope had been stretched across the ice to the far bank of the pond and was tied to the toboggan. Whoever had devised this ploy had used the rope to drag the bear out on the ice from the opposite bank. I bent to grab the rope, thinking I'd show it to Sid.

Suddenly the ice popped. Without further warning, I plunged into frigid water that sucked my breath away. I threshed about underwater holding what little oxygen I'd managed to draw into my lungs before I'd gone under.

I struggled toward what I thought was the surface and banged my head against the layer of ice. I hadn't come up where I'd gone down. I was trapped. My water-soaked clothes pulled me to the bottom. My boots were as effective as bricks tied to my feet. Panic rose in my oxygen-deprived body.

The water was as black as ink. My movements were slow, my brain short-circuiting. I tilted my head. Off to my right I saw a murky glow. A flashlight!

I didn't know if it was the bear's or mine, but I swam a few feet until I was under it. I aimed for the area to the left, where I hoped I'd fallen through. When I stopped paddling, I sank like a submarine. My feet touched the bottom of the pond. I bent my knees and pushed with what strength I had left. I kicked for all I was worth to the surface.

I missed the hole by only a few inches, and my head collided with the ice. The contact jarred my teeth before the ice cracked, and I burst free from my watery near grave. I fumbled for the ice rim and clung weakly. With my head above water, I took deep gulps of air. The pain was intense as I pulled the cold into my aching lungs. I was tired. Too tired to move. Almost too tired to breathe. No. I shuddered. Never that tired.

I took another precious breath before I commanded my legs

to move so I could climb out. They refused to obey, hanging in the water like lead weights. I tried to wiggle my torso up and out of the water, but I couldn't get any leverage.

I screamed for help. Perhaps Topaz would hear me. Or maybe Inez would wonder why I'd left the house and step outside to investigate. Neither happened. Minutes felt like hours as I clutched that shelf of ice. I renewed my screams for help when I saw headlights flash on the trees around the pond bank. Someone had pulled up the driveway to the house.

By the time Sid reached me, my strained voice was a low croak. Sid didn't have my vocal restrictions. Once he'd sized up the situation with his powerful spotlight, he bellowed, "Judas Priest, Bretta! I'll have to go to the car for a rope."

"There's one here."

"How's that?"

I cranked up what little voice I had left. "A rope on the far bank." I tried to point, but my hands refused to let go of the ice. I closed my eyes. They flew open when Sid roared, "Bretta! Focus on me. Listen. You have to keep moving."

"Can't," I mumbled. "Too tired."

Sid didn't answer. Had he left? I didn't open my eyes to check. It took all my energy to keep a grip on the ice. I felt as weightless as the bear. My body was as light as a feather. Unexpectedly, I giggled. Had I stumbled onto a new method of diet control? There's aromatherapy, why not ice-water therapy? I could hang like a Popsicle until my extra weight froze off. Of course, I might lose an important part of my anatomy. A sobering thought, but I found it humorous and tittered.

"Bretta!" yelled Sid. "Snap out of it. Listen to me. The rope is attached to a toboggan. I've pulled it out of the water. It's behind you. Grab hold."

"What about Teddy?"

"Teddy? Who the hell is he?"

"Ted D. Bear," I croaked. I couldn't see Sid's face, but I heard him. So did anyone within two miles.

"Bretta Solomon! Concentrate on what I'm saying. Work your hands around the hole and grab the toboggan behind you."

"Can't," I whimpered. "Don't wanna drown."

"You're not going to drown. I'm here."

"Sid, my fingers won't move." I hiccuped a sob. "I—think they're—frozen." Hot tears thawed a path down my frigid cheeks.

"I never took you for a quitter."

"Reverse—psychology won't—work on—me," I rasped. "I'm not—a quitter. I'm just—"

"A quitter!" roared Sid.

Damned man! So infuriating. Slowly I moved my fingers, then inched my way around the hole. Chunks of ice broke away. Once I nearly went under, but I scrambled for a hold. The toboggan was right where Sid had said. I grabbed it with first one hand, then the other.

I had a nauseating thought. What if he couldn't haul me out of the water? Sid is strong, but I'm—me. Heavy. Heavy. Heavy. After my body left the buoyancy of the water, I pictured myself floundering helplessly on the ice like a beached whale.

"Hold on," shouted Sid.

Before I could draw a full breath, he towed me out of the water. The toboggan sailed across the ice with me bumping along behind like a broken rudder. At the bank's edge, a silent

Sid rolled me belly down on the toboggan, wrapped the rope around his waist, heaved a grunt, and we were off.

Momentum took us down the slope. Steely determination on Sid's part hauled me over the crusty snow to the house. He started his patrol car, then went around to the back and opened the trunk.

I tried to get off the toboggan, but I couldn't move. My icy clothes hugged me with hypothermic eagerness, willing to finish the job the frigid waters had started.

Sid pulled the toboggan next to the car, then wrestled me into the front seat. The warm air from the heater vents caressed my frozen cheeks like a lover's breath. Hastily, Sid tucked a blanket over my quaking body. My head lolled on the headrest. I gazed past him to the house. My room was lit. Inez had a light on in the west wing. The blue-green flicker of the television screen showed on her curtains.

Anxiety stirred in my chest. Panic shot through me. Was I experiencing delayed reaction? Shock? I couldn't think or reason beyond the bitter cold that had seeped into my bones.

I gasped. "House." I struggled against the blanket that wrapped me in a tight cocoon.

Sid shook me. "Stop it, Bretta. I'm not going to take you to the house for dry clothes. I'm rushing you directly to the hospital. Understand?"

The worry in his voice broke through my frenzy. I focused on his face. His eyes were filled with concern, his hands strong on my shoulders.

"Don't go hysterical on me now," he muttered. He reached into the backseat, then pressed something into my arms. "Here," he said gruffly, "I keep a supply of these for children who need a bit of comfort."

He closed the door before I could see what it was. When he opened his door to get behind the wheel, I looked down at my lap. In the flash from the dome light I saw a teddy bear. Button eyes stared up at me. The mouth mocked me with a satisfied grin. I gasped in horror. My world faded to black.

Chapter Eighteen

🌸 I regained consciousness as they took me out of Sid's car and put me on a stretcher. It was an effort to keep my eyes open. I was so tired. Two men rolled me down a hall and into a cubicle. Three nurses swooped in to remove my soggy clothes and wrap me in fresh blankets.

When I got the chance, I raised my head, wondering if Sid had dumped me and left. I caught a glimpse of him outside the curtain doorway. I tried to call to him, but discovered I couldn't make more than a croaking sound. Having a major case of laryngitis threw me into a panic. I squawked like a chicken on its way to the stewpot. I felt as helpless and frustrated as any frantic fowl. I forced myself to take a deep, calming breath, but that action brought on a coughing fit.

"Take it easy, Bretta," said Sid from the doorway.

Exhausted, I rested my head on the pillow, but I raised my hand and curled my index finger, beckoning him closer. I wanted to tell him that I'd been lured to the pond. Someone had meant me serious harm, but I couldn't put those thoughts into words. It was too frightening. I'd come too close to—

Sid leaned toward me. In a frazzled whisper, I said, "Watch house. Doors unlocked."

Sid's expression changed three times before what I said registered. "You think someone might search—I'll take care of it." He spun on his heel and stalked out.

I went limp with relief and let the professionals take care of me. I'd been in the hospital enough times to know that modesty isn't a consideration. I was poked, probed, and pricked with a needle.

I passed the night in a bleary haze of chills. Disjointed thoughts and strange faces peered down at me. No matter how many blankets were piled on me, I was always cold, drifting on waves of icy water. I dimly remember a couple of nurses talking in low tones. One commented that my natural layer of body fat had helped insulate me from the water's frigid temperature. The other agreed that a skinny person would probably be in intensive care or downstairs in the morgue.

My dreams were an erratic mixture of a time long gone and the present. My father took my hand, and we raced to the creek that flowed behind our farmhouse. He was young, lean, and handsome—the way I remembered him, thirty-seven years ago. I was the age I am now, my body encumbered with all the weight I'd once lost. My legs were heavy, my arms flabby. I couldn't keep up with my father. He dropped my hand and ran ahead, looking over his shoulder. I saw his disappointment in me.

I awoke with tears on my face. I fought sleep. I fought the dreams that plagued me when my guard was down. Did I hesitate visiting my father because of my size? Was I worried that I'd be a disappointment to him? I was too emotionally distraught to view the picture clearly. At some point, the medication kicked in, and I slept.

Sunday, the day after my near drowning, passed in a blur. At different times throughout the day my staff paid me visits.

They offered me just enough information to keep me from becoming alarmed, but never enough to satisfy. More than once I asked about DeeDee, about Cameo's murder investigation, about Trevor McGuire's death, but my questions were brushed aside.

I was aware that Cameo's lying in state was taking place. Lois assured me Sid had things well in hand. Chris said my flower shop had gotten the bulk of the orders for Cameo's funeral, though the other flower shops had delivered some fine pieces. I knew from Lew that a crowd was attending. He had been approached with the question of arranging advanced sales on my Christmas merchandise. In a ragged whisper, I'd told him that a lying in state wasn't the place to do business. The prospective customers would have to wait until the open house.

By the second day of my hospital stay, I was feeling better. I had a nasty cold. My throat felt as if I'd swallowed a cactus, my voice scratchy. But I'd been assured that as soon as my strained vocal cords had a chance to heal I'd be as good as new.

Colorful get-well bouquets from friends reminded me of work that needed my attention. A stack of holiday magazines, provided by a hospital volunteer, were a blatant warning that the hours left until the open house were marching on. I had a hundred details to attend to, but I was stuck in the hospital until the next day.

The afternoon paper couldn't hold my attention. I flipped the pages but found nothing current on either Cameo's or Trevor's investigation. Even *Sylvia's Snippets* was humdrum. She was expounding on the need for higher education for public officials. According to her, someone in our midst had slipped through a bureaucracy crater and was holding an exalted position with no more than a high school diploma.

I tossed the paper aside and picked up a magazine. The cover was plastered with pictures of angels fashioned from pinecones, wreaths fabricated from contorted milk cartons, and trinkets pieced together from broken tree ornaments. I shook my head at the inventiveness of crafters before slapping the magazine down on top of the newspaper.

I reached for the telephone and dialed the shop. Lois answered sounding harassed. "Hi!" I said. "It's just me. Are you busy?"

"Gee, I thought it was an obscene call. All that heavy breathing and sniffling and snorting."

"Very funny. Are you busy?" I repeated.

"Nothing I can't handle. Gotta go. Customer is coming in." She plunked down the phone.

I dialed the Henry residence. Darlene answered. "Hello?"

"Darlene, this is Bretta Solomon. Is DeeDee there?"

"My daughter isn't any of your business. Don't call here again." Clunk.

Deep in thought, I hung up. Darlene hadn't sounded worried, only annoyed with me. I hoped I could assume DeeDee was home with her parents. I should take comfort that she was safe. However, any progress I'd made to bring her out of her shell would hit a primary backslide under Darlene's thumb. I shook my head sadly. My heart ached for DeeDee. I cared about her, wanted her to have a life that wasn't ruled by her mother's intense sheltering.

I reached for the phone again and dialed the mansion. Crossing my fingers, I hoped someone other than Inez would answer. Apparently I'd used all my good luck at the pond. Inez picked up after four rings. "Beauchamp-Sinclair estate."

"What?" I rasped. "Inez you know damned good and well that—"

172

"Hello? Hello? I don't know who you are, but stop calling this number." She slammed the receiver down.

I was ready to dial the number again, but changed my mind. Instead I put through a call to the sheriff's department. If Donna was on duty, I might ask her—

"Sheriff Hancock here."

Too shocked to speak, I could only croak.

"Bretta?" he said. "I know it's you. That sniffle of yours is as identifiable as a fingerprint."

"I thought you were overseeing Cameo's lying in state."

His exasperated sigh filled my car. "In case you've forgotten I have an entire county to look after. Your property represents only a fraction of my obligations. I've put two deputies in the house, and three auxiliary officers to help direct traffic. They've had a tow truck out twice to pull people from the ditch. Your driveway is hell."

"I know. I hope we get warmer weather before the open house."

"I assume this isn't a social call. Get on with it. I've got things to do."

I fiddled with the hem of the sheet. "Sid—uh—I want to thank you for saving me and looking after the house."

"I planted myself in that house because you thought someone might try to find those damned letters. I've been in the company of that—that—housekeeper of yours. Lord, but that woman is as cranky as a horny old maid in an asparagus patch."

That stopped me. I had to picture the phallic vegetable before I could appreciate the witticism. By this time, Sid was saying, "—didn't like me in the house, let alone pawing through 'things.' "

"Sid, I didn't just fall through the ice." It was a blunt statement of the facts. I took advantage of his silence to tell him what had happened. When I came to the end of my story, I braced myself for another lecture on minding my own business. He fooled me.

"Figured as much. When I got your message, I called the Henrys'. DeeDee was there, so I knew something was up. I drove out to check on it."

"I'm glad you did."

"On the way to the hospital you kept croaking about a teddy bear. We used grappling hooks and dredged up that bear. Nothing special about it, Kmart sells them by the truckload."

"When I was following the figure, I lost sight of the light and had to follow footprints. Did you see them?"

"Yeah. But they didn't help with identification, if that's what you're thinking. I did use the prints to piece together a scenario. I think the person that lured you to the pond parked at the cemetery, threw everything for the trap over the fence, climbed the gate, and went to the pond where the bear was put on the ice. Once that was done, he/she circled around to come up on the house from another angle, other than the back of the property, so you wouldn't see a bunch of prints in the snow when you took the bait."

I switched subjects, hoping to catch Sid off guard. "How did Trevor die?"

"Don't you read the papers?"

"There was nothing in them."

"That right. McGuire's death is under police investigation."

That statement raised my temperature. "I hate this. I'm not some gossipy old woman. Cameo's dead. Trevor's dead. I was almost drowned. It seems to me I have a right to know what the hell is going on."

"Relax. This case is about to break. Eat your Jell-O and sip your broth. I have things well in hand." And with that he hung up quietly.

I slammed my receiver down. No information. No one to visit with. Nothing to do but lie there and worry. After five minutes of drumming my fingers on the mattress, I made my move. Super careful of the IV needle stuck in my arm, I eased out of bed, slipped my robe over my shoulders, and stuffed my feet into my slippers. I grabbed the pole that tethered me to the bag of nutrients and drugs dripping into my vein and rolled the contraption to the door.

I peeked out. I hadn't been told I couldn't take a stroll. But just in case I wasn't supposed to be out of bed, I gave the nurses' station a wide berth. I meandered down the hall. I would have felt conspicuous except everyone looked like me. Flat hair. Glazed eyes. Shuffling gait. Restrictive pole with bag.

I tagged along behind a couple of patients who seemed to have a destination in mind. It turned out to be a solarium. They sat, but I moved past the chairs to the windows. Weak sunshine and bare tree branches thrashing about in the wind coincided with my bleak frame of mind.

I should have been happy. Sid said the case was about to break. Why didn't I believe him? I didn't have all the facts. But did he? If the case was near an end, then why couldn't I have a piece of information? Deputy Meyer had told me Trevor's death was a sloppy attempt to make it look like an accident. I wanted specifics.

"We'll put the Christmas tree here," said someone from behind me.

I glanced over my shoulder. A group of hospital volunteers were staring at the blank wall off to my left. Their arms were loaded with boxes, bags, and banners.

"I don't know who came up with the idea that our Christmas decorations have to be informative as well as creative," snapped one of the women.

"The administrator, that's who."

"Then let him—"

"Now, Arlene, let's not start this project off by being contrary. If we all pull together, I think we can present an educational display and still make the solarium festive for our patients and their families."

I hid a grin and took a seat. With Arlene's attitude there were bound to be a few heated words exchanged. Since I wasn't involved and had nothing better to do, I decided that I might as well catch the first act.

The six women bustled about unpacking the boxes. A table was covered with a white cloth. A three-foot collapsible tree was plopped in the middle of the table and gaily wrapped boxes distributed around the tree's base. Two of the women worked the tangle of lights into a smooth string and wound them through the branches. Another hung the ornaments. They were laughing, having a good time. I was bored. I'd hoped for a squabble or at the very least, a rowdy discussion. I was getting neither.

I had gotten up from my chair when they posted the first banner. COPING WITH HOLIDAY STRESS. Under this was a smaller sign. "Do the holidays make you feel angry, frustrated, sad, lonely and maybe even resentful?"

"All of the above," I muttered, pausing to see what their solution might be. I knew mine was a piece of deep-dish apple pie topped with vanilla ice cream.

My mouth turned down as I read: "The keys to a joyous holiday season are love, compassion, and understanding."

What a crock! I'd hoped for sudden inspiration to solve my problems. The next banner read: HAVE A SAFE HOLIDAY!

1. Consider an artificial tree for your home.
2. Inspect Christmas lights for broken or cracked sockets.
3. DO NOT OVERLOAD extension cords.
4. Poinsettias are poisonous. So are the berries from mistletoe and holly.

I grumbled all the way to my room. Since the poinsettia is a member of the euphorbia family, the plant bleeds a white, bitter substance. Hardly an inducement to gorge, but every year it's the same old thing. Warnings about poinsettias being toxic flood the public, and I have to answer this question a hundred times a season—"Yes, ma'am, poinsettias are poisonous but only if you eat a handful of the yellow blooms or graze on the foliage. To be on the safe side, I would keep *all* houseplants out of the reach of children and pets."

I was already out of sorts when I reached my room. It didn't help to find Jason seated on my bed, my phone cupped to his ear. Since his back was to me, it didn't bother me one iota to eavesdrop.

"—not here. I guess I can talk to her later. Everything is fine. I told them the truth." He listened, then said, "You're right. That is a loose end that needs tying up, but I don't know how. You can't do that. She's willing. Says she owes me for thirty—" He shifted on the bed and caught sight of me. "Here's Bretta, Topaz—Mother," he amended with a flash of his dimple. "I'll see you later."

Jason hung up the phone and slipped off the bed. "I came by to visit and to bring you a gift." He pulled a flat package from his jacket. "Here's copies of the pictures I took the night of— uh—the—uh—when we were at the mansion."

I stayed in the doorway but nodded to the phone. "Was that Topaz?"

"Yeah. I check in with her every little bit. We're building a good relationship. Thanks to you." His dimple winked. "You gave us time to settle a few things. Thanks for letting us go to the authorities on our own. It was better that the information came from us and not a third party. We told the sheriff everything."

"Everything?" Yikes! Did that mean that Sid knew that I knew—I was getting light-headed.

Jason waved to the bed. "Don't you want to lie down? You look kind of pale."

"No. I'm fine. What did you tell Sid?"

"The truth. I've known all my life that I was born out of wedlock. Two years ago, my father told me the name of my maternal family. I came to River City to meet my mother." Jason shrugged. "It didn't seem right to just appear on her doorstep and announce I was her long-lost son. Instead, I asked if I could take pictures of the Beauchamp estate. It took a lot of nerve on her part to grant me permission knowing Cameo would never approve. I used the time to get to know Topaz and for her to get to know me. I thought I was making headway when she moved out of the mansion and into the caretaker's cottage, but Cameo's influence was too powerful."

"I suppose Sid gave the both of you a thorough grilling?"

"It was rough. Topaz and I are the prime suspects in Cameo's murder." He looked me square in the eye, and said, "But I didn't kill my grandmother."

Chapter Nineteen

🌸 The next day I was released from the hospital with only enough time to shower and change clothes before Cameo's funeral service. My stint in the hospital had netted me a five-pound loss. The dress I wore fit without binding. Not that anyone cared or could see the smooth lines under my heavy coat.

Topaz, Inez, and I were picked up at the mansion in a shiny black limousine. The minister rode in the hearse. The funeral director, Bernard Delaney, and his three associates followed in another car. Our cortege entered the Beauchamp private cemetery by a locked gate, which separated it from the Jackson Memorial Cemetery.

A dead silence had accompanied us on our short journey. Considering our destination it seemed appropriate though hardly surprising. Inez and I weren't capable of idle chitchat. Since I'd last seen Topaz, she'd lost weight, and her face was haggard. I noticed her hand trembled when she brushed her hair back from her forehead.

While the associates took Cameo's casket out of the hearse and placed it on a draped-wheeled cart, we got out of our car. The day was cold and blustery. Snow and ice sparkled like fairy dust scattered over the land. Clouds skimmed the sky, guarding the sun one minute, then setting it free to shine down on us. Giant evergreens crowded the fencerow, circled the clearing, and sheltered us from the rest of the world. The feeling was both peaceful and forlorn.

Dominating the private area was the gray-marble mausoleum. The only entrance into this formidable structure was a steel door, and two enormous urns filled with silk poinsettias flanked it. The men rolled the casket to a stop in front of the door. A gust of wind whipped past as the minister motioned for us to gather closer.

He spoke of life and resurrection, and I let my thoughts ebb. Carl had died in June, eighteen months ago. The weather had been beautiful. Mom had died fifteen years ago this past October. I'd buried her on a crisp fall day.

My father's letter was still in my purse. The dream I'd had in the hospital haunted me. In the light of day, I reasoned it had been a concoction stemming from my anxiety at almost drowning. My weight had cracked the ice. I'd feared Sid couldn't pull me out of the water and might leave me to flounder. Exhaustion had aided and abetted my phobias—overweight, loneliness, abandonment.

Carl had spent the first years of our married life reassuring me that he wasn't going to leave. But after twenty-four years, he was gone. Not voluntarily, but his death had left me with the same feeling of abandonment I'd experienced as a child. After eighteen months of being a widow, I thought I was adjusting very well. I had friends, my business, and plenty of interests to keep me occupied.

If my father had simply sent the box of Christmas grapefruit without the picture, I could have carried on, growing stronger and more self-sufficient with each passing day. But he'd jumped character. After thirty-seven years he was pushing for a more personal relationship.

I wanted to say I hadn't any desire to meet my father, but I did. He was seventy-six. Life is short. I'd certainly learned that lesson. If I didn't take this chance, there might not be another. I studied Cameo's casket. She'd been eighty, but her spirit had been younger. Had she lived, we might have developed a friendship that could have benefited both of us.

Cameo had been a foolish woman to taunt a blackmailer, a brave woman to have tackled the problem on her own. Her pride in her family had made her confront the blackmailer with fatal results. Topaz had said, "Forgiveness doesn't come cheap. The price is usually the cost of our pride." Pride had cost Cameo her life. Pride had cost Matilda Bennett the companionship of her granddaughter, Chris. Pride could cost me the reconciliation with my father.

The minister's words penetrated my thoughts. He quoted John 14:1: " 'Let not your heart be troubled: ye believe in God, believe also in me. In my Father's house are many mansions—' "

I gazed toward my mansion but couldn't see it for the evergreens. The old saying, "You can't see the forest for the trees," zinged into my brain. Carl had believed that the conclusion to most murders was obvious if you concentrated on the facts. Who had the most to gain by killing Cameo?

"Let's bow our heads in prayer," murmured the minister. "Our heavenly Father, we're gathered here today to bid this fine woman farewell, and to deliver her soul into your kind and gentle hands. We pray—"

Jason had said he hadn't killed his grandmother. A part of me believed him. Last night, after he'd left the hospital, I'd looked at the pictures he'd brought. Most were of the house, but a few captured expressions that were revealing. Simon had been caught glaring at Sylvia. Hardly surprising, since Sylvia had something on the man. I'd tossed the close-up of me in the ballroom undergoing a mental meltdown in the trash. Jason had taken a picture of Chris huddled on the staircase.

The rest of the photos had been of Cameo. In one she appeared to be listening to Everett. He'd been frozen in time, with an arm extended in lecture mode. In another she appeared to be preoccupied. From her expression, her thoughts had been melancholy. The picture that brought a lump to my throat was when her gaze rested on me. My pose mimicked Everett's. I'd been gesturing to the secretary, expounding on its beauty. Cameo stared at me with a tender smile of hope.

What did she want from me? Why hadn't she simply asked straight out?

"Amen."

Feet shuffled restlessly in the snow. Pent-up breaths were released with delicate sighs. It was time for the final scene of Cameo's earthly life. With the minister leading the way, we followed the casket into the mausoleum.

The exterior was an uninspiring gray, the interior a deep rose pink—the same shade as the dresses the gems wore in their portraits. Several kerosene lamps illuminated the room. The flames flickered and filled the air with a noxious odor that irritated my nose and made my itchy throat tickle.

The mausoleum reminded me of a giant armoire of drawers complete with handles. Beside each vault was a niche that held a vase. All were empty of flowers except for Amethyst's. Hers held a few stems of mistletoe.

While the attendants positioned Cameo's casket by the vault

that bore her name, I silently read the other inscriptions: Opal Beauchamp-*McNeally*. Garnet Beauchamp-*Lindquist*. Pearl Beauchamp-*Ikenberry*. Amethyst Beauchamp-*Murdock*.

These last names corresponded with the ones on the backs of the men's pictures I'd found in the attic. So I was right in surmising they were the gems' husbands. Where were they buried?

As unobtrusively as possible, I moved so I could see outside. I peered across the snow-covered ground. Looking closely I saw six mounds that could be flat headstones. Jackson Beauchamp's picture had been in the footstool, too. Was his the sixth grave?

Lew had said Jackson Beauchamp was the only male offspring. Land had been donated in his honor for the River City Cemetery. So why was he stuck in an ordinary grave, while the female side of the family rested in splendor?

For that matter, why were the wives sheltered in an everlasting shrine and their husbands in insignificant graves instead of at their sides? Pictures of these same men had been tucked away in a footstool. Didn't the men of the Beauchamp family count?

The kerosene fumes were irritating my raw throat. I tried to stifle a cough, but it wouldn't be suppressed. I hacked once, twice, then couldn't stop. The phlegmy rattle echoed in this marble cavern. The minister paused in his Bible reading. Everyone looked at me.

"Sorry," I managed to gasp. I hurried out of the mausoleum and into the fresh air. Hacking like I was going to cough up a lung, I moved away from the door and to the six mounds. I unwrapped a throat lozenge and popped the medicated disc in my mouth. While it dissolved, I used the toe of my boot to scrape the snow off the markers so I could read the engravings.

Jackson's grave was the first. He'd died at the age of twenty-two. One by one I looked at each stone. All the men had died in their late twenties and early thirties—the height of productivity. What were the odds of this many generations of one family of women losing their husbands at such an early age?

A nearby tree offered me a place to rest. I leaned against the rough bark and looked toward the mansion. The trees hid most of the house, but I saw the west window of the attic. Cameo's rocking chair had faced the west window. Had she sat there rocking and looking at the mausoleum?

The medicine had soothed my throat, relieving my coughing spell. I turned to go back in the mausoleum for another look, but the others were coming out. We waited for Bernard Delaney and his men to extinguish the lamps. They exited, and Bernard locked the door. He shuffled across the snow to Topaz. His wrinkled face was tinged with pink. Nervously, he fiddled with the keys, flipping them with his fingers.

My eyes were fastened on those keys. I wanted them and was already devising any number of devious ways to get possession of them. I could tell Topaz I would supply flowers for the vases. I could say I was worried that the lamps were still hot. I could—

"Miss Sinclair," Delaney said, "the Baughman Monument Company was supposed to be here to seal the vault and add the date of death to the marble tablet. Apparently, there was a misunderstanding about the time." He nodded to an associate. "Leo called the company, but no one is available until two o'clock tomorrow. If you agree, I'll keep the keys and will personally come—"

Topaz plucked the keys out of Delaney's hand. "You've done a wonderful job, Bernard. There's no sense in you making another trip out here." She tucked the keys into my coat pocket. "This is Bretta's land. I'm sure she won't mind dealing with the engravers. For myself, I never want to see this place again. When I die, I'll be cremated, and my ashes scattered over my garden." And that took care of my plotting. Topaz started for the limousine but stopped.

We heard car tires crunching the snow. I couldn't see who it was from where I was standing, but I could see Topaz's face. She was fighting for composure—licking her lips, straightening her shoulders. I stepped around Inez, Delaney, and one of his associates and saw Sid. He and another officer got out of the patrol car and strode purposefully to Topaz.

"Miss Sinclair," Sid said, "I'm arresting you for the murder of Cameo Beauchamp-Sinclair. You have the right to remain silent."

Chapter Twenty

On the ride back to the mansion, Inez sat on her side of the limo with her coattail tucked under her. When I'd entered the car, she'd drawn away from me like I had some dreaded disease. As soon as the car stopped at the front walk, she leaped out. I followed more slowly. My mind was crowded with thoughts, and I wasn't sure which one to concentrate on first. I settled on the most recent.

Topaz's arrest in the cemetery had shocked everyone. Inez had boohooed that "Miss Cameo must be turning over in her grave." Delaney had tried a "Now see here" type of persuasion with Sid. I'd kept my mouth shut. You don't trifle with Sid when he's on official business, even if the nature of that business might be misdirected. I was sure Sid had based Topaz's arrest on the information she and Jason had given him. To my way of thinking it just wasn't enough.

Carl had always said that there were three important considerations when solving a murder. Motive. Means. Opportunity. I'd made my own case against Topaz a few nights ago when I'd been washing dishes. Topaz had motive and means to kill Cameo. It was opportunity that kept the whole thing from coming together. Why pick that particular time to strangle her mother?

I felt reasonably sure that Cameo's murder had sprung

from her announcement that she was being blackmailed. Topaz had said she hadn't known about the letters. I believed her. Someone had feared being exposed by Cameo. Who? Everyone present had something to lose—jobs, respect in the community—if he or she were guilty.

The front door opened and Inez poked her head out. "Phone call," she snapped, then slammed the door.

Wearily, I climbed the veranda steps and went into the house. Pans banged and dishes rattled in the kitchen. I took off my coat and laid it over the chair by the secretary. Cameo had told me to sit here and record my thoughts. Who would ever care to read them? I wondered.

I collected the mail off a side table and made my way across the foyer to the library, where I eased my aching body down on the sofa. I picked up the receiver. "Hello?"

"Mrs. Solomon? Everett Chandler. You didn't keep our appointment Sunday morning. I made the trip to the mansion, only to be turned away at the door by our esteemed sheriff."

I made a face. "Didn't Sid tell you I was in the hospital?"

"He did, but it seems to me someone could have let me know."

"I'm sorry you were inconvenienced, Everett, but I had other things on my mind besides calling—"

His words cut across mine like a machete. "I'm sure you do. You're a blood-sucking leech. I'm giving you fair warning. I'm contesting Mrs. Beauchamp-Sinclair's will. I can't believe I'm saying this, but Sylvia Whitaker was right. You've been involved in the blackmail and murder from the start. I'll see you behind bars," growled Everett, "before you get anything more." He slammed down the phone.

My hands were shaking so badly, it took two tries before I

could replace the receiver in the cradle. I touched my hot face with cold fingers. What had brought on this verbal attack from Everett? Why warn *me* that he was going to contest Cameo's will?

The viciousness of Everett's phone call played in my mind until I wanted to scream. I grabbed up the stack of mail. Right on top was another letter from Texas. I had a wild desire to giggle hysterically, but ripped open the envelope. An airline ticket fluttered into my lap. More pressure to make a decision.

The next envelope held an invitation from the Show-Me Floral Designer's Competition, requesting that I spearhead the spring design show in Branson, Missouri. As an added incentive to accept the position, the letter informed me that the evening's entertainment would be Mel Tillis, a well-known country music star. Mel Tillis, a man known to stutter while speaking but not while singing.

DeeDee. I wished I could be sure it was *her* decision not to come back to work. When Inez walked into the library, I saw my chance to make a subtle check.

Inez asked, "Are you eating or dieting today? I can't keep up with your mood swings."

I wanted to say, "How's this for a mood swing? Get your bags packed and get out of my sight." Instead, I said, "Fix something light. I'm going to the shop." Leaving the mail scattered on the sofa, I got up. "Have you talked to Darlene lately? I don't suppose she's changed her mind about letting DeeDee come back to work?"

Inez shook her head. "Darlene practically has her daughter under lock and key. You want me to call the unemployment office?"

"No. I'll see to it later."

As I passed Inez on my way to the foyer, she warned, "Not much later. I need help or I'm out of here."

"Is that all it'll take?" I murmured, picking my coat up from the chair. Inez went back to her domain, where I assumed she'd indulge in another baking frenzy. I slipped my arms into my coat sleeves and glanced down at the chair cushion Cameo's grandmother had stitched. Lots of ivy vines with—

I'd never taken the time to study the design, but now I saw the ivy surrounded a pastoral scene that featured a miniscule garden with reflection pool and brick walkways. A grove of trees formed the background. As I looked closely I saw that the garden was a riot of colorful knots of yarn representing flowers. However, the tips of the tree branches were capped with snow and barren of leaves. I grinned. Cameo's grandmother had gotten her seasons mixed up.

Then I saw the elegantly draped outcropping of green at the fork of the main limbs. I dropped to one knee and studied the stitches. The yarn was a snarl of fuzzy sutures. The green was unidentifiable. I got up slowly. Pool. Brick walks. The inspiration for this print was right outside the terrace doors. I'd spied the same odd bit of green in a tree the day Cameo had been brought home for a final time.

As I hurried down the hall past the ballroom doorway, I glimpsed the masses of flowers left from Cameo's lying in state. That afternoon the funeral home was coming to pick up the bouquets and distribute them to local nursing homes, churches, and the hospital so the blossoms could be enjoyed longer. Had this been the idea behind the stitched cushion? Preserve the garden in cloth for future enjoyment?

When I opened the terrace doors, the hinges squeaked. I

clicked the latch shut, then picked my way across the icy flag-stone terrace and entered the garden that once had been known as the most elaborately cultivated area in River City.

The picture on the cushion had depicted the trees as sturdy and healthy. These trees were twisted with age. Their trunks decayed, the bark peeling in strips. Brittle branches had snapped and lay on the ground, but the strange bit of green was an oasis in this land of snow and ice.

I made my way down the brick walks. Rose brambles reached out to snag me with their thorny limbs. Birds sang a sweet serenade from their perches high overhead. Suddenly a cardinal swooped down to the patch of green, then flew away with something in its beak.

Rotten limbs barred my way for a close-up inspection, not that it was necessary. The oval green leaves and small pearl-like seeds were very familiar to me. It was mistletoe. I'd seen these same delicate branches reproduced in the wood of the rocking chair and the frames that held the gems' portraits, but hadn't given it a thought, other than decorative carvings. Stems of mistletoe were in Amethyst's vase in the mausoleum.

The terrace door creaked open. Inez yelled, "Lois wants to know when you're going to get to the shop?"

I fingered the mausoleum key that was still in my coat pocket. It wouldn't take ten minutes—but if Lois had called that meant I was needed. "Tell her I'm on my way," I answered.

Twenty minutes later I parked in the alley behind the shop. I climbed the wet steps to the loading dock and went into the back room. Lew looked up from the clipboard where he was copying addresses for his next deliveries. "Natalie Parker wants you to call her," he said.

Natalie was a good friend and probably wanted to meet for dinner. "I'll call later," I said, and started past him but stopped. "Lew, how much do you know about the Beauchamp family?"

"Nothing to blackmail over, if that's what you're thinking."

"How did the Beauchamp family make their fortune?"

Lew laid the clipboard aside and drew his pomposity about him like an overcoat. I smothered a curt comment. I'd broached the subject, now I had to listen to his haughty wordiness.

"There is no *true* Beauchamp fortune, Bretta. The original Beauchamp—the grandpappy of the clan—was a poor tenant farmer. Cyrus Beauchamp came from Arkansas with the clothes on his back and a bundle of apple tree saplings, which he hoped to grow into a fine orchard."

Lois poked her head around the workroom doorway. "Bretta, you've got a man waiting to see you."

I figured it was a salesman. I nodded to let her know I'd heard, but asked Lew, "So where does the fortune come in?"

"I'm getting to that. Cyrus married a woman who was sickly but was able to bear two children—Jackson and Amethyst. From what I understand, Amethyst inherited all the charm, looks, and spirit of the family. When her mother passed away, she took over the care of the house, the cottage that Topaz now calls home."

Not anymore. A jail cell was her new address, but I didn't tell Lew this newsy tidbit. It would redirect his thoughts from the past to the present. "So-o-o," I prompted.

"Don't rush me. You asked about the fortune. I'm getting there. The money didn't grow on trees." Lew chortled. "Fact is, nothing grew on those apple trees. They began to die before they had the first apple on them."

"And the fortune?"

"Mother says the Beauchamp women had a reputation for attracting men with money."

"So Amethyst married well?"

Lew lifted a shoulder. "Well enough. Steven Murdock was Amethyst's husband. The mansion was built with Murdock money. He died soon after the mansion was completed."

"What happened to him?"

Lew scratched his chin. "I don't know. Just died, I guess."

"I saw his grave marker at the cemetery this morning, and according to the dates, he died when he was twenty-eight. That's young."

"By today's standards maybe, but we're talking the late eighteen hundreds. People didn't live to be eighty or ninety."

"Bretta," Lois said impatiently from the doorway, "Mr. Wheeler has been waiting to see you for almost forty-five minutes."

"Wheeler?" I didn't recognize the name. "Is he with one of the wholesale houses?"

"Avery Wheeler," said Lois, crossing the floor to press a business card into my hand.

I glanced down and read: Avery Wheeler, Attorney-at-Law. This was followed by a string of names: Collins, Rinehart, Wheeler and McGuire. The last name leaped out at me.

I followed Lois into the workroom. She went back to an arrangement of roses. Chris was designing a bouquet of red and white carnations. I hurried to the front counter, where Avery Wheeler waited. He reminded me of an old walrus—baggy body, short neck, and a prominent salt-and-pepper mustache under a bulbous nose. His eyes were sharp and intense as they measured my worth. He carried a briefcase in one hand, a cane in the other. His three-piece suit was brown, his shirt the color of froth on a stein of beer.

"I'm sorry I kept you waiting," I said.

"Mrs. Solomon?" he inquired, giving emphasis to each syllable of my name. I nodded. He hooked the cane over the crook of his arm before setting the briefcase on the counter. He released the latches and withdrew a manila envelope.

As he handed it to me, he explained, "There won't be any formal reading of Mrs. Beauchamp-Sinclair's last will and testament. This is your copy. If I can be of any service to you, please let me know." He reassembled his belongings, then walked away. The bells jingled as he opened the door. He paused once to look back at me, dipped his head, and left.

"He waited almost an hour for that?" I muttered. I pried up the seal on the envelope and pulled out a number of legal-looking documents. I scanned the contents for my name. I knew it had to be there or I wouldn't have gotten a copy. When I found what I was searching for, I read the legal phrases and blinked twice before making a beeline for the door.

I caught Mr. Wheeler as he was about to enter his black Mercedes. "Sir?" I called.

He turned. "Yes, Mrs. Solomon?"

I walked closer, rattling the papers, hunting for the paragraph. "It says here, 'all debts to the estate are canceled.' " I looked at him. "That sounds as if I don't have to make another payment."

"Correct."

I rattled the papers again. My trembling hands made the words danced on the page. "What about this? 'All manner of furnishings are given free and clear to the house's owner, Bretta Solomon.' " Again, I looked to him for clarification. "Everything in the mansion is mine to do with as I choose?" At his nod, I asked, "But what about Topaz? Doesn't she want anything?"

"Apparently not. At the writing of this will, she told her mother she's satisfied with her life the way it is."

"But in later years, suppose she changes her mind? What if she decides she wants to give something to her—heir?" I was thinking of Jason.

A sad smile touched Avery's lips. "At the moment, Miss Sinclair has more on her mind than a few personal antiquities. I understand you were present when she was arrested this morning?"

I nodded.

"As the Beauchamp family solicitor I'll represent her. In fact I have to get downtown for her arraignment. She's being formally charged with her mother's murder this afternoon."

"I know you're in a hurry, sir, but how did Everett Chandler know the terms of this will?"

A pained expression crossed Wheeler's face. His mustache twitched. "Mr. Chandler was under the mistaken impression that the museum would profit from Mrs. Beauchamp-Sinclair's death. I'm afraid I had to set him straight when he called my home early this morning, demanding to know when the will would be read."

Something in my demeanor alerted the lawyer. His lower lip protruded in a contrite grimace. "I see. Chandler has already contacted you. I told him the contents of the mansion were in your hands. My mistake, Mrs. Solomon, I apologize."

I dismissed his faux pas with a wave. "Everett would have discovered the contents of the will, anyway. Did he tell you that he's going to contest it?"

The lawyer's eyes glittered. "Let him try," was all he said before he turned to his car.

I felt a pang of guilt for keeping him from Topaz, but I

needed information. "Mr. Wheeler, Trevor McGuire was a partner in your firm."

He smothered his sigh of impatience by clearing his throat. When he faced me again, he said, "The name McGuire actually refers to his grandfather, who passed away several years ago."

"But Trevor had his law office in your building?"

"Yes. Yes, of course." He tossed his briefcase onto the seat and shuffled his cane into his other hand.

"Did Trevor have access to all your firm's files?"

Wheeler's eyebrows drew down. "In what respect?"

"Do you keep files that are a hundred years old?"

"Anything over twenty years is delegated to our inactive files, which are kept in storage."

"Could you tell if a file were missing?"

"I'd have to know the nature of it. Name, date, and such."

I licked my lips. "Edgar Collins was the family attorney to Cameo's great-great-grandmother, Amethyst Beauchamp-Murdock. Would those files be available to anyone who wanted to see them?"

His chin jutted out. "No. Not to just anyone."

"Could I look at them?"

His shaggy mustache was doing a dance—up down, all around. "Mrs. Solomon, the relationship between a lawyer and his client is confidential."

"But all the parties involved are dead." I lowered my voice and took a step closer. "Sir, Cameo was being blackmailed. On the night of her murder she said it was a fact that had been safeguarded for more than a century. Trevor worked at your law firm. Did he have access to files that pertained to the Beauchamp family?"

"I suppose so, but they're in the basement."

"But he could have dug them out?" I persisted.

"If he were diligent enough." Wheeler's dry tone implied this was hardly an accurate description of the late Trevor McGuire's work habits.

"Trevor was ambitious, wasn't he?" I lifted a shoulder. "In a shortcut, who-gives-a damn, kind of way. If he found some information, it wouldn't have been beneath him to use it, right?"

"I'd rather not answer that," was his cautious reply.

I nodded, satisfied. "That's fine. You knew he was trying to get Cameo to name him executor because of some big idea he had for an endowment to the city?"

"I've recently learned of such a plan." Wheeler studied me thoughtfully. "What would you have me do?"

"If you won't let me see those files, will you look at them?"

His shrewd eyes gleamed with interest. "I'll be looking for a motive for blackmail, is that correct?"

"And a motive for murder," I added softly.

Chapter Twenty-one

❧ I went back into the shop and put the envelope of legal papers in my office. The *River City Daily* newspaper lay open on my desk to *Sylvia's Snippets* column. I read the following:

A tittle. A tattle. I had to battle for the scoop on Trevor McGuire's death. He died in the historic section of town. He stopped on a hill. He failed to put the gearshift into park. He stood in front of his car to check under the hood. My question, folks—Why were there acceleration marks on the cobblestones?

Goose bumps raised the hairs on my arms. Sylvia's words painted a vivid picture. The night was cold. The streets deserted in that part of town. Trevor in front of his car, the hood lifted. Suddenly the engine roared to life. Tires squawked on the cobblestones. Trevor's body slammed by the car.

What I couldn't imagine was who'd been behind the wheel. Who pressed the accelerator? Who felt the thud of Trevor's body? Who walked away?

I hung my head and moaned aloud.

Lois peeked around the corner. "You okay?"

"Not so great." On rubbery legs I followed her out of my office. "I just read Sylvia's column."

"I thought you'd want to see it." Shaking her head, Lois said, "You look awful. Maybe you should go home. You just got out of the hospital."

"I'd rather be here with all of you," I said quietly. Her quick hug brought a lump to my throat.

"Avery Wheeler has the reputation for being the best lawyer in three counties," said Lew, coming into the workroom. "You don't look very happy, Boss. Not at all like an heiress."

"Did Mrs. Sinclair leave you something?" asked Chris.

"Mrs. Beauchamp-Sinclair," I corrected automatically. "And no, I'm not an heiress. She didn't leave me money, but the house and all its contents are mine to do with as I choose."

My staff was silent as they digested this news. I used the time to remind them. "We still have to work for a living. I have bills to pay and no inheritance to fall back on. We have an open house in two days. I suggest we concentrate our energy on that."

The phone rang. Lois answered and took an order for Trevor's funeral service, which was set for Friday at one o'clock. I asked Chris, "Have there been many orders for Trevor's funeral?"

"About fifteen or so. Lois says we'll work them up on Thursday."

"I'd better check the coolers for flowers to fill the orders."

"Lois has already done that," said Chris. "She put in a call to suppliers this morning."

I grinned ruefully. "Then I'd better get busy, or I'll find myself out of a job."

Lew waved to an order lying on my worktable. "No time like the present. Mrs. Washburn wants another of your fabulous designs for her bridge party tomorrow. She says only you know how to please her."

"Lavender, purple, and yellow. No mums because they have an aroma. The arrangement can't be taller than fourteen inches high and no wider than twenty inches. Baby's breath for filler. The bouquet has to look like eighty dollars, but she only wants to spend forty." I cocked an eyebrow at him. "Am I right?"

"You got it. I tried to talk her into a Christmas bouquet of red carnations and holly, but she says the colors clash with her home decor."

"What's her Christmas tree look like?" asked Chris.

While Lew described the purple monstrosity, I went to the cooler for the flowers for Mrs. Washburn's bouquet. Instead of standing in the refrigerated air, calculating the number of stems, I grabbed a bucket with an assortment of flowers and hauled it to my workstation. I snatched a low plastic bowl from a shelf, used my florist knife to carve a piece of foam to fit the container and taped it in place. After adding powdered flower preservative and water, I was ready to go to work.

Making floral designs is second nature to me. My fingers know what to do, so my mind is free to search among the facts. Lavender liatris for height; Cameo's murder had been spontaneous. The weapon of choice a handy string of Christmas lights. Purple carnations for line; mistletoe had a special meaning for the Beauchamp clan. Yellow asters for contrast; Trevor's murder had been carelessly executed.

The clues were like flowers in a bouquet. Each fit together to create a design that led the eye to the focal point of the arrangement, or to complete my florist analogy, would lead me to the truth.

I reached for the golden yellow lily that was to be the star of Mrs. Washburn's bouquet. I couldn't shake the feeling that I was being led astray by what had gone before and what was happening now. A scandal in the Beauchamp family had resulted in Cameo being blackmailed. Her announcement that she would expose the blackmailer had resulted in her death. Trevor had said he wanted to discuss a "specific detail of the case" with me. Hours later he was dead. Had he taken his "detail" to someone else?

Lois nudged my shoulder. Startled from my thoughts, I jumped. She pointed to my arrangement. "I realize Mrs. Washburn idolizes your superb talents, but that's pushing it, don't you think?"

I focused on the bouquet. I distinctly remember reaching for the yellow lily. Yet, nestled among the lavender and purple flowers was a garish orange gerbera daisy. As I removed the objectionable blossom, I smiled weakly while my employees enjoyed a good laugh.

I stared at the orange petals of the daisy. Was I subconsciously telling myself that there was more than blackmail at stake? That I needed to look beyond the blackmail for the motive to murder?

I put the daisy back in the bucket. This time my fingers made no mistake. I inserted the stem of the yellow lily into the foam. Topaz had been arrested, but I didn't think she was guilty. The real murderer was out there somewhere.

As I added baby's breath to the bouquet, I gazed around the room at my employees. What were their thoughts on the case? I'd followed Sid's orders and hadn't discussed it with any of them. Even Lois, who'd been my sounding board over the years on a number of different issues, hadn't given me her perspective.

Maybe it was time to pump my employees for information. I could use them just as Carl had used me when he had an investigation that was going nowhere. He and I had worked as a team—airing theories, pointing out possibilities, and sometimes, settling on the truth.

There were too many interruptions here at the shop. I wanted their undivided attention, but I needed an excuse to get them to the mansion. Casually, I asked, "If all of you are free this evening, how about coming to the mansion to go over the last-minute details for the open house?"

My staff was willing, especially when I said I'd furnish dinner—sandwiches and curly fries from Kelsay's.

Before I went to Kelsay's to order the food, I decided to make one last attempt to talk to DeeDee. In this instance, the telephone was useless as a contact. Darlene held the record for being the fastest phone-slammer in town. Besides, I wanted to see DeeDee and make sure she was okay.

The note I'd supposedly sent still bothered me. I also wanted to know if she had seen something the night of Cameo's murder. While those were valid reasons for visiting her home, the fact was I missed her.

Since she'd come to live at the mansion, I'd grown fond of her, and I was sure she felt the same about me. I suppose that's why it was difficult for me to let it go. I had to know from her that she didn't want to come back to the mansion. If she were being forced to stay away, I'd have to do something about it. I just wasn't sure what.

The Henrys lived on Rockaway Drive in a well-kept ranch-style house. The roof and shutters were black, the siding white clapboard. Streetlights lit my way up the shoveled drive. I walked along a sidewalk that skirted the front of the house.

The draperies hadn't been pulled across the picture window, so I was afforded a view into the living room. Darlene was watching television. DeeDee sat in the corner of a sofa with her legs tucked under her.

I positioned myself so that if DeeDee looked up she would see me. Now all I had to do was get her attention. I made like a windmill, whirling my arms. Didn't work. I jumped up and down. Nope. I tried a combination of both—hopping and waving my arms like I was performing a regime of calisthenics.

Soon I was out of breath. I huffed and puffed, sucking frigid air into my abused lungs. This brought on a coughing attack. I stopped leaping to whoop and hack. I figured the reverberation would trigger porch lights to flash on up and down the street. Only one flickered into use. It was just over my head.

The Henrys' door was flung open, and Darlene craned her neck for a gander outside. She spotted me. *"You!* What are you doing here?"

I leaned against the porch railing, trying to catch my breath. "Came . . . to see DeeDee," I managed to say.

"David!" yelled Darlene. *"That* woman is here."

"I just want to . . . tell DeeDee I'll miss her."

Darlene spoke, but the wicked tone was gone. "Sweetheart, go on to your room. *She's* leaving."

I shifted, hoping to see DeeDee, but her mother blocked the door. I wanted to tell Darlene that she was making a mistake. Treating DeeDee like a child wasn't right. It wasn't fair. At twenty-three, DeeDee needed to make her own decisions, live her own life, not the life her mother thought she should lead.

Topaz had said, "Parents and family are at the root of more psychological problems than any other aspect of our lives." Wasn't that the truth?

Shaking my head, I trudged down the driveway to my car.

Seated behind the steering wheel, I looked back at the house. Darlene was hanging out the door; her steely gaze fastened on me, making sure I was on my way.

A flicker of a curtain in a corner bedroom caught my eye. I saw no one, but a small hand was pressed against the glass. DeeDee. The forlorn gesture broke my heart. I drove to Kelsay's with tears on my cheeks.

I placed my take-out order with a waitress, then looked around the crowded room, wishing I'd phoned ahead. My gaze lighted on Natalie Parker, who grinned at me like the Cheshire cat. Lew had told me she'd phoned, but it had slipped my mind to return her call. I tapped my forehead in an "Oops, I forgot" gesture and made my way to the table she shared with her husband, Dan.

Natalie is short, and chunky, and wears her dark hair in a Dutch boy's bob. Dan is the typical absentminded professor—black-rimmed eyeglasses, shaggy hair, and a dreamy expression in his eyes. His large commercial wholesale greenhouse supplies the tropical and blooming potted plants that I sell at the shop.

I sat in the chair next to Natalie. "How did you know I'd be here?"

"When you didn't call, I phoned back and talked to Lois. She said you were stopping by to get food for a staff meeting. I told Dan this might be the only chance we'd get to see you before the open house."

Dan likes his meals at home, where he says he can think in peace. Coming to Kelsay's had to be Natalie's idea. I waved my hand at our noisy surroundings. "When Natalie forced you kicking and screaming through the door, did you attract any attention?"

Dan grimaced. "We had a perfectly good meat loaf at home, but Natalie wanted to see for herself that you were all right."

I grinned. "I'm fine."

"You don't sound fine," said Natalie.

I endured her questions about my throaty voice, the hospital stay, and why I was having a staff meeting instead of tucking myself in bed with a heating pad. Finally, I called a halt to her inquisition by directing a question to Dan. "How's business?"

He brightened considerably. Natalie muttered, "Now you've done it."

"We've got a new slogan for the greenhouse. Flowers Bring—"

"Wait," interrupted Natalie. "Let's keep her in suspense, though with all that's been going on in her life, the words to our slogan won't keep her on pins and needles."

Ah! Now we get to the real reason why Natalie dragged Dan to Kelsay's. The murders. If I could have talked without further straining my vocal cords, I might've been tempted into a discussion. Besides, my food order would be ready shortly.

To head off another round of Natalie's inquiries, I asked Dan, "What do you know about mistletoe?"

For a moment, Natalie looked disappointed, then she pursed her lips and made kiss-kiss noises. "It makes for a great ice-breaker," she said, batting her eyes.

"Thanks, but I'd rather hear Dan's definition."

Dan stared at me. "The last time you asked me for information you ended up in trouble. As I remember, it involved a murderous fiend intent on doing you—"

Inwardly, I shuddered, but for him I waved a hand airily. "Christmas. Holly. Open house. Decorations. Get the picture?"

"Oh," said Dan. "What's there to know? Hang a branch out of the reach of kids and animals. The berries are poisonous."

"I know, but isn't it like the poinsettia? Wouldn't you have to eat a bunch?"

Dan shrugged. "Since mistletoe is a parasite, its sucker root takes what it needs from the tree where it's attached. Some trees give off toxins that might affect the berries. To be on the safe side, Bretta, add your ribbons and doodads, then hang the mistletoe away from curious fingers."

Thinking of the carvings on the rocking chair and portrait frames and the stems of mistletoe in Amethyst's vase, I asked, "Is there a symbolism connected with the plant?"

"The common name, mistletoe, is derived from the fact that it's propagated from bird droppings. 'Mistel' is the Anglo-Saxon word for 'dung' and 'tan' is the word for 'twig.' When you put it together you get 'dung-on-a-twig.' Symbolic?" He chuckled. "I guess it depends on what you're looking for."

I saw my waitress carrying a bulging bag to the front counter. It was probably my order. Getting up from the table, I gave Dan the names of the books Cameo had substituted for the ones Lois had chosen for the secretary. "Do any of them sound like they'd have something to do with mistletoe?"

Dan shrugged. "*Christmas Poems*? You'd have to read it. The book on compost is out. Most people have a sentimental picture of mistletoe when actually it's a pest. It can threaten the survival of any tree where it takes root. Mistletoe sets seed from October to December. With the first snowfall, propagation begins in earnest. Birds hunt out berries because the snow covers their usual feeding area. The seeds pass through the birds' digestive tract and the droppings—"

"All right. All right," said Natalie. "Enough is enough. What about Cameo's—"

My waitress waved the check. "Gotta go," I said. "My order is ready."

"You might look at that mythology book," said Dan. "Seems to me there's a myth about a god named Balder who was killed with an arrow tip of mistletoe. Can't remember much else."

We said our good-byes, and I paid for the food, then hurried out to my car. While I waited for the engine to warm, I thought about what Dan had said, "most people have a sentimental picture of mistletoe." I had proof that the Beauchamp family considered it important. They'd re-created the plant's likeness in wood. Had put stems of mistletoe in the mausoleum. Why? Especially since the plant is classed as a pest—a parasite.

"That's what Cameo called the blackmailer," I said aloud. "A parasite."

Carl's voice was in my ear. "Piece it together, Babe. Take one train of thought and carry it through."

I smiled, happy to hear Carl's voice, then frowned at his advice. "Swell, but where do I start?"

"At the beginning. Where else?"

"The beginning?" I licked my lips. "Cyrus Beauchamp came to Missouri from Arkansas to grow an apple orchard. The remnants of that orchard still exist if you count the rotted stumps and dead branches. Mistletoe is on the survivor, but I can only surmise that it killed the other trees. What does that have to do with anything—"

"Keep going, Babe," encouraged Carl.

I put my elbow on the steering wheel and propped up my chin. "—except that the mistletoe was symbolic to the Beauchamp family. Amethyst was sole owner. She married well. I've seen her portrait, and she didn't look the type to need a man to protect and care for her."

Carl chuckled lustfully. "I know it's been a while, but a man has other purposes besides protection."

Tears filled my eyes. "Oh, Carl, I can't think about that. I remember the last time we—"

"Stop right there. You're getting off the subject."

I swallowed a sob, then took a shaky breath to steady my raspy voice. "Amethyst hooked herself a well-to-do husband, built the mansion with his money, and he died very young." Uneasiness stirred in my stomach. "He died young," I repeated. "All the Beauchamp husbands died young." I paused, then whispered, "Carl, I don't like what I'm thinking."

"Tell me, Babe."

"At the cemetery it struck me that the men of the family didn't count because of the simple grave markers. Their photos were stuck in a footstool along with a blue bottle that had ridges molded into the glass. When I talked to Topaz, she said that type of bottle was used in the eighteen hundreds as a warning that the contents were dangerous."

"But she didn't use the word 'poison.'"

I shook my head. "She said 'restricted dosages,' but there's the mistletoe. It's important. It's poisonous. What if a tincture was made of the berries? I smelled alcohol when I opened the bottle. Would a concentration of mistletoe berries prove fatal? What if it was used on a husband who'd fulfilled his usefulness?"

"Whoa, Babe."

"Why? You're the one who told me to follow a train of thought to the end."

"You might have the wrong train. Hell, Babe, you may even have jumped the damned track."

I laughed out loud, then looked out the passenger window

and saw a man and a woman gaping at me. A nearby street-light had showcased my animated one-sided conversation.

I waved jauntily before I put the car in gear. As I drove out of the parking lot, I muttered, "You're going to get me committed, Carl." His deep haw . . . haw . . . haw echoed in my ears. That much-loved sound soothed my troubled thoughts, but it didn't make them go away.

Chapter Twenty-two

🌿 Fifteen minutes later, I crept up my icy driveway. Lois and Lew had arrived. Their cars were parked near the front walk. I pulled around to the concrete apron in front of the garage and hit the control on my sun visor for the door. Chris's car lights flashed behind me. I eased into the garage, cut the engine, and got out.

"Come on in," I called, grabbing the sack of food. When Chris was inside, I touched the button to seal out the cold. "No sense in you traipsing around to the front."

"It's bad luck to enter a house through one door and leave through another," she said. "I'll have to come back out this way."

"Keep that in mind. Let's not tempt fate. If you've got a rabbit's foot on you, give it a kiss for luck." I opened the door into the house. Lew's deep bellow of laughter greeted us. I nodded toward the sound. "Or you could rub a bald man's head. That's supposed to be lucky."

Chris hung back, and whispered, "I don't know what I'm going to do, Bretta. I'm not romantically interested in Lew. I don't want to make an awkward situation at work, but I can't date a man I'm not attracted to, just to keep the peace."

"No one expects that, Chris." I lowered my voice. "Be pleasant, but don't encourage him. He'll get the message."

"I hope so. He's nice, and he does comes from a good family." She sighed ruefully. "I suppose I should be honored that he's attracted to me, but I can't pretend I care for him."

"You're too tough on yourself. Why shouldn't he be attracted to you? You're bright, pretty, and come from impressive stock yourself." As the words left my mouth, I wanted to grab them out of the air. "Chris, I'm sorry. I shouldn't have said—"

"It's okay. You're right in fact, just not substance. It's hard to associate myself with my mother's side of the family. My grandmother never acknowledged my birth. I used to think it was because I resemble my mother so completely—hair, eyes, voice. Matilda's treatment of me has stolen much of my self-worth." She gave me a shy smile. "But I'm working on changing that."

"Good for you. And who knows? Your grandmother might change, too."

Resigned, Chris shook her head. "If Matilda Bennett couldn't forgive her own daughter enough to attend her funeral, nothing's going to faze her."

"She might still come around," I said, thinking of my father's continued pressure to get me to Texas. "Time has a way of making the hurt less painful. Someday your grandmother will wake up and realize she's wasted her life by being unforgiving."

"I'll believe that when I see it," muttered Chris bitterly.

I jiggled the sack. "Let's eat." I raised my voice. "We're here, and we've brought curly fries."

Lew and Lois came out of the dining room. Inez peered around the kitchen door. She eyed the grease-spotted sack distastefully. "If I'd known you wanted oily potatoes, I could've made them. I've got a can of lard in the freezer." She gave a disapproving sniff and disappeared into the kitchen.

I spread the food on the dining-room table. Inez brought a tray of ice-filled glasses and a pitcher of tea. Without a word she left, only to return with a carafe of coffee, mugs, and a plate of brownies glazed with chocolate and sprinkled with black walnuts.

"I'm not complaining," said Lew, slathering Miracle Whip on his tenderloin sandwich, "but why are we here? I thought all the details for the open house were done."

"They are, except for these." I pulled a notepad from my pocket. While we ate, I delegated last-minute chores to each of my employees. We had a lively discussion on who was going to man the cash register, and who was going to help customers carry their purchases out to their cars. By the time we finished our meal and polished off the brownies, we'd reached an agreement and were ready for an inspection of the house.

In the foyer, I turned to the horseshoe-shaped staircase. "The poinsettias are being delivered tomorrow. I want them positioned on the steps to discourage any wayward shopper from going up. I'll use the elevator or the back stairs to get to my room."

"Do you want me here to help unload the plants?" asked Lew.

I shook my head. "The delivery is planned for one o'clock. I have to be here anyway because the monument company is sending someone to seal Cameo's vault, and I have the key to the mausoleum. I'll leave the poinsettias in the foyer. We can check them for water and position them on Thursday."

"What about that box of handblown glass ornaments you were going to hang on the Victorian tree?" asked Lois.

"The box is in my room. I'll bring it down tomorrow."

"Want me to get it?" offered Lew.

"No. The box isn't heavy, just cumbersome. Let's go into the ballroom."

We moved down the hall. My hand trembled slightly as I clicked on the overhead lights, then turned to my employees. "I've gotten you here under false pretenses."

"I knew that sandwich was going to cost me," said Lois, rubbing her stomach. "But I was thinking of a sleepless night because I ate too much. What do you want?"

"I'd like to talk about Cameo's murder. Get all of your ideas on a few things. Carl and I used to do this when he had a case that wouldn't jell."

Lois grinned. "If I know you, you've already got a theory. Go ahead. I'm sure we can poke a few holes in it."

"On the night of her murder, Cameo said that the senior member of Trevor's law office had been her ancestors' solicitor. She also said the secret was more than a century old. What if Trevor found this data and blackmailed Cameo? Topaz says Trevor wanted Cameo to make some sort of endowment to the city with him named as executor. Maybe he used this information to pressure her."

"If we can believe Sylvia Whitaker's column, McGuire was murdered. If he killed Cameo, then who killed him?" asked Lew.

"I don't know, but I think someone else acted on the same information he had."

Lois's eyes widened. "You mean she was blackmailed by two different people?"

"Cameo said the blackmailer came onto the property and mentioned an amicable solution. She said there were three letters, each mean-spirited and cruel. What changed the black-mailer from amicable to cruel?"

"Maybe nothing," said Chris. "Maybe he got impatient or desperate."

I shook my head. "Don't you all see? If there were two blackmailers, and Trevor was one, that leaves the other as his killer."

"They could have been working together from the start," offered Lois.

That was true, but I still liked my theory best. Rather than pursue it, I said, "The flower shop grapevine has let all of you down on the latest happening."

"What's that?" asked Lois.

"After Cameo's funeral this morning, Sid arrested Topaz for murder."

"Good Lord," said Lew. "I wonder if Mother knows."

"You don't agree with Sid?" asked Lois.

"No. I don't think Topaz killed Cameo."

Chris said, "Since she was arrested, that must mean the authorities have evidence against her."

"I'm not saying Sid didn't have a good reason. I just think he's giving the wrong interpretation to what he's got. Jason is the one who should have been questioned more thoroughly."

"Jason?" said Lew. "Why him?"

"He's her son," I said bluntly.

Lois pursed her lips. "Well, I'll be damned. You're kidding?" She eyed me closely. "You're not kidding. Girl, you're a fountain of information."

"How do you know he's her son?" asked Chris.

I skimmed the highlights of the how and why of my deductions. I ended by saying, "Jason visited me at the hospital and told me that he came to River City to get to know his mother. He purposely made her acquaintance, but didn't tell her who he was. He kept dropping less-than-subtle hints for Topaz to draw her own conclusions. He hoped she'd accept him because she wanted to, not because he had miraculously landed on her doorstep."

"I see where you're going with this," said Lew.

Were Lew and I on the same wavelength? I traded glances with Lois. She gave me a sly wink. Curious, but a little uneasy, I asked, "Where is that?"

"Jason was here the night of Cameo's murder."

Chris frowned. "Big deal. So were we."

Lew's face registered hurt at Chris's sharp tone, but he continued. "Yes, but none of us had a motive for wanting the old woman dead."

"What makes you think Jason did?" asked Lois.

Before Lew could speak, I said, "Cameo was in Jason's way. Topaz might have admitted he was her son much quicker if it hadn't been for Cameo. He said when Topaz moved out of the mansion, he was sure she was on the verge of telling him, but she didn't. He said Cameo's influence over her daughter was too powerful."

Lew nodded. "It's a well-known fact that Cameo has kept Topaz under her thumb. Topaz should have left a long time ago," he added piously.

This observation was laughable coming from Lew. His mother dominated him body and soul. I caught the amusement in Lois's eyes and quickly frowned a warning not to say something we might regret.

Chris said, "From what you're saying the police were right in arresting Topaz. Topaz was the one who had to deal with her mother. Jason could have gone away if things didn't work out."

"I still don't think Topaz killed Cameo," I argued. "Whoever killed Cameo was at the end of his or her rope. Cameo's death was spur-of-the-moment because of what she'd said at the dinner table. The blackmailer was being pressed into a corner. His or her identity was going to be exposed. The killer had no choice but to silence Cameo before she could say any more."

Lois yawned. "I'm sorry, Bretta, but this is too involved for me. I think I need to sleep on it. Maybe by tomorrow I can offer you some fabulous insight into the whole mess, but right now I'm exhausted."

I nodded wearily. It had been a long, long day. Lois and Lew moved out of the ballroom. Chris followed, explaining why she was leaving by the garage door. Lew cautioned both women to take it slow on my slick driveway.

I agreed, told them good night, then walked with Chris to the garage. She paused. "Thanks for dinner. It's always a pleasure to come here. This house is so beautiful. Living here must make you feel special." She slowly shook her head. "I can't get over Cameo's will. All of this is yours, and you did nothing."

I was jolted out of my preoccupation. I'd done nothing? I thought of the work. Of the money I'd spent—money from Carl's life insurance, a misnomer if ever there was one. I thought of the lonely nights. Of the times I ached for an encouraging hug, and he wasn't there to give it to me.

I took a deep breath to ease the lump from my throat. "I wouldn't say I did nothing, Chris. The price of this house was pretty damned steep. Fact is, you could say it has cost me dearly."

Her eyes widened. "Oh, Bretta, I'm sorry. I forgot about Carl's—"

I opened the door and led the way across the garage. "I know. Go on home. I'll see you tomorrow."

I waited until she'd turned her car around, then went back to the foyer. Inez stomped out of the kitchen, saw me, and harrumphed. Without so much as a good night, the old rip went back to the kitchen, and I hoped, on to her bed. I wanted some peace and quiet. I needed a good night's sleep, but I had a couple things on my mind that would have to be cleared up before I could rest easy.

I went to the secretary and pulled the Norse mythology book out from under the others. Using the index I looked up the god, Balder. I found the name and flipped to the correct page. Too tired to hunch over the secretary for the lengthy read, I nudged the chair out from under the desk. After giving the stitched cushion an apologetic glance, I plopped down.

I wiggled. Sid was right. The cushion was uncomfortable. It felt like it was padded with cardboard not—Cameo had told me to sit here to record my thoughts. *Sit here.* I jumped up like my butt had made contact with a cocklebur.

The cushion was attached to the chair by two pieces of cord tied to the backrest. My fingers fumbled with the knots, but once I had them untangled, I picked up the cushion and flipped it over. A heavy second layer of fabric had been sewn across the back to form a pouch that was secured with a button. I slipped the button from the slot and upended the cushion over the secretary.

Six small books fell out. They were each the size of a pocket dictionary and were made of black tooled leather. Stamped in gold on the lower right-hand corner of each book was the name of its owner—Amethyst. Pearl. Garnet. Opal. Cameo. Bretta.

Bretta? I brought the book cover almost to my nose and saw that Topaz's name had been scratched out and mine superimposed.

I took my find to the library and sat down on the sofa. My heart was pounding as I reached for the book bearing my name. I flipped the pages but all were blank. I picked up Amethyst's book.

On the inside flap was a faded drawing of a necklace. The sketch was amateur, but each stone was identified with its name. Puzzled, I checked to make sure I was reading Amethyst's book. If she were born first, then how did she know each consecutive child would be female? What if a male child had been born?

I shivered and almost tossed the book aside. Maybe I didn't want to know the secrets of this family. I had an idea that my illusion of Cameo being a sweet, kindly old woman was about to be blown to smithereens. I weighed the pros and cons of reading the journals. Curiosity won out.

My Dearest Ones: I embrace each of you with love. As a plant sets seed to sustain life, so must I. Drastic actions are sometimes necessary. If you are reading my words, then you have taken the sacred vow of the Beauchamp women—preserve our heritage at all costs.

Papa thought himself a visionary. But as is true with most men, his sight was limited. I foresee a dynasty built from this land that turned against him. If you are to survive—if our strain is to remain pure—you must learn to take what has harmed you and reap the benefits.

I had the gist of Amethyst's philosophy, so I skimmed the pages looking for her explanation of "drastic action" and "preserve our heritage at all costs." Since I'd already figured mistletoe was important, the word leaped out at me.

When Papa came from Arkansas with his apple tree saplings, unbeknownst to him seeds of the mistletoe were anchored to the bark of these ill-fated trees. The mistletoe sprouted and grew, suckling the very life from Papa's dream. My brother, Jackson, a stupid man, thought that by cutting the mistletoe from the trees he could make it go away. Such was not the case. The plant flourished as birds ate the seeds and redistributed them to fallow sites.

Learn from nature. Make use of what it offers. The mistletoe destroyed Papa's vision. I shall use that same mistletoe to secure our rite of passage. The first snow is magical, my beloved. It signals the production of our special elixir. Gather the pearly white mistletoe berries. Steep. Stir. Strain. Use only the ridged bottles and store them away from prying eyes.

My precious family, you can employ this potion only once a generation. I used it three times but only to procure our future. Jackson inherited the land and was about to be married. His offspring would have been next in line. Today, I'm sole owner, just as each of you shall be. When it comes your time to use the elixir—be generous with the dosage. Jackson lingered. A doctor was called, but to no avail. Jackson died after another measure of elixir.

This fine home was built with all of you in mind. I used the elixir a third time to make it possible for me to be the sole owner again. Resist the urge to erase minor inconveniences from your life. Its use is reserved for keeping the Beauchamp dynasty in our hands. The male members of our society will want to wrestle the reins of ownership from you. Marry wealth. Take the man's name. Bring forth a daughter and name her as I've instructed. Never let your husband control the Beauchamp dynasty.

"Lord have mercy," I murmured. The book slipped from my fingers. Amethyst had been a diabolical woman. Had the other ancestors followed their mentor's instructions? Had Cameo accepted Amethyst's plan without reservation?

Slowly, I picked up the book that bore Cameo's name. I skipped and skimmed until I came to a paragraph that made my heart lurch.

I'm rarely able to write in my journal. Hiram is so jealous, so demanding. He wants to know what I'm doing every minute of the day. I long for pregnancy so I can be free of my fanatical husband.

"And she called him a fanatic?" I muttered aloud. The history of the Beauchamp women had brought on a thundering headache. I needed my bed. Bleary-eyed, I turned to the last pages of Cameo's journal.

Some of the narration was boring. Most of it had to do with regrets over Topaz's continued resistance to adopt the Beauchamp ideals. "You go, girl," I mumbled. "Hang tough." I was ready to close the book when my own name caught my eye. I read the paragraph with a mixture of anger and humiliation.

I've found my surrogate Beauchamp. Bretta Solomon is past childbearing years, but she loves this house and will cherish it. I'm sure I can bend her to do my bidding.

My breathing was erratic, but I turned the page.

Outside forces are pressing me. Another blackmail letter came today. Bretta's doing a wonderful job restoring the house, but she's busy and time is running out. The tingle at the nape of my neck is as you each described. My death is imminent. I have to rid myself of this blackmailer so I can make Bretta understand the importance of our accomplishments.

I turned the page.

Christmas is coming. A holiday greeting from an old friend was enlightening. I've discovered the identity of my black-mailer in a most unusual manner. Even as I write this, I am smiling. In honor of you, Great-grandmother Pearl, your art of double-dealing will come into play. I shall blackmail a blackmailer. I have no intention of going to the law. I will take care of my parasite and watch it shrivel from lack of nourishment. A dinner party, a revelation, and the path will be cleared of obstructions. My precious family, please forgive me for failing you in the vital area of preserving the Beauchamp line, but I'm about to make amends in the best way I can.

The last entry.

Bretta is at her shop. I'm free to wander my home, and gather strength for the upcoming revelation. To celebrate this won-drous occasion, I've had Inez take me to the mausoleum. I've placed mistletoe in Amethyst's vase as a remembrance, but also to signify the dastardly scheme that almost brought us to ruin.

Chapter Twenty-three

❧ Sheer exhaustion took over. I closed my eyes and didn't open them again until a loud noise in the foyer awoke me. I stumbled to my feet and went to the doorway. Inez had her coat on and was peering impatiently out the front glass. A suitcase was at her feet.

"What's going on?" I asked.

She whirled to face me. "I won't stay another minute in this house with a—a—conniving—" She gulped air. "Last night, I heard you say that 'the price of this house came pretty damned steep.' Then you said, 'it has cost me dearly.' How right you are. It's going to be damned pricey when you're tossed into jail, and Miss Topaz is freed."

"It's too early in the morning for riddles, Inez. What are you talking about?"

Instead of answering, she crossed to the entry closet and jerked open the door. Triumphantly, she flipped my purple jacket. "See? Here's the proof. I knew it was you blackmailing Miss Cameo. I didn't hear everything, but I heard you say your 'plans for the house were an amicable solution to a disagreeable problem.' You plan on turning this fine old home into a boardinghouse. Miss Cameo denied it was you on the terrace, but I saw that purple jacket. Next thing I knew, you were parading around this house like you had every right to it."

I heard her rambling, but I zeroed in on one fact. "You saw the person who blackmailed Cameo?"

"I saw you!"

"No, Inez, you didn't." I took a step toward the housekeeper. "You're in a position to solve Cameo's murder. Put what you think is my involvement out of your mind, and concentrate on what you actually saw."

On the driveway tires crunched through the snow. A horn honked. "That's my taxi," Inez said. "I'm on my way to the police."

"Good. Tell Sid—"

"Ha! The sheriff is a friend of yours. I'm going to the River City police."

"Inez, for your own safety don't tell anyone except the authorities what you've told me." I took another step to reiterate my warning. She brought her handbag up to her chest like a black-leather shield.

"Don't come any closer. I've put my set of house keys on the kitchen counter. The freezer is full of pies, cakes, cookies, and casseroles. There's fried chicken and potato salad in the refrigerator." She scoffed nastily. "Stuff yourself. I've worked my fingers to nubs cooking and baking just to have the pleasure of seeing your weight climb higher and higher."

I blinked in confusion. "You've been sabotaging my diet? I thought you loved to cook and that's why you—" I couldn't finish. I was struck dumb by the vindictiveness of the woman.

Inez smirked. "Miss Cameo said I was wrong about you. She told me to stay and get to know you. I promised her I would, but even she wouldn't expect me to stay with the person responsible for her—"

"It's best you go," I interrupted, "but I want one thing

straight." I waved a hand to our elegant surroundings. "My husband's life insurance paid for this, or I could never have afforded it. This house cost me dearly, Inez, but not because I had to resort to murder. But because Carl is dead, and this is all I've got." I watched for some softening, some trace of understanding. Inez stared at me, unmoved. "Your cab is waiting," I said. "Don't let me keep you."

She grabbed the handle of the suitcase, opened the front door, and stepped onto the veranda. Gently, I closed the door. Once again I was alone. I should have hated the house for what it represented, but it was merely a shell, a façade like the human body. What you see on the outside isn't necessarily what's going on inside. Cameo and her ancestors had proved that. They'd been socially acceptable but morally corrupt.

The silence of the house was so tangible I felt I could reach out and touch it. I gazed at the beautiful oak wood that had been bought and paid for time and again with murder. I shook my head sadly. This building wasn't a home. It had never been one. It was merely a storage place for furniture and gewgaws from past generations.

Disgusted, I crossed the foyer and went into the kitchen. The first thing I saw were Inez's keys lying on the counter. I opened a cabinet door and took out a box of cornflakes. The box was new, and I couldn't get the plastic pouch opened. It should have been a simple task, but I fumbled and fought until tears of frustration filled my eyes. In desperation I yanked open a drawer, snatched a knife from a multitude of sharp objects, and ripped at the plastic seam. It split, and cornflakes exploded across the floor.

What followed illustrates how distressed I was. I tossed the box in the trash, threw the knife on the counter. I proceeded to stomp the cornflakes into a pulverized powder that coated the floor. When my theatrical performance came to an exhausting end, I stalked out of the kitchen without a backward glance.

In the hall I smoothed my hair and took a deep breath. "Carl, I can't do this alone. I need someone in my life. I need companionship. I need to feel loved. I want to matter to someone. Tell me what to do because these pressures are getting to me."

I waited expectantly. I squeezed my eyes shut and concentrated. Carl's voice was eluding me. "Damn it, Carl," I cried, "it was bad enough when you died. Don't abandon me now when I need you more than ever." Again I waited.

"Fine," I choked back tears. "I'll handle this on my own."

"I know you will Babe, I never doubted it," was his gentle reply.

As I drove to the shop, I thought about Inez. Regardless of what branch of the law she told her story to, I knew Sid would hear it, and I could expect a call from him. At ten o'clock, I answered the phone.

"Bretta," said Sid, "have you stepped out of line?"

"Not in the last hour, though I did hike the price of a dozen roses to a customer. He wanted style and elegance. In my present mood they don't come cheap."

His gusty sigh whistled through the receiver. "That housekeeper of yours has been down at the city police department telling some tale about you being the killer. Where'd she get this idea? What the hell is she talking about?"

Right off the bat I set him straight. "Inez isn't employed by me any longer." Then I gave him the flat, abridged version of my remarks to Chris. When I finished, he mumbled, "Oh," then asked, "Will you be at the shop all day?"

"No. At one o'clock an order of poinsettias is being delivered to the mansion. At two, I have to unlock the mausoleum for the monument company."

"A blizzard is on the way. Heavy snows are already being reported up north. Get your work done, then get inside. I'll be around to check on you."

"Fine," I said absently. I wanted to search the mausoleum for the blackmail letters. "Make it later, Sid. By that time I'll have my ducks in a row."

"What the hell is that supposed to mean? Sounds like cryptic soap-opera-detective lingo. Spit it out, Bretta. What are you up to?"

"I'll tell you later. Gotta go." I hung up, then scurried across the floor, putting distance between me and the phone.

Amused, Lois asked, "What ducks are you putting in a row? Lame ducks? Sitting ducks? Dead ducks?" Her smile faded to a frown. "What's going on?"

The bell—the telephone bell—saved me from having to answer. Lois picked up the receiver, but kept her eyes on me. I gave her a smile before I turned to my next order.

After that we were too busy to have any personal conversations. With a major storm threatening, business picked up. Each call began the same: "I'd planned to visit my—friend—mother—neighbor, but with this storm coming, I'm going to stay at home. Will you deliver a bouquet of flowers for me?"

Sure. We love bad weather. For a florist neither rain, nor snow, nor sleet—blah, blah, blah. The flowers must go through.

The avalanche of orders, combined with the weather forecast, heightened my nervous state. I kept my eye on the clock. It was just after eleven. If I left at noon—

"Call for you, Bretta," said Chris. "It's Baughman Monument Company. This man says they want to seal the vault immediately. Can you meet them?"

Before I could answer, Lois turned from the other phone. "This call is for you, too. It's Dan Parker. He says his delivery truck is stuck in a snowdrift forty miles from River City. He says not to worry about your poinsettias, the driver has the heat on, but he'll be late. Will you be home?"

I pointed to Chris. "Tell Baughman's I'll unlock the gate in an hour." I nodded to Lois. "Tell Dan to deliver the poinsettias whenever possible. I'll be at the house." When each woman had hung up her phone, I said, "We're calling it a day. No more orders. Go home as soon as you've helped Lew load his last deliveries and finished up here."

By the time I had completed the bouquet I was working on, answered Lois's and Chris's last-minute questions, and driven to the mansion, I had half an hour left to get to the mausoleum. The wind cut through my jacket and made me shiver as I hurried up the front walk. Instead of driving to the mausoleum, I decided that it would be quicker to take the shortcut across the west edge of my property. But first, I had to find something warmer to wear. The first snowflakes had begun to fall, creating a dazzling display that was as perfect as a Christmas card setting.

I paused on the veranda steps. Cameo had written in her journal: *A holiday greeting from an old friend was enlightening. I've discovered the identity of my blackmailer in a most unusual manner.* Holiday greeting? Christmas card? Something was bugging me, but I was running out of time.

I hurried inside and up the stairs to my room. Buried in the back of my closet was an old snowsuit I usually refuse to wear because it makes me look like a stuffed white rabbit. Fashion wasn't a top priority. Warmth was the name of the game. I dragged the quilted suit from a box and undressed, fighting my way out of my work clothes and into the bulky snowsuit.

As I zipped the heavy parka up to my chin, I decided I'd better not wait for Sid to put in an appearance. Once I had the letters in hand, I would deliver them to him. I might have been a bit overly confident, but from the way Cameo had worded the last line in her journal I was sure she'd hidden the letters at the mausoleum.

The back stairs were closer, so I raced down them. If I was out chasing Sid, I'd better call Lew and tell him to come to the mansion to accept the poinsettias. Caught up in my thoughts, I misjudged the bottom step and had to reach for the doorframe to catch myself. My finger hit the elevator button. The machine whirred into action. I slapped the button to make it stop.

In the kitchen I dialed the shop. Chris answered, and I relayed instructions. "When Lew gets back from deliveries, tell him to come out here right away. I'm leaving the terrace doors unlocked so he can come inside if I'm not here. Tell him I want him to wait for the poinsettia order."

As I talked, I turned, then stopped unable to believe what I was seeing. The cornflake fiasco had been cleaned up, and the floor shone as if from a recent polishing. I stretched the phone cord so I could open the drawer. The knife I'd used on the plastic pouch was there with the others. The trash had been taken out.

Chris was saying Avery Wheeler needed to see me. "Tell him I'll talk to him later. I'm running late." I hung up and yelled, "Inez?"

I heard a door slam upstairs, and muttered, "She's crazy if she thinks she can waltz back in and expect me to forgive and forget." I wasn't going to deal with the old rip right then.

I hurried out of the kitchen and down the hall to the terrace doors. I clicked open the latch and stopped on the threshold to gasp in disbelief. Since I'd come into the house, Mother Nature had unleashed her fury on this part of the world. By the looks of it, she'd gone stark-raving mad.

Chapter Twenty-four

❧ I tied the parka hood in place and pulled the door shut behind me. I stood still and allowed my brain to follow an obstacle course of clues. Christmas card. Christmas card. Cameo had written—*A holiday greeting from an old friend was enlightening.* The whirling snow blew images across my mind. They danced and wavered and changed places. Parents and family are at the root of most psychological problems. Actions, conversations, and impressions rolled from my memory like film from a projector.

Sleet mingled with the snow—fluff and substance. Hard, round iridescent pearls of ice. After Cameo was murdered, I'd seen the pearl ring in her lap. Had Cameo pulled the ring off her finger as a clue to the duplicity of her killer?

I hurried toward the mausoleum. Pellets of sleet pecked my face. Snowflakes landed on my eyelashes and made me blink. I pictured the scene in the dining room. Everyone had been on edge from Cameo's comments in the library. I examined every word of the conversations, looking for nuances, double meanings. A horn honked three sharp beeps. I picked up my pace, rounded the last bend, and saw a truck parked on the Jackson Memorial Cemetery side of the fence. I waved, and two men climbed out.

They were dressed in green insulated coveralls with the name BAUGHMAN MONUMENT COMPANY printed across the backs. Stitched in yellow thread above their respective breast pockets were the names, Ernie and Russell.

Russell held the padlock steady so I could insert the key. When the padlock clicked free, he pushed the gate back. Ernie stood with his hands in his pockets and watched us as if we were a spectator sport. Russell went to the truck for the necessary equipment to do the job. I unlocked the mausoleum door and stepped inside.

"Wow," said Ernie, from behind me. He aimed a flashlight around the room. "This is the biggest danged crypt I've ever been in."

"Hell of a storm," said Russell, stepping through the doorway pulling some apparatus on a two-wheeler. His reedy voice bounced off the marble walls. "Worst one I've seen in years."

"You say that every time a snowflake falls," grumbled Ernie.

"Do not.

"You do, too. In the summer you say 'this is the hottest day I've seen in years.' "

"I don't either," said Russell.

"You do it all the time."

Their bantering came from a close association. On the night of Cameo's murder, I'd heard a similar "did not" "did too" exchange in the library. "I'll be over here out of your way," I said, moving closer to Amethyst's tomb.

"Job won't take but twenty minutes from start to finish," explained Russell. "First we'll cut a stencil, then we'll start up that machine." He pointed to the apparatus. It was about thirty inches tall with an attached black hose that ended in a ceramic nozzle. "It's a combination generator, air pressure tank, and sandblaster. We'll cut the deceased's date of death"—he pulled a slip of paper from his pocket—"into the marble drawer front. After that we'll seal—"

Ernie scoffed, "She ain't taking lessons, Russ. Give her some earplugs, then let's get on with this so we can go home."

I took the offered plugs and put them in my ears. I waited until the men were bent over the stone tablet before I turned to the vase behind me. I removed the mistletoe, then surreptitiously reached inside. My grasping fingers touched something. Behind me the sandblaster roared to life. I pulled out a parcel of papers that were rolled into a cylinder.

Quickly, I looked at my discovery—three typed letters and one Christmas card. I opened the card and saw the signature: Matilda Bennett. I waited for the staggering information to register. Other than a tremendous sense of sorrow, I remained composed.

I turned my back to the men and stashed the papers under the waistband of my snowsuit. With the plugs in my ears, I was alone in my own world. Was there something I could have done differently? If there had been signs, I'd either missed them or given them a misinterpretation. I'd thought Sid's conclusions were erroneous when he'd arrested Topaz, but I had him beat when it came to misjudging the facts.

"Ma'am," Russell shouted, "you can take the plugs out. We're done."

I removed the foam absently. We stepped out of the mausoleum into snow that fell so thick and fast I couldn't see six feet in front of me. The two men waited while I locked the mausoleum door.

Russell asked, "You want us to give you a ride to the

house?" He tugged the flaps on his cap down over his ears. "This looks like a whiteout, what with the snow coming down so hard."

"It'll be faster if I walk." I waited until they had all their equipment on the Jackson side of the cemetery, then locked the gate and trotted off.

The wind's velocity buffeted me along. All sign of my prints were gone. While we'd been inside the mausoleum more than an inch of snow had fallen. At this rate—that's right, I thought, think about snow piling up.

Don't think about familiar hands twisting the string of lights around Cameo's fragile neck. Think about how cold it is. Don't think how easy it was for the killer to sneak down the back staircase and reach around the doorframe to push the button for the elevator. Think about getting back to the mansion and calling Sid. Don't think about how the pain of rejection can eat into your soul. How it can consume any feelings of self-confidence and make you question your own worth.

I ran from my thoughts, tears stinging my eyes. Wet snow clung to my boots. My footsteps slowed, and my breath came in painful gasps. The mansion suddenly loomed in front of me, and I assaulted the terrace like a trooper, threw open the glass door, and burst into the hall like a deranged person.

When my snow-crusted boots made contact with the polished floor, my feet shot out from under me and I fell with a bone-jarring crash. I got up slowly and closed the door. I limped down the hall to the kitchen and reached for the phone. It was gone.

I shook my head in disbelief. The phone didn't miraculously appear. I had to blink several times before reality sank in. I pushed the hood from my head and stripped off my mittens. Straining my ears, I listened but couldn't hear anything except the roar of the wind.

The partially closed knife drawer caught my attention. I eased it open. Only slotted spoons and spatulas. Like a woman possessed, I pulled open drawer after drawer. Anything that might be used as a weapon was gone. Fear pumped blood through my veins at a dizzy speed.

There's a phone in the library flashed in my brain. I hurried out of the kitchen, crossed the foyer, but stopped at the library doorway. There was no need to go any farther. The table was empty, the phone gone. I turned to the fireplace. Those tools were missing, too.

A shoe scuffed the parquet floor. I pivoted on my toe and frantically scanned the upper balcony, the hallway, and the foyer. Something glittered at the base of the staircase. I moved closer and saw the box, which had contained the handblown Christmas ornaments, lying empty—every fragile decoration smashed.

A movement in the shadows caught my eye. I peered across the foyer. Her name slipped from my lips like a woeful sigh. "Chris."

"You were carrying that box downstairs," she explained quietly. "In the dusky light, you lost your footing and fell. I found you. I called 911, but it was too late. You were already dead."

I shook my head.

"Oh, yes," she replied, sadly but coolly. "Once I have your body arranged to my satisfaction, I'll plug the phones in. I'll return the knives to the drawer and put the poker and shovel by the fireplace. But first I have to get you upstairs." She stared at me. "I don't suppose you'll go peacefully?" I backed away, and she sighed. "I thought not."

Chris reached into a large silk arrangement by the dining-room door and pulled out a butcher knife." She pointed the tip at me. "Move!"

"Lew will be here—"

"Sorry. I didn't give him your message."

"Lois might—"

"Wrong, again. She's gone home."

"Don't do this, Chris. You need help. Let me call Sid. Let me—"

"You've done more than enough, Bretta. I knew the dinner party was a mistake. I didn't want to come, but you insisted. I was afraid Cameo would recognize me because of my resemblance to my mother. I tried to change my appearance. I curled my hair, put on those dreadful high heels to make me look taller, but as soon as you introduced me, I knew Cameo had made the connection. What I didn't know was that Trevor had been trying to blackmail her, too. He wanted money. All I wanted was a chance to be accepted by my grandmother."

"What could Cameo do?"

"When I discovered that the Beauchamps had a scandal in their family, I hoped to use the information to force Cameo to let me live here as her personal companion. If Cameo appeared to accept me, then Matilda might also. But Trevor's letters made a mess of everything. Cameo thought I'd sent them. I wasn't going to let her brand me with his disgusting plan, too."

I wanted to move farther away, but was afraid any action on my part would bring our conversation to an end and result in a scramble for my life. I kept my feet glued to the floor, but said, "I suppose the law office where Trevor worked was one of your father's cleaning accounts. You found the blackmail information in Trevor's office when you worked for your father."

"Aren't you smart? Trevor figured it out, too. That's why he said someone went past him in the ballroom. He told me he was giving me an alibi, but that I owed him hush money. He thought Cameo had paid me, and that's why she ignored his letters. He was slick," she said with a shudder.

"Chris, we've become friends. I'll help you. I know what you—"

"Shut up!" she cried. "You don't know anything about me. That day in the shop when Matilda slighted me was just another example of the blank wall she'd erected between us. When I was in first grade we were told to invite our grandparents to school to show them around the classroom. Mother told me I could invite Matilda, but not to be disappointed if she didn't come."

Tears welled up in Chris's eyes and ran down her cheeks. "I worked for days on my grandmother's invitation, and I hand-delivered it, but the bitch wouldn't come to the door. Her servant said she wasn't there, but I could see her." Chris's voice rose in outrage. "I could see her sitting with her back to me, but not once did she turn and acknowledge me."

She dashed a hand across her face. "When I found that information in Trevor's office, I thought I'd take it to Matilda and show her that her highfalutin friends had secrets and scandals in their family, too. But after thinking it over, I changed my mind. I wanted Matilda to come to me. I dreamed of her crawling to me, begging forgiveness for all the pain she'd caused my mother and me." Her voice trembled. "Do you know what Mother's dying words were? 'Tell Nana I've never stopped loving her, though she stopped loving me.' "

My heart fluttered with compassion. My gut told me to wise up and get control of the situation. Chris seemed lost in thought. I shuffled one foot forward. The knife came up with the point aimed at my midsection.

"Do as I say, Bretta."

I crossed my arms over my chest. "I'm not going up those stairs. What will that do to your plans?"

Chris took a step forward. "Nothing. I'll have to be more inventive." She thought a moment. "You took this knife upstairs to open the box. It was in your hand when you fell. It was a dreadful, freak accident."

"Like Trevor's death? You screwed up, Chris. A rolling vehicle doesn't leave acceleration marks. I thought you were more clever than that."

"Leave her alone," said another voice from above me.

My neck popped as I yanked my head up. Jason stood at the top of the stairs.

Chapter Twenty-five

🌸 "I've been waiting for you to put in an appearance," I said quietly. "I thought you might be a coconspirator in this deadly affair."

"Chris told me you were on the verge of piecing it together."

"You worked at ingratiating yourself into Topaz's life, but Cameo was the stumbling block. Was murder on your mind from the start, and Chris beat you to it?"

Jason's voice rose. "Hell no. I told you I didn't kill my grandmother."

Jason hadn't produced a weapon, but that didn't mean there wasn't one. I turned the conversation down another avenue. "How did the two of you hook up?"

"Happenstance," said Jason. "I was taking pictures of the grounds when I overheard Chris's chat with Cameo. When Chris left, I followed her." He smiled tenderly down at Chris. "I could sympathize because of her grandmother's rejection. I'd experienced some of those same feelings when my father told me my mother hadn't wanted me. It might be too soon to say, but marriage could be in the future. As my wife, Chris would get the acceptance she needs and deserves."

"A bastard son-in-law would hardly impress Matilda Bennett," I commented recklessly.

Jason scowled and took a step down the staircase. "Who gives a damn about Matilda Bennett? My family is every bit as influential as the Bennetts and the Beauchamps. They'll accept Chris."

I smiled coldly. "That performance in the library concerning Chris's hair barrette was an impromptu production to alibi both of you."

"Are you wasting time, Bretta, or are you trying to impress us with your wisdom?" asked Jason sarcastically.

I looked at Chris. "You lured me out on the pond. Did you hope I'd drown?"

"It would have solved several problems," she admitted.

"And the note to DeeDee? You sent it?"

"In the library she acted like she wanted to say something. You'd told us at work that she never talks on the phone, yet the next day when I answered, she asked for you. I knew then that whatever she had on her mind was important."

"Which one of you killed Trevor?"

"That doesn't matter," said Jason, taking another step down. "Chrissie and I are in this together."

"Chris, you knew Trevor called the shop and told me he had a 'specific detail' he wanted to discuss with me. Is that when you decided to kill him?"

She trembled with anger. "All he was interested in was money. I promised to meet him with a payoff. Before I left the house, I called Jason to tell him what I was going to do. He tried to talk me out of it, but Trevor would have kept on until he either laid all the blackmail on me or bled me dry. I couldn't allow that to happen."

Her tone turned bitter. "Trevor swooped down the street in his fancy car. Got out with that disgusting swagger. While he was bent over the briefcase, ogling the money I'd scraped together, I hit him on the head."

The knife dipped and wavered as she talked. I inched forward. "Then what happened?"

Chris shuddered. "Jason arrived. He was going to stop me, but he was too late. We dragged Trevor into the street, opened the hood of his car so it would look like he had car trouble, then we propped him against the headlight. Jason got behind the wheel—" She sobbed. "The sound. That horrible sound of his body . . . being . . . crushed."

"That's enough, Chris," said Jason.

I swung my gaze up to him and saw movement in the shadows by a bedroom door. Who was it? My heart fluttered with hope, and then lurched with fear, when Jason took another step down. I wouldn't stand a chance against both him and Chris.

"Stop!" I screamed. My sudden outburst caught Jason by surprise. "You—uh—don't want to get glass in the soles of your shoes." I quickly ad-libbed, "Staging accidents isn't exactly your forte. You were sloppy with Trevor's murder. If you step in that glass, you'll grind it into the soles of your shoes. Sid will look at everything very, very carefully. He's my friend. He won't let my death pass without a close scrutiny."

"She's right," said Chris. "I'll hold the knife on her. Use the back stairs and come around that way."

"It could be a trick to get you alone."

Chris straightened her shoulders and swiped at her tears. "I'll be fine. I have the knife." She raised it for emphasis.

I wanted to sneak a peek toward that bedroom door and see if the shadow was still there, but if I had help, I didn't want to jeopardize it.

Jason slowly backed up the stairs, his eyes on me. Chris

advanced with the point of the knife aimed at my vital organs. I wasn't thrilled with the situation, but a gun, making a sudden appearance, would have struck terror in my heart. So far the only weapon in sight was the butcher knife. Though it was deadly, enough space separated us—for the moment.

I'd make my move once Jason had disappeared. Behind me was the front door. I hoped I could wrestle it open before Chris stabbed me. It was a flawed plan because it left my back exposed, but it was the best I could come up with.

Jason hesitated at the head of the staircase. "I don't like this," he called to Chris.

Before she could speak, an eerie voice floated on the air, "Y-y-y-ou k-k-k-killed m-m-m-me!"

"What the hell?" murmured Jason.

"Y-y-you k k-k-killed m-m-m-me!"

DeeDee! My heart leaped in my throat.

Rapid footsteps crossed the floor above. I saw a flash of rose-colored cloth. I glimpsed a veiled hat. Jason misjudged his location on the stairs. He stepped back, lost his footing, and fell. His arms flailed uselessly as he rolled down the stairs. I heard the sickening crack of his skull as it made contact with the wooden steps. His lifeless body finished its descent and sprawled at the foot of the staircase.

Chris's head swiveled with disbelief from Jason on the floor to the figure at the railing, then back to Jason. Her eyes widened. Her mouth opened. A scream welled up in her throat with an intensity that raised the hair on my scalp. She took a deep breath and cut loose again. This wail climbed the musical scale like an opera singer checking the range of her voice. From the depths of Chris's diaphragm anguish resonated. The guttural sound traveled higher, gaining volume until it emerged in a primeval roar.

I glanced up and saw DeeDee was gone. Where was she? My God, what was she up to now? I looked back at Chris. Her agony was difficult to watch. Years of being denied, of being ignored, had solidified into one cancerous mass. Jason's friendship had put the disease in remission. His death had unleashed it. Any healthy tissue that remained was being devoured. Desperation became her driving force.

Her chin came up. Her gaze caught mine. In that moment when our eyes met, I knew I was going to die. I broke visual contact, hoping to restore some measure of my own rationality. My attention went to the knife in Chris's hand. Her grip was loose, her thumb and index finger wrapped closest to the hilt. She dipped the point. With a flick of her wrist, she repositioned the handle, grasping it like a dagger.

I'd seen enough. Whirling, I was at the door in four long strides. I wrenched it open, letting in a blast of arctic air. An old man hurried up the walk, his neck hunkered into the collar of his coat. He raised his head, and I saw the walrus mustache.

"Run!" I screamed at Avery Wheeler. "She's got a knife!" I saw the "huh" on the old lawyer's face. He looked past me. From the way his eyes dramatically widened, I knew, if I was going to save myself, I'd better move. I twisted sharply to the right. The knife blade sliced the nylon fabric of my snowsuit. Blood didn't spurt, so I kept going. I bellowed at the lawyer, "Get in your car! Go!"

I lost track of him as I ran the length of the veranda. With Chris behind me, where was I going to go? Avery's presence complicated things. I'd planned to run down the drive for help, but I couldn't lead Chris to the old man. I couldn't go back in the house because DeeDee was there.

A horn honked furiously. I risked a quick look. Avery was in his car, the engine running and the passenger door wide-open. He gestured to me. I stopped suddenly, pivoted on my toe, and flung out my arm as hard as I could. I caught Chris in the rib cage and knocked her against the house.

I leaped the railing in a single bound, a feat I could never have accomplished if a killer hadn't been on my tail. I fought my way out of the branches, jumped up, and ran for Avery's car.

Younger and more nimble, Chris came off the veranda and ran diagonally across the yard to cut off my escape. I beat her by a whisker, slamming the door in her face. She was on the vehicle in a flash, hacking at it with the knife, gouging the paint.

"Drive!" I screeched at the attorney. "Get us the hell out of here!"

Avery's hands were shaking so badly, it took two attempts before he could grasp the gearshift lever. He put the car into reverse, but the tires spun. The engine roared as he pressed harder on the gas pedal. Under the useless turning of the wheels little potholes were being dug in the ice.

"Don't press so hard on the accelerator," I instructed breathlessly. "Give the tires a chance to grab hold." He eased his foot off the gas. "Do you know how to rock a car?" I asked. His answer was a blank stare. "Do this?" I flipped the gearshift into drive, back to reverse, back to drive. His eyes grew round as the gears shrieked a protest.

"I can't do that. It might damage the transmission."

Before I could make the obvious reply, the windshield shattered in a spiderweb of cracks. A brick from the fountain rested on the hood of the car. Chris reached across, picked it up, and got ready to heave it again.

"For God's sake, Avery—"

I didn't have to finish. The old man grabbed the lever and

ripped it up, down, up, down. The rocking motion did the trick, but not before my side glass was smashed. I have to hand it to Mercedes, they put out a premium automobile, but nothing except a tank could have withstood the abuse Chris generated. I whimpered as she beat on the fragmented window.

"Go, Avery!" I shouted as the splinters of glass showered in on me. The window gave way, and the knife appeared. The blade raked my jacket again before the car moved.

Avery Wheeler might've been a great lawyer. He might even have been brilliant when it came to deciphering complicated legalese, but he didn't know jack-squat about driving on ice. He had absolutely no control over the car, yet he continued to press the accelerator, increasing our speed down the slippery drive. The tires spun, the rear fishtailed, and the ditch loomed as a foregone conclusion.

I twisted on my seat so I could look out the rear window. Like a bionic woman Chris ran behind the car. I faced forward and saw where we were. "Slow down, Avery," I cautioned. "We're getting to the end of the drive."

I wasn't sure if he heard me. My face burned from cuts I'd gotten from the flying glass. A drop of blood dribbled into my eye. In the brief moment it took for me to wipe it away, three things happened. My warning about the driveway sank in. Avery reacted by slamming on the brakes. The delivery truck with my poinsettias turned into the drive. It looked like a head-on collision. I braced myself.

Avery surprised me with a spurt of astuteness. He took his foot off the brake, gunned the engine, and brought us out of the tailspin. He wrenched the steering wheel hard to his left. The car responded like a pro. It leaped forward, and then like a cow on ice it fought for traction. We spun out of control. I made brief eye contact with the driver of the truck as we did a pirouette in front of him. I saw his astonishment, saw him wrestle the steering wheel. We breezed by him, missing the truck's bumper by inches before we landed in the ditch.

I heard Chris scream. The sound was followed by a thud, then silence. I assured myself that Avery was still breathing. He waved a limp hand in response to my inquiry. I climbed weakly from the car. The first thing I saw was Dan Parker's new business slogan on the side panel of his delivery truck: FLOWERS BRING PEACE OUT OF CHAOS.

Epilogue

❧ I tucked my stocking feet under me and tugged the comforter closer around my shoulders. In the hearth, flames licked the pile of logs. The heat was there, but I was cold, chilled to the marrow of my bones. It was Sunday. Three days had passed since Chris's and Jason's deaths.

I'd canceled the open house. In a move that might put me into bankruptcy, I'd donated all the perishable Christmas merchandise to River City families in need of some holiday cheer. I closed my eyes. Tears seeped from under my eyelids and washed my cheeks in a salty bath.

Past events had left me physically ill. I ached in a place nothing or no one could touch. Sleep revived the horror, so I spent my time on the sofa in the library, staring at the fire, remembering everything with absolute clarity.

Topaz had been released from custody. She'd packed a bag, closed her cottage, and accompanied Jason's body to New Orleans. We hadn't exchanged a word, but I knew she wouldn't be back.

On Saturday, Simon had requested a library board meeting to announce his resignation. Another piece of the puzzle had found a home. Simon had been the person Sylvia had accused of "holding an exalted position with no more than a high school diploma." Sylvia had used Simon's secret as leverage against him. The library board had gone to Milo, the newspaper's publisher, and Sylvia had been fired.

Avery had come to the mansion that fatal day to tell me he'd found the Beauchamp file stashed among some papers in Trevor's office. A personal notation made over one hundred years ago by Edgar Collins stated that he was disturbed by the unexpected death of Jackson Beauchamp. Collins had written that he suspected foul play, but nothing could be proved.

Avery and I had spoken several times since Wednesday. I'd found a good friend in the old lawyer. We'd survived a vicious attack, and we shared a very nasty secret—the truth about the Beauchamp family.

I opened my eyes and glanced to my right. On the side table were the journals. Each was small enough to hold in the palm of my hand, yet held reams of human decay. As the mistletoe sends down its sucker root to steal the vitality from its host, so had the Beauchamp women. They were parasites one and all. Settling on a victim, stealing his wealth, and finally, destroying him. And they'd done it all in the name of *family*.

I leaned my head against the sofa and stared at the ceiling. Maybe it was safer to be alone. Tears blurred my eyes. But sometimes, being alone hurt, too. "Oh, Carl," I murmured, "I wish you were here to make the pain go away."

DeeDee came into the library bearing a small tray. I sat up and scrubbed the tears from my cheeks. She was my one bright spot. Already she was showing herself capable of running my household. I'm not sure how well Darlene is handling this new and improved version of her daughter, but so far the only interference has been six or eight phone calls a day. I can live with it.

Thanks to DeeDee, in fact, I'm able to live—period. I've

since learned that she saw Chris in the hall, *after* her trip to the powder room. DeeDee knew the woman hadn't been on the staircase the entire time, but she didn't know how important that fact was.

DeeDee had been in the attic the day I'd come home to change clothes to go to the mausoleum. She knew Cameo made trips up there with Inez, and hoped to find something that would end this nightmare. While she hadn't unearthed anything, she'd been in a position to overhear Jason and Chris discussing their plans for me, and she'd seen them hide the telephones in an upstairs bedroom. She'd donned the dress and hat, then waited for the right moment to use her disguise to the best advantage. Afterward, she'd gotten one of the phones out of hiding and called 911.

The uniform was gone and she was dressed in a pair of blue jeans, a white blouse, and a red vest. I nodded to the tray in her hand. "Hot chocolate?" I asked. It had become a game we played. To tempt me, she'd bring hot cocoa in different containers—thick mug, silver chalice or a paper-thin porcelain cup. I'd let the cocoa sit untouched until a film congealed the surface.

"N-n-n-no. H-h-h-hot t-t-t-toddy."

I raised my eyebrows. "Liquor, DeeDee? I'm amazed. Where in the world did you learn to make a hot toddy?"

She didn't speak but looked over her shoulder. A man in an overcoat stepped through the library doorway. "I didn't hear the doorbell," I said, frowning. "I'm really not up to company."

"I'd forgotten how rotten Missouri winters can be," said the stranger.

I caught my breath. I bunched the folds of the comforter into a tight wad against my chest. A knot the size of a grapefruit filled my throat. "Oh," I breathed.

The face was creased with wrinkles. The dark hair had turned gray. He was heavier than I remembered, but the slow, gentle curve of his lips was the same. Thirty-seven years hadn't diminished the power of his smile.

"Daddy?" I whispered as I stumbled to my feet. The years fell away, and I was that young child of eight again. I held out my arms and surrendered my bruised heart into his care.

"Death hasn't diminished Chloe's beauty," said Robbee. "That silver-blue casket was a great choice, Bretta. Too bad her eyes are closed because their fabulous color would mirror the finish."

I ignored him so I could study the funeral bier without distraction. As the florist in charge, I searched for any minute detail that was out of sync. A bank of floral tributes surrounded the casket and perfumed the air to an intoxicating level. Behind me two hundred empty chairs waited for occupants.

To my critical eye the bouquet on the left overpowered, but the traditional spray of flowers across the lower half of the casket was elegantly styled. The freesia's creamy color matched the satiny lining. The melon-pink tulips, royal-blue iris, and yellow daffodils were the right seasonal touch. It was April, and spring had blossomed in Branson, Missouri.

Robbee lowered his voice. "So young and so-o-o sexy. I had great plans for her, but now I'll have to turn my sights on someone else." He leaned closer. "Maybe someone older and more experienced."

His suggestive tone grabbed my attention. Before I lost one hundred pounds Robbee wouldn't have given me a second glance. I'd never be a skinny-minny, but I had a waistline, and I could cross my legs with ease. For someone who's never experi-

enced "thunder thigh syndrome" the latter might seem insignificant. I knew otherwise. Sitting in a chair and having the option
of flinging one leg over the other is damned important.

I wore a blue T-shirt with the tail tucked under the waistband of my jeans. Since the room was ultra cool to preserve the
condition of the flowers, I'd added a plaid flannel shirt. There
was nothing unique about my clothes and that's what thrilled
me. Gone were the polyester pants and oversized blouses that
had been the basis of my wardrobe.

The experts say it takes twenty-one days to develop a habit.
At forty-five, I'd had plenty of time to perfect a routine of
overeating. My new figure was almost two years in the making. Twenty-two months ago, I'd become a widow. These facts
were tightly woven into the fabric of my spiritual and physical
regeneration. Carl's death had raveled a portion of my soul
that could never be mended. Other areas had grown stronger
in his absence.

Robbee's breath stirred the curls near my ear. "You smell
wonderful, Bretta. Let's go—"

I didn't let him finish. My self-esteem could use a boost, but
not here and not now. "Shh!"

"Yes, Ms. Solomon," he said, clamping his lips tightly
together. He pretended to turn an imaginary key in an imaginary lock on his generous mouth. With an elaborate gesture,
he rolled the phantom key in his hands, then seductively
tucked it down the front of his shirt, taking great pains to
expose his chest for my appraisal.

I'd seen better, but it had been a while. At thirty-two,
Robbee's lean good looks paved the way for his brazen manner. His long brown hair was pulled into a ponytail and tied
with a strip of rawhide. He had more lines than a Broadway
actor, but I was immune to his prattle.

I shook my head at him. "With all the florists in Missouri, I don't know why I've been saddled with you for an assistant."

Before he could speak our "corpse" sat up. "I want out of this thing. I've laid here so long it's beginning to feel comfortable."

"That's not your line," said Robbee. "You're supposed to say, 'Welcome to the first annual Show-Me Floral Designers' Competition and Conference.' "

"I know what I'm supposed to say, but I need a break."

"Help her, Robbee," I said, nodding to the dearly departed, whose leg was draped over the edge of the casket.

Robbee folded his arms across his chest. "If I wait, the show's gonna get better." To prove his point, Chloe's dress inched higher, revealing a shapely upper thigh. He waggled his eyebrows. "See what I mean?"

The casket teetered on its stand. "Go," I said, "before she tips it over and we have a bona fide use for the damned thing."

He sighed but strode up the aisle. Once Chloe was safely standing, she smoothed her navy dress into place over her trim figure. Petite, fair-haired, and lovely summed up her physical appearance, but her personality was harder to define. Chloe is quiet and reserved in a group. With me, she acts as if she's found a surrogate mother.

At twenty-five, she's the youngest of the six competitors in our design contest and the most naive. Robbee's flirtatious smile had brought a rosy glow to her cheeks. I sighed. Anyone who thought all male florists were gay should see Robbee in action. He could charm the pistil from a cactus flower.

But a person can take only so much frivolity, especially when that person is in charge of the first floral contest our association has held. I'd been asked weeks ago to be the coordinator. Scuttlebutt had it that my name had been nominated because I hadn't attended the St. Louis design semifinals and couldn't flat-out refuse. I'd accepted the job because it was an excuse to get out of River City.

Since Carl's passing, I'd thrown myself into my flower-shop business with a vengeance. I needed a change of scenery, and the chance to visit Branson was too good to pass up. However, after a day and a half with a bunch of egotistical, competitive florists, I was beginning to doubt the wisdom of my decision.

I rotated my shoulders to lessen the stress. When this weekend was still in the planning stage, I was sure Robbee and I could handle making the display bouquets and setting up the contest area. Before I'd left home, I'd worried myself into issuing a last-minute invitation to the contestants to participate in the behind-the-scene preparation. From the moment they stepped through the hotel's doorway I'd heard rumblings of discontent, with my abilities as contest coordinator their biggest beef.

In a cover letter to all the contestants, I'd made it clear that the design categories would remain a secret until Saturday when the competition began. I wanted the premise to be inter-pretation plus ingenuity—creativity under pressure. Now it seemed that the pressure was on me to reveal those categories. So far I'd stood my ground but tension was high.

Today was Thursday. Tomorrow the festivities would com-mence. I'd thought the conference fee was rather high, but two hundred eager florists had signed on to be entertained as well as educated by guest speakers who had made a name in the flo-ral industry. Add in the cost of lodging at this pricey hotel, and the weekend would be danged expensive. Since I had a major role in the production, I wanted to make sure my colleagues got their money's worth.

But for now, all work would have to cease. I was starving. I glanced at my watch. It was after two o'clock. No wonder.

As I walked to the back of the conference room, I saw some floral supplies that had been left on a table. "Janitor, mother, contest coordinator," I muttered as I swept the mess into my oversized handbag. "Is there no end to my duties?" The pint of flower preservative was a tight fit, but I squeezed it into my purse.

At the door, I called good-bye to Chloe and Robbee. Neither looked around. They lounged against the casket as if they were in a singles bar. Robbee was such a tease, I hoped Chloe wouldn't take him seriously. But that's not my problem, I told myself as I entered the lobby of the Terraced Plaza.

The hotel is a five-year-old structure of glass and concrete and is part and parcel of an estate known as Haversham Hall. The old residence, with its palatial gardens and unique botanical conservatory, sprawls across a bluff overlooking Table Rock Lake. The hotel, located at the base of the bluff, was built to accommodate the surge of organizations needing a place to hold their conventions since Branson had become a vacation hot spot.

Yesterday when I walked in the front door, I'd been tempted to tuck tail and scurry back to my car. For someone who's afraid of heights this hotel levitates my phobia to a new stratosphere. The structure is nine stories high and each floor has a balcony that circles the interior of the building. An adventuresome guest can step directly from her room and look over the railing to the lobby below or across the heart-stopping abyss to the opposite tiers of rooms.

Glass-enclosed elevators bob up and down the walls like fishing lures, beguiling would-be victims. Thirty-foot trees, festooned in clear twinkle lights, shade the lobby with an ambience that's congenial and refreshing. Brick planters filled with tropical foliage edge ramps that carry foot traffic to different levels or terraces. A lounge, a café, and a souvenir shop were tucked into alcoves. The floral conference had access to numerous meeting rooms on the ground floor with storage for the mass of donated flowers in the basement.

A formal restaurant topped the building, and I'd been told the view was breathtaking. Tonight I'd have my chance to witness this dramatic display when officers and contestants came together for the introductory dinner. But for now, I was happy to have my feet firmly planted on the lower level of the hotel.

I saw Alvin at the front desk and made a quick detour over to him. Before I went up to my room, I needed to see if my last contestant had arrived. Yesterday, Angelica Weston, or Gellie, as she's affectionately known, had car trouble on Interstate 44 just outside of Springfield.

Alvin's gaze was locked on a computer screen. A young woman hung over his shoulder. I stopped at the counter and heard the woman say, "If you can find a 'Mrs. Carol Salmon' registered, I'll quit harping at Daphne. But I still say she didn't try to deliver these messages. They've been on my desk since yesterday, waiting for me to do her work."

I figured Alvin hadn't seen my approach. I was wrong. Briefly he held up a pudgy hand. "Wait a second, Bretta," he said, then continued typing.

Alvin's official job title is "Hotel Event Specialist." He's in his thirties, with thick chestnut hair and skin the color of an unbaked biscuit. He looked as if he never did anything more strenuous than pecking the keyboard. He wore the hotel uniform—teal slacks and a white crewneck shirt. The knit material hugged his love handles like cream over a plump strawberry. I licked my lips. A gnawing hunger was taking over my brain—biscuit, cream, and strawberry.

In the past few weeks, I'd visited with Alvin a number of

times on the phone as we hashed out details for the floral contest. He'd listened to what I needed in the way of chairs, tables, refrigerated space for the donated flowers, huge trash containers, handy access to water, the casket from a local mortuary, and an ample supply of patience.

Alvin had met each of my demands and then some. It had been his idea to make optimum use of the hotel's banquet facilities by dividing the main meeting room, where we'd set up the funeral bier, from the actual contest area. For added drama, he'd suggested that the florists be asked to wait in the lobby and be admitted all at one time for the opening ceremony. That way Chloe wouldn't have to endure a lengthy stay in the casket before welcoming the visitors to the conference, and the attendees would have the full effect of the body in the casket as they made their way into the room. I was in agreement, so events were moving along.

Alvin finished typing and threw up his hands. "I give up. She isn't registered. In fact, there isn't anyone named Salmon here. I'd say toss the messages."

"I can't do that. The McDuffys are guests here. I'll just make a note that when they return, someone—named Daphne—has to let Vincent know the messages weren't deliverable." She peered at the slips of paper in her hand. "And everyone says my penmanship is atrocious."

She walked off muttering, and Alvin swiveled his chair to face me. His mouth curved into a welcoming smile.

"So," I said, leaning against the counter. "How's tricks?"

Alvin gave a mock shudder. "In this stellar hotel we avoid the use of that word."

I chuckled. "Just for the record, the service and your staff have been superb."

"Things are running smoothly?"

I thought of all the potential problems and sighed. "Let's just say that everything in *your* power is fine. I'm still a bit dubious about my part in this soiree." I gestured to the keyboard. "Could you tell me if Angelica Weston has arrived? She was supposed to be here yesterday, but she had car trouble. If she's stranded in Springfield, I need to know so I can rearrange my schedule and go get her."

Alvin clicked a few keys. "Yes, ma'am, she's here." He grinned. "See? Another worry resolved. You've got to have more faith, Bretta."

The telephone buzzed before I could give him my personal opinion of faith versus hard work, perseverance, and plain old bullheaded stubbornness. I waved farewell and moved on, giving the lobby a sweeping glance.

A good-looking man seated on one of the sofas peered at me over the top of an open newspaper. I got the impression he'd been giving me a thorough inspection. When I turned my attention to him, he met my gaze with a direct stare before raising the paper.

The brief glance we exchanged wasn't much, but I sucked in my stomach and wondered who I was trying to impress. I didn't recognize him as a fellow florist. He was simply an attractive man sitting in the lobby, but I'd responded to him like a flower taking up water after a drought. Confused by my reaction to a total stranger, I ignored the glass elevators, opting for the stairs.

It was a long climb to the fifth floor, but I needed the exercise. At the door to my room, I slipped the plastic card into the key slot, waited for the little lights to flash from red to green, and then turned the handle. The door met with a bit of resistance before swinging open.

What I needed was a cool drink and a snack. Before I left home, I'd fortified my suitcase for just such an occasion. I hauled my bag out of the closet and flipped back the lid to reveal my cache of goodies—diet style.

I groaned. "What was I thinking?" Fruit and fat-free cookies when I yearned for cashews in caramel or pecans in fudge. "Stop it. Think thin. Think chic." I savored a vision. "Chic . . . ken fried to a crusty, golden brown."

I passed over the apples and bananas and grabbed a peach. While munching the succulent fruit, I opened the draperies, taking care to stand a few feet away from the floor-to-ceiling window.

Haversham Hall had rounded out its tourist complex with a miniature golf course that was in the final stages of completion. The theme "The Wonders of Missouri" was played out in Lilliputian detail: a small-scale version of the St. Louis arch. From Mark Twain's *Tom Sawyer* a partially whitewashed board fence. A log cabin portrayed Laura Ingalls Wilder's *Little House on the Prairie*. A natural cave was rumored to be a real tourist treat, but it was the distant, natural view that inspired me.

The Ozarks were beautiful in the spring—miles and miles of country overlaid with trees. Stark branches were budded with nubs that would soon open and flourish under the warm Missouri sun. Cedar and pine spiced the vista with hope of life everlasting. White dogwoods looked as if they'd been caught in a freaky snowstorm, their four-petaled flowers bursting into a frothy cloud of bloom. Redbuds appeared like a rosy mist, rising from the earth, spreading color to a forest of greens and browns.

In crowded spots the trees rose tall and spindly, their limbs spaced farther and farther apart as they competed with their neighbors for room to grow. Others less pressed for space were compact; their limbs set at intervals that showed good nutrition as they maintained their correct cycle for maturity.

Breathing deeply, I allowed the true reason for this trip to surface. I'd come to Branson to get away from all that was familiar, so I could concentrate on what I wanted to do with the rest of my life—a life that didn't include Carl.

My flower shop in River City made me a good living and gave me an outlet for my artistry. I'd used Carl's life insurance money to buy an old mansion and was renovating it into a boarding house. I had friends. I had work. I had a fabulous home in the making. But I wanted—no—I needed more.

In the two years since Carl's death, I'd jumped from one project to another—always busy, always working, always on the move. I gave those tall trees another speculative look. Was I like them? Trying to reach new heights by stretching myself beyond limits that weren't healthy? During the next storm would I splinter because my foundation was weak from having tried to cover too much space in too short a time?

Carl had been a deputy with the Spencer County Sheriff's Department. He'd made me privy to his investigations—everything from assault to murder. My interest in his job and his trust in me had cemented our marriage as a partnership. Carl had used me as his sounding board by laying out the facts of a case he was working on. We'd discuss the evidence, and I'd point out possibilities or weak links. My lips twitched. Carl hadn't always agreed with my assessment—he could articulate with the best—but after I'd been right a few times, he'd listened to my theories and publicly given me credit.

After his death, I'd been drawn into doing some amateur sleuthing on my own, which had almost gotten me killed. Abruptly I turned from the window and tossed the half-eaten peach into the trash.

The afternoon sunlight streamed into my room and highlighted a five-by-seven manila envelope lying on the floor by the door. I hadn't noticed it when I walked in. My mind had been on food.

Before picking up the envelope, I pushed a portion of it under the door. Tight fit, but I figured that's how it had been delivered. A note had been taped to the outside, and when I caught sight of the salutation, my eyebrows winged upward in surprise. It had been twenty-two months since anyone had referred to me as:

Mrs. Carl Solomon:

Last month my wife and I were in your shop buying flowers for our daughter's funeral. A nice lady helped us with our order because you were on the phone. We shamelessly eavesdropped on your conversation and learned that you would be in Branson this weekend for a floral convention. We've timed our trip to coincide with this event.

Your husband, Deputy Carl, was a fine man and a thoughtful officer. My wife and I live in the outer reaches of Spencer County, and when he was on patrol, he would stop in and visit with us. He often spoke of you and told us how you helped him with some of his investigations. We've since read in the River City Daily *that you were instrumental in assisting the sheriff's department in solving two murders.*

We don't have enough evidence to take to the authorities. You, Mrs. Solomon, are our only hope to right a terrible wrong. Please keep this envelope safe for us. If we haven't retrieved it by 7:00 A.M. on Friday, you have our permission to open it and assess its contents.

> *Our highest regards,*
> *Vincent and Mabel McDuffy*
> *Spencer County, Missouri*